**Scribe Publications**
**THE LIMIT**

RIIKKA PULKKINEN was born in 1980 and studied literature and philosophy at the University of Helsinki. She is the author of *True*, which was published in seventeen countries and shortlisted for the 2010 Finlandia Prize for Fiction. *The Limit*, her debut novel, was a bestseller in Finland and the Netherlands, and won the Kaarle and Laila Hirvisaari prizes.

LOLA ROGERS is a freelance translator living in Seattle. Her published translations include *Purge*, a novel by Sofi Oksanen; Antti Tuomainen's thriller *The Healer*; and numerous works of poetry and fiction for *Female Voices of the North*, *Words without Borders*, *World Literature Today*, and other publications. Her translations of *The Rabbit Back Literature Society*, by Pasi Jääskeläinen, and *Compartment Number 6*, by Rosa Liksom, will appear in 2014.

# RIIKKA PULKKINEN

*Translated by Lola Rogers*

SCRIBE

*Melbourne • London*

..ck, Victoria, Australia 3056
..ns Walk, London, EC1R 0LU, United Kingdom

Gummerus Publishers with the Finnish title *Raja* in 2006

published in the English language by arrangement with
O.      up Agency, Helsinki

Published by Scribe 2013

Typeset in 11.5 / 15.5 pt Dante MT by the publishers
Printed and bound in Australia by Griffin Press

The paper this book is printed on is certified against the Forest
Stewardship Council® Standards. Griffin Press holds FSC chain
of custody certification SGS-COC-005088. FSC promotes
environmentally responsible, socially beneficial and economically viable
management of the world's forests.

This work has been published with the financial
assistance of FILI — Finnish Literature Exchange.

Quote on p. 25 from 'Leaflet' by Tomas Tranströmer, from *New Collected Poems*,
trans. Robin Fulton (Bloodaxe Books, 2002). Reproduced with permission.

National Library of Australia Cataloguing-in-Publication data

Pulkkinen, Riikka, 1980-

The Limit / Riikka Pulkkinen; translated by Lola Rogers.

9781922070340 (pbk.)

894.54134

scribepublications.com.au
scribepublications.co.uk

*For my mother and father,*
*who taught me to read and write.*

*For my sisters, Johanna and Marikka,*
*thank you for letting me grow up with you.*

*For my friend Ilona,*
*my most critical reader, who is mild and wild in*
*this life like no one else.*

# Anja

ON THE DAY Anja Aropalo decided to die, the weather was as sweet and dense as a web of sugar. It was August, and still hot — even the nights were hot, but dark, like summer in the south. Anja woke up in the morning with a clear thought: her plan had to be carried out today. No more hesitation or cowardice. Today was the day.

Anja Aropalo had been lonely for two years. Loneliness like a stabbing pain under her breastbone ever since her husband left. She could feel it spreading into her whole body; a longing like a strangely physical hurt, a peculiar pain that she couldn't pin down, a continuous ache. It didn't usually make her cry, except sometimes at night, when she rolled onto her side and groped at the empty space beside her. Mostly it just ached.

Anja was walking home from the store. The thought she'd had in the morning had, over the course of the afternoon, strengthened from an idea to a decision. She had run her usual errands in town, stopped at the grocery and the pharmacy on her way home. Bread, cheese, milk for her coffee, some meat for dinner. And Doxal. The pills were at the bottom of her purse. Ninety pills, each one in a clean blister pack. *Depression*, the prescription said.

It had been surprisingly easy to get the medication. She had made an appointment, gone to the health center, and told the doctor about her life. The doctor had suggested antidepressants and Anja had nonchalantly mentioned that she'd prefer the older type of medication — Doxal, perhaps, or Triptyl. "The new depression drugs make me feel really ill, I'm afraid," she said. "Side effects." They exchanged a look of commiseration.

The doctor wrote a three-month prescription for Doxal. "It's nice to have a patient who knows what's good for her and takes responsibility for her health," the doctor said as they shook hands. Anja avoided his gaze, walked out of the room and out of the health center without looking back, sped up, and walked quickly along a road lined with blooming horse-chestnut trees until the shame started to fade.

The visit to the health center had been in June, and now it was August. Something had made her put it off. First there were the lilacs in bloom. She ought to see them. Then two weeks for the strawberries — till the end of June, she thought. No one wants to die during strawberry season. Now the air was turning heavy under the weight of the approaching autumn. Extravagant banks of peonies swaggered along the side of the road, their ponderous white heads too large for their thin stems. The thought of how trivial it all was still lingered at the edge of her consciousness, but the warm sunlight reduced it to a faint trace. This is my reality, she thought. This is what I'll leave behind: a whole life of walking to the store and walking home again. Autumn will come, and winter and spring and summer again, along with everyday tasks like these, always the same.

But the trees. The birches with their slender white trunks and the apple trees that had blossomed in May, painfully vivid.

There had once been a thick forest here with just a footpath through the moss, then a cart road. Now it was a gravel road, and only a few of the old spruces were left, their tops stretching toward the deep-blue arch of the sky. What did it matter whether a person made a path for herself? She'd still be in the woods. You're supposed to cut a path for yourself through time; to find some meaning, some way of making sense of life even as it slips through your fingers. Then just when you're becoming yourself, when you reach a place that defines and delineates your life, you're supposed to give it all up and reach for something else. Anja sighed and stopped to look in her shopping bag for something to drink. I'll water the roses as soon as I get home, she thought, feeling guilty about the buds drooping in the heat of the veranda.

The sun was burning Anja's neck and making her ears ring, and she felt infinitely weary. Life was full of these heavy moments, just waiting for time to pass, to get home, to close the blinds and make the food she'd planned to make, and eat it, and then wait for night to come. But night wouldn't come now, not for her. First I'll water the roses and make something to eat, she thought. Then the pills.

She was met at the front door by a flood of sunny, dusty stuffiness. The houseplants were wilting. She hurried to open the living-room windows. The air stood like a humid wall just outside the glass, hovering over the glowing geraniums. It was perfectly quiet. The clock on the wall ticked, each second spreading outward in a circle. Anja wiped the sweat from her forehead. The roses. She got the watering can from the kitchen cupboard and went back onto the veranda. She turned on the spigot next to the porch. The water sputtered through the hose, finally gushing into the watering can, sparkling in the sun. The roses seemed to sigh as they received the water. Drops fell like tears from their velvety petals. A bee, fat and clumsy with midsummer nectar, buzzed at one of the buds as if in a trance.

Her husband's rubber boots were still in their usual place in a corner of the veranda. Anja shoved her feet into the boots. A pair of gray socks, felted from many washes, had been left inside them, still shaped like his foot. On winter mornings he would put his socks and boots on and sweep the snow from the driveway on his way to get the newspaper.

Anja stepped onto the lawn, the grass flattening under her feet. This is how I leave tracks, how I claim this space. I have this body, its outlines and open spaces. She walked across the yard to the vegetable garden and looked at the cabbages. The soil of the vegetable beds had lightened and cracked in the heat.

She hooked up the sprinkler and set it in the middle of the garden, next to a row of carrots. The lettuce and snap peas needed the most water. She picked up a bucket that lay moping at the edge of the field and sprayed it clean, then filled it with a few summer squashes and carrots. She could put the pea pods in the salad — and radishes, of course. The lettuce leaves looked wilted, but she picked a few of them, too. And onions.

ANJA UNDRESSED in front of the mirror in the upstairs bedroom. At fifty-three years old, she was still slender. Her legs were strong and smooth, her stomach tight. Her breasts were lower than they'd been when she was young, a little stretched, but still beautiful. She liked her collarbones and neck the most: when she was younger, their straightness and angularity had made her seem boyish, erect. Now the boyishness had disappeared but the posture was still there, a certain openness in the shoulders. There were lines on her face that she cherished like old friends. They were the mask that experience had formed for her and she felt a deep affection for them.

She looked at the tan line marking the boundary between her arm and her shoulder. Her arms and neck were toasted a copper color, the area around her breasts paler. The mirror drew another line, too, another shape from within this middle-aged woman's image, a figure forgotten by the years but nevertheless drawn out in dim outline from within the reflection. The curve of the hip a little straighter now than back then, the down on the skin coarser. And the face had a deeper expression — the flesh's knowledge of the nature of reality. Other than that, this woman was the same one her husband had fallen in love with years ago; the frame of her skeleton carried the outlines of the same young girl he remembered even when he'd forgotten everything else.

How had it all begun, the forgetting? When had she first begun to sense a change? There had been so many summers like these, so many autumn evenings and icy winter days together, early springs with their rosy sunsets, melting snow and shared walks into the springtime woods. And then some inkling that everything was not as it should be — had he said or done something, or was he just different? — and soon afterward that inkling became a fact and then a certainty: there was no going back to what was beloved and familiar.

Anja washed her feet and put on her white summer dress. She put her hair up in a rubber band and went downstairs to the kitchen. The first breeze of the day fluttered the thin drapes as the seconds still ticked on, spreading inward. She took out the Doxal and put each packet in its own spot on the table. She walked to the counter and looked at the row of pills from a distance. The white tablets looked back at her — innocent, naked eyes.

She sliced the onions while the oil heated in the pan. There was a safe, deep peace in the scent of the frying onion. She remembered a feeling she'd had as a child, a peace that settled gradually into her whole body after a very long wait. Her mother coming home from work, the two of them making dinner together; her father would be home soon. The fragrance of frying onions drifting through the kitchen. She remembered the roughness of the hem of her mother's skirt and the black cast-iron pan, the voices of children playing in the yard. Her sister had been outside with the others and Anja had these precious moments with her mother all to herself before her father came home.

Anja chopped fresh peppers and tomatoes and a large zucchini and fried them with the onions. She cut the meat into pieces and browned it lightly in butter in another pan, picked fresh herbs from a pot on the windowsill and put them in the pan with the meat, added carrots and onion. The potatoes were simmering. She went to the cellar for a bottle of white wine. Red wine would have been better with the meat, but the thought of red wine in this heat was too heavy. She poured herself a glass. The bottle felt cool in her hand; the wine sparkled in the glass and tasted slightly pungent in the back of her throat. She remembered the taste of the wine during the first May with her husband. She had been in her first year at the university. He was already in his third year, older than her, and Anja had felt a shy gratitude when he showed interest in her. The weather that year had been unnaturally warm as early as May Day. And then, in the middle of May, it felt like spring deepened into summer overnight. They celebrated all night long, and in the wee hours, as they waited outdoors for the sunrise, it started to rain, and he tugged her under an apple tree and kissed her. The kiss tasted like wine — pungent, like lemon and spruce needles and a promise of happiness that even then, under the apple blossoms, already contained some element of that quiet certainty of sadness. She had interpreted it as fear at the time, but now she knew what it was: the silent realization that happiness is at its most powerful in possibility, when everything is within reach but nothing is yet promised. And as soon as happiness puts out its hand and you dare to take hold of it, the knowledge of its impermanence rises up in front of you.

Anja got a pen and paper from a drawer and sat down at the table. She had to write her farewells. To her sister Marita at least, and a separate one to her niece, Marita's daughter. She jotted some words on the paper. There didn't seem to be any point in trying to explain. *There's stew in the fridge, seasoned with rosemary. Eat it. Don't throw it out. I'm sorry I couldn't cope. You can take any of my things that you want. Give the rest to the Salvation Army. The money in the bank is for my husband's care.* She read through the message. It sounded blunt, but she didn't know how else to say it.

She wanted to write something for her niece, Mari, that would be useful in her life. Life instructions. She flipped through her notebook. Nothing suitable there. *Forgive me*, she wrote on the message to her sister after a moment of thought.

When she'd eaten some of the rosemary beef stew and potatoes and drunk two glasses of wine, Anja pushed the tablets through their foil backing and onto the tablecloth. She decided to have one more glass of wine. She arranged the pills into words: SHIT. Then DOXAL. She switched the L and D and rearranged some of the pills: LOVER. Rearranged them again: ALONE.

She put the A in her mouth: LONE. Then the first arm of the N: LOVE. She picked up the LOVE and swallowed it.

She'd taken quite a few tablets by this time, so she thought she might as well take the rest. She scooped them all into a pile, crammed them in her mouth, and washed them down with white wine.

Who would even miss her? If her sister didn't notice she was missing, they wouldn't notice her absence at the university until she didn't show up at the reception for the department head in a couple of weeks.

She thought about how she wanted to be found. Should she go lie on the bed? Dressed or in her night shirt? Under the sheets or on top of the bedding? If she went upstairs to her bedroom somebody could come into the house and still not find her. She must be out of town, they would think. Then she thought: They won't find me until I've started to stink. She thought of tabloid headlines: *Mummified Woman Rots in Bed for Weeks*. No, no. She shouldn't go upstairs to her bed. It occurred to her that she could tape a note to the staircase with an arrow beside it pointing up. The thought of an arrow to direct you to the body was amusing. She could put another arrow pointing upward on the head of the bed: *Gone to heaven*.

The thought made her laugh. The laugh made her flinch. The sound of her own laughter in the empty house at a time like that was grotesque. This was no laughing matter. She was about to die, after all.

She noticed that she was slightly drunk. It seemed inappropriate. It wasn't the kind of solemn moment she had planned for her departure. On the other hand, perhaps death ought to be greeted with a little levity. There was no harm in that.

Anja lay down on the kitchen floor. She pressed her cheek against the yellow stripes of the rug and felt slightly dizzy. Her stomach hurt a little. She closed her eyes and let her consciousness slip further away, until it reached the edge of awareness and beyond, to a cradle of dense forest.

There were ferns in the forest. The colors were bright, unreal, piercing. Anja walked deeper into the cool, arching vault of the trees. Sunlight filtered through the criss-crossing branches. A fine, gentle moisture radiated from beneath the ferns.

A magic forest.

Anja could see herself and her sister. They were small, wearing braids, running down the forest path and out of sight. The expanse of June surrounded her, and a bird fluttered back and forth above the tops of the spruce trees. Then the woods closed in on themselves, and she drew away from the cradling forest, back toward the feeling of nausea, the kitchen floor, the yellow stripes on the rug where her head was resting. She flung her eyes open and felt the waffle weave of the rug on her cheek. There was slobber on the rug. Nausea came in insistent waves along her jaw.

Anja took a deep breath.

It didn't help.

She sat up.

Her stomach felt awful now. She was definitely going to throw up. She dashed into the bathroom and just managed to reach it before she vomited it all up: the rosemary beef stew; the wine; the Doxal tablets, still undissolved. She gasped for breath between retching coughs. Vomit went into her nose. Water ran from her eyes. She got up, sobbing, and flushed the toilet. The sobs sounded ugly and wheezing in the tiled space of the bathroom. She sank down to the floor again, next to the toilet brush. Tears flowed freely. Her mouth tasted like vomit and salty tears.

Anja got up and rinsed her mouth out. It occurred to her that she hadn't thrown up in decades. The last time was when she was eighteen. She had thought she was pregnant at the time, but it had just been some kind of food poisoning. They had never had any children.

She went back into the kitchen. The smell of the food was revolting. She felt dizzy. She sat on the floor, thinking she would rest her head for a moment; then she lay down next to the spot of slobber and closed her eyes.

SHE WOKE UP to the sound of the neighbors' lawnmower. Her head felt heavy. Her mouth was sticky. She sat up carefully, then stood. She felt shaky. She turned on the tap, let the water run until it was cool, took a glass from the cupboard, and drank four glassfuls. Her head was pounding. She still felt like throwing up. She listened for a moment. Got the sick feeling under control.

The empty pill packets were on the table. She didn't throw them away: that would be destroying evidence. For some reason it seemed important that the evidence of her attempt to die remain, if only for herself. But she couldn't die today. Suddenly she felt a vague tenderness toward her floundering life. It was no good trying anymore today. Dying would have to be postponed.

She would have to kill her husband instead.

AS THE AFTERNOON turned to evening, clouds piled up against the sky, as they often did in hot weather. The warm air floated up to make room for the wind. The slanting sunlight still shone warm as Anja closed the door to her house, but when she came to the bus stop the sky was already covered in a threatening graffiti gray. A wedge of the gradually yielding sunlight sliced through the grayness. The heat was making way for rain. A willow warbler still sang in a tree. Its sweet song took on a threatening tone against the color of the sky.

It was already pouring as Anja stepped onto the bus. Always the same route: the bus curving away from the small residential area and speeding up as it reached the motorway. Halfway there she felt the usual reluctance, almost a fear: I don't want to go. She had to encourage herself, rebuke those negative thoughts, tell herself, You simply have to. Every time, as the bus passed close to downtown, she had an almost irresistible urge to get off, change to the tram and ride it to Kaivopuisto, buy some ice cream from a kiosk, and just walk and forget everything.

The first clear sign of the illness had come by surprise one day when her husband came home in the middle of the afternoon. Anja was working at home. He had stopped at the store on the way home and bought ten cartons of strawberry ice cream.

She remembered the look on his face — a bewildered, wary expression with fear glimmering behind it. He had stood at the front door with his arms full of strawberry ice cream melting and dripping quietly onto his shoes. She remembered laughing at first, thinking it was a joke. Then she asked why, why all the ice cream, and he said he didn't remember, couldn't remember at all.

"What's happening to me?" he said, and Anja didn't know what to say; she just went and hugged him. To touch another person is the only way to partake of their pain and fear. It's the only way, but it's not enough.

The bus turned onto a narrow road and Anja got off. The rain shower was over and the sun slipped through the clouds in bright rays. The small white-brick building always looked the same. The people in it always looked at Anja the same way, with the same expression on their faces. The vanished memories, forgotten lives, and solid asphalt walkway that led to the entrance were always the same, hot from the sunshine a moment ago and now steaming with the fragrance of rain. Earthworms lying smashed on the ground, puddles and rose bushes lining the path. The wall of intoxicatingly dense, damp air after rain, the leaves blazing in the fall, and finally the crisp crust of frost, the soft absolution of snow. Inside the nursing home there were always the same faces, the forgetfulness, and the smell of meat broth, apricot pudding, pea soup on Thursdays.

She opened the front door. Her footsteps on the lobby floor echoed against the white walls. Ferns nodded by the window at the back of the lobby.

At some point she'd been forced to recognize the seriousness of the situation. He couldn't remember anymore. Someone had asked them at a party how long they'd been married and he couldn't even remember that, and soon afterwards he forgot how to brew coffee. A vivid image: her husband helplessly folding a paper coffee filter in his hands; and her in the kitchen doorway, surprising him at the mouth of the tunnel of oblivion. The realization that lashed out at her consciousness as she stood there.

Gradually all of his everyday tasks — brushing teeth, tying shoes, reading the paper — started to require much more time: everything had become harder. Their time had slowed down.

He took sick leave from his work as an architect, and their shared memories, the ones he could still reach, became more important and meaningful. They gathered up their memories together; she told him what she remembered and he told her his memories out loud — the smells, the curls she had as a young girl years ago, the curve of her hip. What did it matter if he'd forgotten his work, all that had once been his calling? He still remembered the curve of her hip, a particular scent from the past. When he had forgotten the shape of his own body, there was still a memory of the color of the sky on a certain spring evening, a memory of the downy fuzz on his beloved's cheek. We have our memories, she thought, and our selves through them. Memories more important than the body that delineates our selves. My body may start to wither and rot, it may turn against itself and eventually fade away, but my memories will still be alive, even after my body no longer obeys my wishes. And then they, too, will fade, or be transferred to those left behind.

Anja walked down the linoleum of the hallway to the day room, greeted a nurse she knew as they passed each other. The light in the day room was striped by the blinds, bands of light shining in the shape of a cross against the wall. Her husband was sitting next to the window, opening his mouth for a nurse to feed him.

"Oh, hi!" the nurse said cheerily.

Was it Annika or Anniina? Anja could never remember her name.

"Would you like to finish up?" Annika or Anniina said. "He's had a good day today. He's enjoying his meal."

Anja nodded and stepped closer. Affection flooded her body and made her shoulders shake. She laid her hand on his and squeezed it gently. His hand was warm, pale, trembling.

"Hi. It's just me, Anja."

"Oh, yes. Anja. Just Anja," he said hoarsely.

His gaze wandered, trying to find her face, then moving away again. Finally he looked into her eyes and she saw an excruciatingly familiar expression, as if all this were just a brief sleep that he could wake from at any moment. If she just found the right words to wake him, the right doorway into memories, then everything would open up. But no. He opened his mouth like a baby bird and looked at the food. There was still some gravy on the plate. Anja picked up the spoon and fed him. He ate, breathing loudly through his nose. She gave him a drink of juice from a lidded cup.

"Look, a squirrel," he said, and pointed to the spruce tree outside the window.

A squirrel sat on a branch of the tree, nibbling something with its paws in front of its mouth, as if it were praying.

"Look at that," Anja said. "It is a squirrel."

"And there's a horse, scratching at the top of the tree," he said, looking up.

"Really? A horse?" Anja said. "All right then." She gave him a drink of juice and wiped his mouth.

"Thank you," he said, and looked into her eyes, through her eyes, past them. His face was like a mask spread over his familiar features. There was no longer any sign of suffering there, no longer a shadow in his gaze that had made her cry in the evenings two years ago, when he was only at the nursing home during the day and still slept next to her every night. No longer that gaping horror that had opened up in his eyes that night years before, when he had leaned toward her and said the thing that had placed a burden on her — a burden that no one could refuse to bear for the ones they love. A clear knowledge, a lucid moment in the night, and simple words: *I can't bear to live through this. Help me.*

Now that abyss of horror was gone from his eyes. All that was left was a different kind of gaze: friendly, a little hesitant, uncertain. He patted Anja's arm.

"And who might you be?" he said. "You sure are a nice girl."

Anja stroked the fuzz on top of his head.

"It's just me," she said. "Just Anja."

"Yes, yes. Anja," he said. "Just Anja."

ON HER WAY HOME Anja leaned against the cool window of the bus, still covered with rain. The drops trickled down the window, sometimes changing direction, forming random streams. It was almost a kind of unobtrusive, arbitrary work of art, the flow of the water, its apparent aimlessness hiding a pattern that followed some kind of hazy logic. *And who might you be? You sure are a nice girl.* His words echoed in her mind, their hoarse timidity, like a child and an old man in the same voice. He was talking to his wife. You sure are a nice girl. A nice girl.

THE DOXAL PACKETS were still on the table at home. Anja stopped in the kitchen doorway and stood watching the setting sun as it disappeared behind the trees in the yard. An idea came to her, faint at first, wavering in the shadows of all her other thoughts, but then becoming stronger: a request like that can't be passed up. There are no facile words, no half-hearted approaches to it. The meaning is always complete, the responsibility absolute. You don't do it out of nobility. You do it out of humanity. Words with that responsibility in them, with that weight of mutual trust, can never be made into something easy, something painless.

And Anja had to recognize the inevitable: she couldn't die. Not now. Someone else had to die instead, someone who had asked something of her. A responsibility had been placed on her, a request. Under its crushing weight, the idea of her own fate became as light as laughter.

# Mari

SOMETIMES — QUITE OFTEN, in fact — Mari thinks about dying. It's a game she plays. She might play the game anywhere at all, usually when she's bored — on the bus or the tram, in history class, waiting in line at the store to buy some lip gloss or strawberry yogurt.

The dying game progresses chronologically.

First Mari imagines how she will die. She has numerous variations.

Maybe she'll be run over by a car. Suddenly, on some ordinary Tuesday, a car will come toward her, speed up like it's mentally deranged, aiming right at her, and she'll go flying into the air. It will be a lovely arc, in slow motion, almost like a dance: her legs moving in the air like a ballerina's, graceful and controlled; her arms sweeping through the air in amazing, elegant patterns. Then a thud, and she'll be turned into a shapeless heap, human mush. People on the street will stop in horror, call an ambulance, although they'll know it's no use. *So young!* someone will shout. *And so pretty, too!* someone else will say. *What a tragedy!* another will add to the chorus. But Mari won't hear them. Her eyes will be open but will no longer see, will never again look at the world. Her open eyes will just reflect blue sky between drifting clouds.

Or maybe she'll end her days herself, die by her own hand, end it all, do herself in. Maybe she'll slit her wrists open and watch the sweet blood swirl and flow along the seams between the tiles and down the shower drain. Or maybe she'll fly, jump from somewhere, opening her arms as if she could spread her wings and soar. From a roof? The limb of a tree? A cliff? It doesn't matter. The result is what's important — she will no longer exist.

The most thrilling one is to catch some rare, fatal disease. Weird symptoms, dizziness, difficulty breathing, then the final, fateful diagnosis. She'll languish and suffer, unable to walk, lying on pale sheets, with her friends and family around her weeping helplessly until she takes her last breath, says her last words in a trembling voice. Sometimes she practices in front of the mirror. *Life is beautiful*, she'll say. *I loved life so much. I loved all of you. I'll carry all of you in my heart for all eternity.* This is what she practices saying. She puts a catch in her voice, tears in her eyes, her hands trembling. She thinks about her mother and father, the rest of her family. She struggles to breathe, just barely able to say her last words before her breathing stops and she becomes holy, forever young, untouchable, more beautiful than life itself.

The funeral, of course, has its own chapter. Mari imagines herself small, beautiful, and stiff, lying in a white coffin. The people at the funeral recite poems and are too sad to eat the lemon-cream tart served with coffee at the memorial afterward. Her parish pastor might say a prayer, and her confirmation class will play the guitar and sing. Mari herself will be silent, lying in the coffin with an eternal smile on her lips.

Thinking about the funeral doesn't give her much satisfaction. She plays with the funeral idea a little, imagines the coffin lowering into the ground, the speeches, the flowers — single red roses thrown on top of the coffin before the first shovel of earth — and the tearful expressions on the people's faces. Then she tires of it. Sometimes she starts over from the beginning — run over by a car, flying, illness — and sometimes she jumps ahead to the obituary in the newspaper, the reactions to the news of her death.

Thinking about death is a game. Of course Mari doesn't actually *want* to die, for the most part. For the most part she wants to live. But she doesn't want to entirely close her mind to the baffling possibility of death, the incomprehensible idea that she could cease to exist. It could happen that there would be no more Mari. In a month, a year, next week. It could happen. It's her private thought, hers alone. It gives her great happiness.

AGE: SIXTEEN YEARS OLD. Name: Mari — just plain old, two-syllable, dull Mari. A good girl's name. A girl called Mari is hardly likely to do anything big or special in her life, hardly likely to elope, become a street artist, rescue a child from a burning house, or develop a cure for an obscure disease. No, a girl called Mari draws flowers in her notebook in grade school like the teacher tells her to, right in the middle of the page, to the millimeter, so that every petal points in the right direction. A girl called Mari eats all her chicken fricassee, even though it makes her want to throw up. A girl called Mari does everything she's supposed to do: she goes to grade school, middle school, high school, university; she studies to be a dentist or a day-care teacher or an optician; she gets married, takes care of the children, comes home from work and fixes dinner and makes love to her husband after the evening news in the blue glimmer of the bedroom.

But this bearer of the name, this Mari, this self, is sixteen.

Mari is in her first year of high school. She has little breasts with budding nipples, and hips that might be stealthily spreading. She ought to check that. She ought to check everything, there's no letting up for even a minute, all her minutes and thoughts and feelings are devoted to it. Mari is getting a nine in math and biology and everything else except language and literature, where she has a perfect ten.

Mari is afraid that she smells. In fact she's absolutely certain that she smells, and that the smell doesn't go away when she washes. Once in a while in the shower she scrubs her skin with a rough shower mitt, or maybe a fingernail brush, or even a scrub brush like you use to scrub rugs. But the smell won't go away. She rubs herself down with aloe-vera cream to cover the smell. What does it feel like to put a rough shirt on over that? The cream sticks to her skin, the skin sticks to her shirt, and the smell sticks to everything.

Mari lives in a large stone building on the western edge of the city with her mother and father. Spring, summer, fall, and winter, the same graceful birch trees with their thin arms line the road that leads to the space contained within those rough stone walls — living rooms where safe, thick curtains frame many-paned, arching windows; kitchens where everything is as it should be, liverwurst and butter and milk in the fridge, cereal in the cupboard, and rye bread in the bread box. Mari wakes up in the morning and studies for her Swedish test while she eats bread and cheese and drinks cocoa. She gets dressed, combs her hair, closes the heavy wooden front door that always clicks shut behind her in the same way, walks two hundred and sixty-three steps to the tram stop, and rides the tram downtown. She waits for the green light on the corner and walks through the crisp morning toward a school building made of light-brown stone. The street slopes gently downward and there's a hum in her ears as she listens to the fragments of the morning conversations of the people she passes.

She crosses the street without looking to the left — she only ever looks to the right. She leaves the left side of her field of vision an open possibility, the road opening out from it, a door to oblivion, emptiness. She walks the rest of the short trip along the shadowy street, the cold of the morning reaching from her stiff fingers to the soft, delicate hair on her neck, and opens the school door. In the lobby is the kind of smell that will become very, very familiar through the years to come, although it hasn't yet. The smell of the day, the smell of shelves full of listening-comprehension workbooks.

Mari is thinking about how nothing in her life has its full weight yet. Everything is still empty. Everything is still open. Everything is still possible. There's only one thing this can mean: there's something — something she doesn't know about — still to come.

As the September-afternoon sun paints the walls of the classroom, Tinka lets down her golden-red hair and flicks it behind her in a way that makes it look as if her whole head is ablaze. Tinka and her hair. And her smile. Tinka's smile can turn any man, young or old, to a pillar of salt. She knows her power, and smiles often — always — particularly now, during language and literature class.

Mari has known Tinka for two weeks. Tinka came to talk to her in the hall during the very first week of class, and announced right away that Mari was her new best friend. Now Tinka wants to sit next to Mari in every class, and Mari wants her to, because the approval of a girl like Tinka is something to be grateful for. The only thing Mari worries about is the smell. Whenever Tinka approaches her, Mari draws back, afraid Tinka will notice it. Tinka definitely doesn't smell. Her faint fragrance is a mixture of rose milk and lavender, with an aroma of apples in her hair and a hint of something Mari can't quite name.

Tinka: a secretive, playful name — a conqueror's name. A girl called Tinka could get the boys to fall in love with her even in kindergarten; date the handsomest boy in the class in her last year of grade school; smoke cigarettes in the middle-school back lot in her tight jeans; lose her virginity at the age of thirteen with the soccer player that the whole school was lusting after; go to high school, smile her way through her thesis and final exams; get into drama school or political science or anything she wanted; screw the richest, best-looking, smartest man, and give him two beautiful children. And she definitely wouldn't smell.

But right now Tinka is sixteen and it's language and literature class and they're going over their homework. Tinka, with her fragrance of roses, leans closer to Mari and whispers, "Look at that teacher. Don't you think he's a hunk?"

"What?" Mari whispers stupidly.

"Don't you think he's good-looking? The teacher?"

Mari looks at the teacher. He seems young, boyish somehow. His light hair curls a little on his neck and over his ears. Straight-backed, with the eyes of an intelligent animal, both predator and protector. He's explaining something, turns to write on the blackboard. Mari looks at his neck, his back, his butt.

"You're staring," Tinka whispers.

Mari looks down at her desk, blushing.

"There's one essay I want to particularly highlight, because it's so good," the teacher says. "Which of you is Mari? Sorry, I don't remember everyone's name yet."

Mari flinches. Tinka smiles. Mari gestures hesitantly.

"Ah, there's Mari. Your text was really remarkably interesting. Where'd you get ideas like that?"

Mari blushes and can't say anything.

The teacher looks at her.

She smiles back at him, puts on her brightest almond-eyed smile.

"We've got a real thinker here," he says, and winks.

His statement hangs, echoing in the air. There's no rising inflection at the end. Mari, he said. Said aloud like that, it's a definition. He says the name Mari and places the bearer of that name at a precise point on the axis of space and time, the place where she belongs. Something feels like it matters. The teacher smiles at her. They both smile.

"How was school? How do you like your classes? Have you made any new friends yet?"

Mari's reading a magazine at the kitchen table and her mother has put on her mother face, dressed herself in solicitude like she does once every week, often on a Friday, like now, when she's left her work in the shiny, expensive briefcase in the front hall and has some time to be interested in her daughter's life. Mari gives a snort of feigned disgust, but she also feels a distant tenderness: it reminds her of when her mother asked her about her first day of grade school, in just the same way. And there are other memories:

striped socks and a pleated skirt, the school building and its smell of rye crisp and hamburger soup even when it wasn't lunchtime. Her mother's warm hand, safe, before she went to look for the desk with her name on it. And ice cream. Vanilla ice cream in a cardboard cup, the kind with an eye of jam in the middle. You ate it with a disposable wooden paddle, and sometimes as you were eating it you would taste more wood than ice cream.

"So how are things going at school?" her mother asks again, setting the teapot on the table to steep.

"Uh, good, yeah. I did meet this one girl, Tinka."

"What are your subjects?"

"Lang and lit. And history. And, um, foreign languages, and something else."

"What are your teachers like?"

Mari feels her face flush hot and her heart start to pound. She takes the croissant her mother offers, tears it into pieces, and pops them into her mouth nonchalantly. She's been thinking about the language and literature teacher. She's been finding things out about him. He's twenty-nine years old and his name is Julian Kanerva. Julian. Nailuj. Like a character in a novel. Mari feels like repeating that name, savoring its every contour. But the students don't call him Julian, they call him Kanerva. All of the girls in the upper grades drool over him just like Tinka did, but he has a wife and two kids. Mari has decided to stay after class the next time and ask him for reading recommendations. Maybe he'll notice that she's not just an ignorant little girl.

"Jeez, Mom. They're just, you know, normal teachers," she says, and turns the page of her magazine.

THAT EVENING, Mari goes into her room and closes the door. She looks at herself in the mirror. The dying game is beckoning again, and she invites it in, lets the thoughts come. Her hands find their way to the ticklish outlines of her body and she urges herself to think how amazing, how incredible it is, that this "me" exists.

She puts on a gossamer-thin, pale-blue nightgown, which her mother gave her for her sixteenth birthday. Her nipples poke out like buds under the delicate fabric. Her long dark hair falls to the lower edge of her shoulder blades, its shorter tendrils framing the white skin of her face.

She steps in front of the mirror, stands very close to it. This is a girl who's going to die, perhaps very soon. This is a girl who can die. A tear rolls down her cheek. First one, then another. Mari licks the tears up into her mouth. The thought of death comes easily. Now she's flying again, through the air, maybe tossed by a car, maybe because she jumped.

*One day we shall loosen from everything*
*We shall feel death's air under our wings*
*and become milder and wilder than we ever were*

And Mari opens her hands, there in front of the mirror, as her Winnie-the-Pooh clock ticks on the night table and a juniper branch scratches at the window. One day she'll come loose from everything, this girl. One day, perhaps very soon.

"*We'll become milder and wilder than we ever were,*" she says slowly, reciting the lines from a book of poems she got at the library.

Mari sighs, glances at herself in the mirror once more before going into the bathroom to brush her teeth. The children's toothpaste tastes like candy, cloying strawberry, thick, until it gets nice and foamy.

# Anja

"Do you mind telling me what these are?"

Marita was waving two slips of paper in front of Anja's face. It took a second before Anja realized what they were. Her goodbye notes. Inexplicably, she had left them on the table. They had been there for a week while newspapers and junk mail piled up on top of them and she had completely forgotten about them. Now Marita had found them.

Anja looked at her sister, whose tone was openly accusatory. She was standing in the kitchen with her shoes and coat still on. The silence was emphatic. The look on Marita's face was reproachful, with a hint of helplessness behind it. Anja could see her hands shaking. Marita's hands never shook. She was always calm, her face an even color, her voice melodious. But now she was trembling and her voice was tense.

Anja didn't say anything. She knew better than to try to explain, or to defend her privacy. Marita thought everything that happened around her was automatically her business.

She had come over unannounced. The harmony of the afternoon was thrown out of balance. She stood in the middle of the kitchen, not saying a word, her whole being projecting a force that had shoved its way into the brittle solidity of Anja's little world. Anja looked at Marita's shoes. Expensive, well-chosen shoes. Her sister was the kind of person who thought that expensive shoes were a sign to the world of her attitude, showed that she was serious about her ambitions in life. Shoes and home decor.

Anja sometimes thought about how precarious Marita's sense of her own life was: her daily routine at work, stopping at the store on the way home, dinner alone, watching television and waiting for her daughter to come home so she could go to bed. When Anja dropped by on one of those evenings, her sister would offer her tea from an expensive teapot and they would watch the evening news or a quiz show without talking, her sister leafing through decorating magazines, lifting her head now and then so Anja could see her gaze fixed on some faraway dream. Longing, sadness, hope were somewhere else, far from this life that had become tedious without her realizing it.

Of course Anja understood that Marita's interference was purely the dictate of kindness. She wanted to help her, to define the nature of the emergency and come to the rescue. That's the way it always was. Marita came and put things right. From Marita's point of view the matter was a simple one: people had to be rescued. From themselves, from the world, from their circumstances.

Anja purposely hesitated over her explanation. She felt like just saying nothing. Her sister had sat down at the table and started to pull herself together.

"Is this how low you've sunk?" she asked in a strangled voice.

Anja snorted. She registered the shame bouncing around somewhere in her stomach. She tried to quiet its ruckus with hauteur.

"How low I've sunk? Who are you to decide what my situation is? You don't have the slightest idea what's been going on."

"Well, these notes give me a pretty good idea what kind of difficulties you're in."

Anja just snorted again. The shame was overwhelming her. Her sister had collected herself, was reprising the attitude she'd had since childhood, redrawing the invisible lines between them that had always defined them: Marita was the one who decided the course of events, the one who knew how to handle things.

"We can't just drop the matter," she said crisply. "I have to make sure you get appropriate treatment, therapy ..."

"A lot of good therapy is. As if there weren't enough medical treatment around here already, with my husband under twenty-four-hour care."

"I'll make an appointment for you myself," Marita said through tight lips.

"I won't go," Anja said.

"Yes, you will."

＊

AT THE END OF SEPTEMBER the light was already at a slant, ponderous and ripe like an old woman's wisdom. The bus slowed as it came to an intersection. I have clear boundaries here, Anja thought. I have to keep the fear outside me. Draw the line at my skin. Hope can stay in the pure space within my body. Everything else is dirt, meaningless dross that doesn't belong inside me.

She got off at the edge of downtown. She watched her

feet as they continued along the wet road toward the hospital building across the street.

She stepped through the sliding doors into the building. The broad linoleum horizon of the hospital lobby opened up in front of her. The woman at reception was typing at her keyboard with a tense expression. Anja went to the counter.

"Excuse me. I'm here for an evaluation."

"Take a number, please!"

The woman didn't raise her eyes from the computer screen. Anja looked around in confusion. She didn't see anyone else waiting.

"But," she said uncertainly, "there's no line."

The woman took an inordinate amount of time before looking up from her screen, to make it clear that she was annoyed. She screwed up her mouth with an exasperated air, lowered her chin, and stared at Anja from under her eyebrows. An undisguisedly artificial smile spread across her face, expressing the utmost condescension.

"It's not about lines, it's about order," she said sharply.

Her smile didn't curdle. It was like a plastic doll's smile. It gave Anja the creeps. She let out an off-key laugh to ease the tension, but saw immediately that it was a mistake.

"There's nothing funny about it. Just take a number," the woman repeated, like a tape recorder.

"All right. Sorry."

Anja walked to the other side of the lobby and took a number from the feed. Twenty-six. The woman bent over her computer again and Anja was left standing there with the number in her hand. The digital number display on the wall showed twenty-three. The woman behind the desk pressed the bell. *Bing!* Anja took a couple of cautious steps toward the counter. The woman raised a forbidding hand and shook her head, her mouth a straight line. Anja retreated dutifully. The woman looked through her with a blank expression on her face. The second hand of the clock on the wall ticked five steps forward. The waiting room was empty. The only sound was the steady pumping of the filter in an aquarium built into the wall. The woman at the reception desk opened her mouth and paused significantly. Anja glanced at the number on her slip — yes, it was definitely twenty-six. The woman pressed the bell again. *Bing!* The number on the display changed to twenty-five.

The aquarium bubbled. Anja felt the sweat roll down her back. Her heavy coat was too warm. The slip of paper with the number on it trembled in her hand. She had to look at it again. *Bing!* The number display flashed twenty-six. Anja walked hesitantly to the counter. The woman smiled her plastic smile.

"We have rules, you see," she said. "We have to wait five seconds between numbers."

"Right. Rules," Anja said, defeated.

"What is your reason for coming?"

"It's, um, psychiatric. I have an appointment at two."

"And what would the name of the attending doctor be?"

"I don't ... I don't remember," Anja sputtered.

She was overcome with dread. Why couldn't she remember the name? Was it Valtimo? Laskimo? She shouldn't try to guess, or the receptionist would think she was making a joke at her expense.

"Well?" the woman said.

"I can't remember," Anja said unhappily. "But my name is Aropalo, Anja Anneli Aropalo."

"We can't be messing around with patients' names here!"

the woman said, with obvious relish. Anja was trapped again, a prisoner of her ignorance.

These people, she thought — people like this woman — rule the world. They're always throwing the book at someone, always have, even when they were little girls and boys, and then they grow up and become teachers and tax auditors and receptionists and they're everywhere, throwing the book at people for anything they do, making anyone who opposes them squirm under their thumb and beg them for the right to exist. Where did these rulers of the world come from? Maybe their parents had humiliated them so much when they were growing up that they had to put themselves in charge, to make other people pay for the way they were treated as children. Or maybe there was something in them, some inherently evil element that no manner of exorcism or incantation could uproot. A demon working through them, spreading its perverted fruit.

The receptionist was just getting started.

"Ma'am, how do you think it would be if every Aropalo in town made an appointment at the same time? We would have a hundred Aropalos here, every one with a different problem. You would come with a mental-health problem and be sent to chemotherapy, and some unfortunate cancer sufferer would be given antidepressants! How do you think we would sort out a mess like that? All hell would break loose."

"Uh-huh. All hell. Right," Anja said, sinking into a hole in the ground.

"So please give me your social services identification number."

Anja gave her the number.

"You see?" the receptionist said in a teacherly tone, typing the number into the computer. "Now we're getting somewhere.

You are Anja Anneli Aropalo and you have suicidal thoughts and your sister made an appointment for you. And here's your doctor's name. Anna-Liisa Valtimo. Your number tells us your identity and your whole situation."

"Right," was all Anja could say.

"So, you'll be down that hallway. The door on the end. Go in there and wait until your name is called."

"Thank you."

Anja trudged toward the double doors. She felt outside of herself as she walked. She went through the door and found another waiting area. The walls of the room had the same bands of light as the day room at the nursing home. It was quiet. The door of one room was ajar. Restless, Anja stood up and examined the door. Should she just wait here until she was called? She heard quiet voices from a distance, and the low gurgle of a coffee maker. There were fluorescent lights set into the ceiling, shaded by thin, pastel-colored fabric. They reminded her of stage props, like a scrim. Anja felt anxiety rising. She looked at the door again. Her appointment was for two o'clock, and it was already five minutes past.

She got up and walked warily toward the door. The soft sound of her own footsteps was almost startling. She opened it a little: the room was empty. She opened the door wider and stood on the threshold. Suddenly she flinched: in the corner, in a narrow section of the room that the door cast into shadow, there was an armchair, and in the armchair sat a woman. The woman looked at her with interest, as if she'd caught Anja in some childish misbehavior. Watchful triumph shone from her face like an exclamation point. Anja felt the tremble that followed alarm; the embarrassment of being surprised caused a flash of shame to redden her face.

"Oh, uh ..." She coughed. "I didn't know you were in here. I was waiting in there."

The woman still didn't say anything. There was a trace of a tight sort of smile on her lips, which seemed to Anja like nothing but ghoulish mockery after what had just happened.

"So is this ... are you a psychiatrist?"

"What do I look like?" the woman said in a friendly voice.

"I didn't mean ... I just thought ... I see."

Anja went quiet, her explanation smothered in its insignificance. She didn't want to say anything inconsiderate, to make the woman draw any conclusions about her.

"Would it be easier if I called myself the on-duty consultant?" the woman asked, still dubiously friendly.

Anja sat down in the chair across from her.

"So," the psychiatrist said.

"So," Anja said.

"I understand you're going through a period of change in your life."

"Yes."

The woman was silent. Anja didn't speak. What was there to say? Nothing noteworthy came to mind. It really is the same kind of light, she thought, trying to think of something to say. *Presence is never mute*, it said on a framed card on the desk. There was also a basket of tissues. People came here, cried bitterly about where their lives were, and wiped their noses on the tissues placed thoughtfully next to their chair; closed the door behind them, went to the store, bought some chicken legs and ground beef, went home, and watched the evening news. *Presence is never mute.* Is it an empty or full feeling, mute or clamorous, to yearn for something with all your senses, sleeping and awake? Mute. Above all, mute.

"How do you feel about your sister making this appointment for you? What kinds of feelings does that bring up?"

Anja's lips narrowed to a thin line. "My sister has her own ideas about things."

"And now her idea seems to be that you're in need of help."

Anja was quiet. It didn't matter one way or the other to her. The psychiatrist was silent again for a long time, then she said, as if starting over, "What things do you see as meaningful in your life? What's most important to you?"

"Nothing," Anja said blankly.

She sounded like an obstinate child who hadn't got her way. *Nothing.* It echoed in the room with a bright sound, ricocheted from the walls and hit Anja in the back of the head. The worst part was that it wasn't a lie. Not that nothing mattered to Anja. It was just that the most meaningful thing was the gaping emptiness that echoed in every hollow second. Or was it the weight of the seconds? All that had been and was gone made the moments heavy, made it difficult to breathe.

She had an urge to disrupt events somehow, their randomness, their meaninglessness.

In the first years of the illness, when the signs were already there but there was no diagnosis yet, and neither of them had the information, or the courage, to recognize the seriousness of the situation, Anja had thought that her husband had another woman. He had started to come home late in the evening, a little later every week.

ONE THURSDAY her husband doesn't come home until late at night. Anja's waiting in the dark kitchen, trying to act nonchalant.

"Hi," her husband says, as if to a co-worker.

Anja pauses before answering. "Hi yourself."

He turns on the light and puts a bag of sweet rolls on the table. Dallas rolls with butter filling. She can tell from the bag that he bought them at a gas station along the highway. Anja draws her own conclusions; she doesn't trouble herself to remark on them.

He goes to the cupboard and takes out a pot lid. What's he going to do with that? she wonders. A pot lid on Thursday night at one a.m. He takes out the rolls and puts them on the lid. There are seven of them.

"So you're thinking of having some rolls and coffee?"

"Yes."

"You're thinking we'll have rolls and coffee in the middle of the night."

"That's right."

"Have you been at work?"

"Yes, at work."

"And was it a long day?"

"It sure was."

He takes out the cheese cover and puts it over the rolls. Anja watches his actions, surprised. He takes the coffee pot from the coffee maker, fills it with water, and pours enough in the coffee maker for ten cups.

"What the hell are you doing, getting ready for a coffee party?" Anja says. "You don't come home till the middle of the night, and now you're going to make some coffee? Have a nice cup of coffee with your wife to end the day? Don't think I don't know what's going on."

"Damn it," he roars. "What's your problem? I'm making coffee in my own kitchen."

Anja feels like crying. Her question comes out wrapped

around the first inevitable sob, sounding more forlorn than she intended:

"Where have you been?"

He relents, approaches her. For the first time, Anja sees a lost look in his eyes that she didn't notice in her anger. He strokes her hair with his fingers. His hands are shaking.

He tries to smile, but his voice is squeezed to a narrow, frightened snort. "I took a wrong turn."

"What? Where?"

"I don't know."

"What do you mean you don't know?"

"I don't know. I just don't know. I got lost."

He smiles an agonized smile, a pained grimace pierced with a certainty, and Anja suddenly wants to say something, anything, to make him stop smiling like that.

What does she say? What does she do? Maybe she says what her husband wants to hear, what they both want to hear. Maybe she kisses him and laughs, teases him for his absent-mindedness, tries to break through the armor of fear that has surrounded them. *You're so scatterbrained*, she might say, gently pinching him.

There they sit, husband and wife, eating rolls and drinking coffee on Thursday night at one a.m., and neither of them says anything about the fact that there are seven rolls, and that they're on a pot lid under a cheese cover.

Neither of them mentions that.

THE PSYCHIATRIST was looking at Anja with a stupid, sympathetic look on her face.

"So what do you say we make an appointment for another visit?" she said in a patient tone. "How does next week sound?

Maybe on Tuesday at two again?"

Anja said nothing, indicating assent. They shook hands and Anja closed the door behind her. When she got to the end of the hallway her anxiety faded, and anger mixed with shame took its place: she wouldn't be coming back.

SHE SPENT THE REST of the afternoon at the library. At first the events of the day rattled around in her head and made her heart race. But the musty peacefulness of the library gradually settled her mind.

On the way home she saw a waxwing in a tree. It was standing on a branch, silent. It wouldn't sing again until the spring. The afternoon was already darkening a little; the last light of the sun had come down from the sky and flowed in a red haze from the tops of the naked trees and down their trunks to the ground. In the fall, everything turned pink like this just before dark. There was no snow yet to lend its glow of cold, sharp light. And any ice there was on the ground filtered through the soil's own frosty darkness in a soft shimmer, painted a gentle purple by the extinguishing light of the sun. Sky and land, and between them a person breathing the air. A waxwing perched on a rowan branch next to a bus stop, as if it were keeping watch over the descending darkness, the sky and land.

When she got home, Anja took the groceries out of the bag and put them on the kitchen table and turned on the television. The comforting theme music of the early-evening news soothed her. She took one of her husband's shirts out of the closet and sat down on the sofa. She closed her eyes and read her husband's familiar smell from the folds of the shirt — it still lingered there in the clinging lint, along the seams. She felt herself stepping back where she belonged, as if this were the axis around which her being turned. Safe in the familiar smell, she let the longing descend from the throbbing hollow of her temple and flow through her shoulders and into her limbs and rest there, like a weight.

# Mari

SATURDAY EVENING at Tinka's house before the school social. Tinka is in front of the mirror, drawing a line around her eyes. Mari is sitting on the bed, reading *Cosmopolitan*. Tinka is dressed in a short denim skirt and fishnet stockings. The crossed straps of her wonder bra, like the ones the models are wearing, are visible under her mesh-like blouse.

Mari is nervously scanning the magazine's tips on intimate contact: kisses, sexual positions. Tinka seems to know so much. Mari feels like she has a lot to learn.

"Do my boobs look all right?" Tinka asks, agonizing over her reflection. "Don't they look kind of flabby?"

"Don't be silly," Mari says. "Everybody stares at them. They're just right."

"Hey!" Tinka says. "Wanna borrow my Gossard tonight? Let's make you look so good the men will hit on you!"

"Uh ... nah."

"Yes, yes!" Tinka screams, searching the wardrobe for her other bras.

Mari looks in horror at the bra dangling from Tinka's hand.

"Just put this on, and some eyeliner. You'd be so pretty if you just dressed up a little," Tinka says.

"OK."

Mari undresses shyly, the cool air of the room puckering the tips of her breasts into dark rosettes. Tinka looks the other way, but Mari can see her watching in the mirror. The wonder bra's cups are too big: they look like tea cozies, their rigid lace domes loosely covering her pale breasts, centimeters of space between their arched edges and her skin.

"Maybe you could put some toilet paper in them," Tinka says.

She wads some tissue into pads to fit inside the bra. Mari puts them in and looks in the mirror. Her artificial breasts puff out in front of her.

"I dunno," Mari says.

"No, you should wear them. And we'll give you devastating eyes," Tinka says with enthusiasm.

She paints bright almond eyes on Mari and fluffs her hair. Mari looks different: in the mirror is the outline of an unknown woman. Tinka smiles fondly at her in the mirror.

"Look at you now. You're pretty."

"Oh."

Pleasure flashes down from her shoulders, lingers around her ribs, then curls up to pulse sleepily in the region of her lower abdomen.

Tinka opens a bottle of wine she got somewhere with the practiced air of an adult.

"Where'd you get that?" Mari asks.

"My parents think they're wine connoisseurs. They have dozens of them. They never notice if one's missing."

"Is it expensive wine, then?"

"I dunno," Tinka says, lifting her slender shoulders and taking a swig. "Drink up."

Mari takes a drink, too. The wine tastes bad, sour. A haze of secrecy wraps itself up inside the two of them.

THE PARTY IS in a room on loan from a university club. Only students from the high school are supposed to be there, but Mari can see that there are a lot more people than that. She doesn't see any chaperones. There's a boy with dreadlocks vomiting pink bile into the potted torch just outside the door. Mari is scared. The toilet-paper breasts poke out from under her Gossard bra, two unconvincing lumps, even under her coat. Tinka is immediately at home, starts flirting with a group of boys as soon as she walks in the door. Someone offers her a one-liter soda bottle filled with a pink mixture, the same color as the stomach contents of the dreadlocks boy, splattered onto the snow a moment ago. She pays no more attention to Mari.

Mari wanders around the drunken crowd looking for faces she knows. A boy from her chemistry class comes up to say hi, staggering, smiling drunkenly.

Mari doesn't know what to say.

"So, hi," the boy says. "What was your name again?"

"Mari. Just Mari."

"That's right. Mari," he slurs, swaying toward her. "Mari, may I say something?"

Mari feels a familiar sinking feeling in the pit of her stomach. The boy bends over toward the base of her ear and grabs one of her breasts.

"You got a hell of a nice rack there," he whispers, with a mucousy snuffle.

Mari backs away, alarmed, and runs through the crowd to the bathroom. Safe within a cubicle, she swallows her tears and pulls the tissue out of her bra. Her hands are shaking and sobs escape into the air.

Baby, she thinks, scolding herself. You're such a sissy-ass baby. What are you whimpering about? You knew what would happen.

Someone pounds on the door of the stall and insists it's their turn. Mari takes a deep breath. She's got to pull herself together. Be a big girl.

When she gets back to the party room, Tinka rushes up to her.

"Where've you been? I've been looking for you," she whispers. "I've got the perfect man for you."

"No, I don't wanna. I really don't."

"Don't be childish. I spent hours on your hair for just this thing."

Tinka pulls her onto the dance floor and there's nothing she can do but go along. The lights start to flicker and Tinka pushes her toward a boy standing nearby. Mari can't see anything in the flickering light, but she can feel the roughness of the boy's cheek and his damp t-shirt stuck to his back. He comes closer and grabs her butt. They dance, pressed against each other, slowly swaying, although the music is still fast.

Mari can feel his hardening organ under his jeans.

He shoves his tongue in her mouth.

She tries to remember *Cosmopolitan*'s advice about kissing. The boy's mouth tastes like beer and cigarettes. Your tongue shouldn't be too stiff, she remembers, and you should keep your mouth moving. She tries to kiss the way the magazine recommends. He pushes his tongue farther in until she feels like she can't breathe anymore, and has to move away.

He smiles.

"Would you like something to drink?" he says. "We could go sit somewhere if you like." She can see his eyes for the first time.

"Sure."

MARI SIPS A GREEN DRINK through a straw. The boy swigs a beer. People are even drunker now, some of them hanging on to each other in front of the door.

"I know a nice spot in that building over there," the boy says. "Wanna see it?"

They walk across the courtyard to a red sauna house. He opens the door with his own key. It's dark and stuffy inside. There's a low, worn table surrounded by an old, dark-green plush sofa set and a fireplace in one wall, its white bricks blackened with smoke. There are corks mixed in with the firewood, shining among the dry bark like forlorn, impudent eyes.

The boy sits down on the sofa. "Come here."

"How come you have a key?"

"Let's just say I know the right people."

"Ah."

Mari sits down next to him. It occurs to her that she hasn't asked him his name. She swallows uncomfortably and draws a pattern in the carpet under the table with her foot. The carpet has black shapes like salmiakki lozenges, paler in the middle than on the edges. The boy slips his hand under her blouse.

Mari lets it happen.

He skillfully unfastens the hooks of the borrowed bra and cups his hand over her breast.

"I've always liked women with small breasts," he says. "Little fairy creatures like you."

Mari listens, testing her feelings. There's a vase of dried wildflowers in the window. Someone picked them in the summer, maybe for midsummer. She doesn't really feel anything. The boy sucks on her breast and unfastens his pants with his other hand.

"Will you ... can you suck it?" he asks hoarsely.

Mari looks at his penis. She bends over and tastes it hesitantly. It doesn't taste as bad as you'd imagine. It doesn't really taste like anything. A salty, slightly musty aroma. She sucks on it gingerly and thinks about strawberry ice cream and mint chocolates, pear soda, raspberry popsicles that you could only get at the store in the summer when she was little. The popsicle was shaped like a hand with the index and middle fingers held up and you always started by biting them off.

Frosty raspberry, she thinks, to keep herself from gagging.

"Don't just slobber on it. Suck a little harder. *See voo play.*"

Mari starts to feel nauseated. She tries to think of nice things.

Grapes.

Licorice drops.

He pushes his penis deeper into her mouth, pokes it against the back of her throat.

Strawberries and whipped cream in July.

Dried pineapple and lemon meringue.

It isn't working. Mari sits up and runs to the porch to get some fresh air. She feels dizzy, like she might throw up. Her bra is hanging from her left shoulder by one strap. She gasps for air to keep from vomiting. The boy comes to the porch, snapping his pants up, disgusted.

"Yeah, sorry. You coulda told me you weren't experienced."

Mari is quiet, looks away.

Beyond the terrace is a wooded area, and beyond the woods a stream glimmers. You can run there to swim after a sauna in the summer, Mari thinks. First a really hot steam, then a plop into the soft, cool water. The summer night caressing your bare skin, like sweet, pale velvet. She can't think of anything important to say. She looks at a bend of the stream covered with a crust of ice. There's a dock and she can see ducks underneath it. They're very still and quiet, as if they're stuck there.

"So. Think I'll go have a smoke," the boy says.

"Yeah. OK."

"See ya."

MARI WALKS HOME. The temperature has dipped below freezing. On a fall night like this it can start to snow, the rain hardening into snowflakes that drift gently to the ground and cover everything up, make everything softer and quieter.

She thinks about the boy at the party, about the sucking. Anyway, she's done that now, tried it at least, had a little taste of it.

The light-hearted feeling she has surprises her: she's experienced now — not very experienced, but a little.

She puts the embarrassment and shame behind her. This is a good thing. Definitely a good thing.

Mari gets home, takes off her coat, and climbs the familiar stairs to her room. She opens a dresser drawer, the one where she keeps her underwear. Under a pair of Winnie-the-Pooh underpants she has hidden a small kitchen knife. The thought of marking herself is exciting. It's also a game. She has stroked the outlines of her skin, drawn the boundaries of her pale flesh with her fingers and thought: There are girls who do this — keep themselves wounded, keep themselves open. Maybe there are boys like that, too; she doesn't know. But there are girls like that, anyway. The idea fascinates her. It may have first come to her when she was in the sauna and accidentally ran into the stove door. And there it was: a burn, a brand; indisputable proof of her existence in the world. Or maybe she'd been slicing bread with a sharp knife and — oops, one false move, a gash in her smooth skin. Blood flowing bright along her pale flesh, tracing the line between herself and the world. She doesn't know whether she'll like this game. She doesn't know if it's right for her. But she wants to try.

She takes the knife out of the underwear drawer with a trembling hand. She's prepared: she has gauze and bandages. She sits in the corner, rolls up her sleeve, takes hold of the knife. She doesn't know how it's supposed to feel. Should she feel tormented? She doesn't feel particularly tormented. She tries to listen, tries to invite a feeling of anguish. There are girls — and maybe even boys — who take their longing to their skin this way, girls who draw themselves, draw themselves out with a knife, a razor blade, a shard of glass. There are girls — and maybe even boys — who put themselves in the moment this way. Maybe they're tormented, maybe they're always longing to be somewhere else. Mari isn't tormented. But she does feel a longing, definitely a longing. For something, someplace else, somewhere inside herself. The longing is reason enough. The longing is permission.

Mari presses the knife against her wrist. For some reason her wrist is the first place she thinks of. Of course she can't cut herself there — not on her wrist. She presses the blade of the knife against the translucent skin of her wrist just to try it, just to sense the nearness of death, its incontrovertible possibility. She presses slightly, just a little bit, enough to make a little scratch in the skin. How strangely fragile it is, the pale skin that covers her flesh and veins, pale skin that forms the boundary that contains the totality of this life. Up close, the shreds of skin torn by the blade of the knife look like lace.

Mari turns her arm over, rolls her sleeve up higher. Carefully, feeling her way, she presses the knife against the skin of her left upper arm. The knife sinks into the flesh but doesn't break it. She doesn't know if she has this in her. Maybe this is a mistake. Maybe she ought to go to bed, dream about summer and ice cream, wake up in the morning, eat toast with marmalade and watch Sunday-morning cartoons. Maybe she ought to be someone other than this girl sitting in a corner of her room with a knife in her hand. But she wants to try this game, to try it on like an unusual-looking coat glimpsed in a department store.

She holds her breath, lifts the knife a little distance away, and slices a quick, sharp gash into the skin of her arm. She flinches, hears her own groan, hears how her voice cuts through the soft repose of night. Her own voice astonishes her. It's a strange, entirely new voice, strange and new like it is at the height of passion, groaning as she touched herself the first few times, finding her most sensitive spots. She cuts another gash with the knife. There's a hot throbbing around the wounds. It feels good. This is pure, this is where the thing is that says me. Suddenly it's here, this moment, just this moment and a sweet pain. No longing. If longing is a cloak, it's slipped away now, rolled up into a little throbbing knot at the open place on her arm. She takes a deep breath. This suits me, she thinks. It's right.

She takes some gauze from the drawer and wraps it around the cuts. She puts on a long-sleeved shirt and goes into the

bathroom to rinse the knife. The blood mixes with the water —
her own blood. It mixes with the water and disappears down
the drain. This is right for me, she thinks. It suits me.

MARI IS HIGH on a stairway that leads steeply downward —
too steeply, reaching farther than the eye can see. The stairs
aren't really stairs, they're bleachers. Mari is standing on the
bleachers, high up, and the bleachers sway and there's a noise
all around her. She stretches one foot toward the next level
down but she can't reach it. The bleachers are swaying and
she can't get down. Kanerva is next to her, has been there the
whole time. Kanerva is her rescuer. He looks at her without
smiling and says something in a muffled voice. Mari can't hear
him. She reaches out to him. Kanerva puts his hand on Mari's
breast, cups it in his hand and says, his voice clear now, that
everything's allowed, you just have to watch the flow, make
sure it doesn't reach flood stage. The flow? The smell, you
mean? Mari says. No, the flow, Kanerva answers, and smiles.
The tower has changed into a classroom and he tells her to
watch the doorway, still cupping her left breast in his hand.
Everything is all right as long as the flood doesn't reach this
high, as long as no blood flows over the threshold.

# Anja

"WHERE ARE WE GOING? Do we have to go somewhere? They have fruit pudding here. As much as you want."

Anja's husband sat meekly on the bed in his room. Anja was bent over his feet, tying his shoes. She was planning to take him home for the afternoon to look at the changing leaves. They had talked about a trip home many times, and he had always been enthused at the idea and even remembered the things around their house — the large ash tree at the end of the garden walk, and the forest trail at the back of the yard, where you might see a hare in the evening. But now he didn't want to go, had been harping for two hours on all the reasons it would be better to stay at the nursing home. Anja tried to channel her annoyance into bustling activity. She tied his shoelaces a bit tighter than she intended, and wiped the saliva at the corner of his mouth with a quick flick of a tissue.

"No, we're definitely going," she said crisply as she combed his sparse hair with brisk strokes. "We've been talking about it for days."

The change of place had to be stressful for him. Strange sights and the noise of the city, and always the same cab driver who talked to them about this and that without realizing the nature of his condition, glancing politely but curiously at her husband's reactions in the rear-view mirror. "How come they lowered the tax rates? They go down and our health benefits go down with them," the driver would chatter, her husband nodding uncertainly. "Yeah. That's right," he always said, shy and helpless, not knowing what he was talking about, or to whom. The last thing she wanted to admit was that she was ashamed. And she didn't admit it. All she felt was a crackling rage toward all the stupid people who wanted to test her husband's fuzzy understanding.

As they stepped out of his room and into the hallway, a relative of the old woman with dementia who lived in the neighboring room walked by and greeted them. He was a little over forty, and Anja had sometimes wondered if he was the old woman's son. She hadn't yet formed friendships with any of the other residents' families, although she'd heard that the nursing home had an active family association. There was nothing she desired less than to identify herself with that peculiar, random group of people, united only by their helplessness as they watched the inner selves of the ones they loved stripped away day by day.

Without thinking, Anja turned back to look as they passed each other and noticed that the man was looking back at her, too. The stranger's gaze felt inappropriate somehow, made her uncomfortable. He wasn't smiling, just looking. The second stretched interminably, layered between them into years, until Anja turned her head and took her husband's hand to help him over the threshold.

THE YARD WAS FILLED with an invisible mist — the damp scent of the end of October. Anja hadn't raked it enough: new leaves had dropped from the birches and the neighbor's maple tree, and the rain had turned them into a dense, fragrant mat. She and her husband used to take care of the yard together. Now she did it alone, and didn't have time for it.

He stood on the porch and looked at the yard with an unfathomable expression on his face.

"What? What do you see?" she asked.

"Nothing. I was just thinking," he said, almost shyly, "that I know this place."

Anja's heart leaped. These fragile flashes of memory were heart-wrenching. He turned to her, and there was something roguish, teasing, in his expression. Sometimes it was hard for her to believe that he really didn't remember. Sometimes an absurd thought would come to her: What if he's just pretending, playing a joke on me? Sometimes his face would freeze in a good-natured grin, his eyes flashing. The kind of expression he used to have when he told a joke or poked fun at something. What if he was testing her? But of course she knew he wasn't.

When they got inside, he went to the kitchen and took out a wineglass from the cupboard.

"Would you like some white wine?" he asked, as if they were on some kind of date.

Anja was baffled. What was he thinking about? Was he going to try to get her drunk? Did he want to get drunk? But he wasn't thinking anything. It was just another distant memory.

"Yes, let's," she answered.

They cordially opened a bottle that had been set aside for his sixtieth birthday. It occurred to her that there wouldn't be any sixties for him. The fact was a desolate knot in her belly. They went into the living room. His stride had become a shuffle. Even though she knew it came from his medication, she found it annoying. Shamble-footed. And it wasn't going to get any better. Some wine spilled from his glass onto the living-room rug. He never would have spilled it before, she thought.

He sat down on the sofa and patted the cushion next to him convivially, inviting her to sit there. She sat down. He had an odd look on his face.

"How long have you had this place?" he asked, taking a sip of wine.

"This place? I guess you don't remember. This is our home. We've lived here for twenty years."

"I see," he said.

He was quiet for a moment, sipping his wine and looking out the window. Soon he turned back to her and put his hand on her knee.

"So, if we agree on one whole night, would fifteen hundred marks be enough?"

Anja looked into his eyes and saw that their two worlds had become separated from each other. Orbits that had once intersected, now light years away. Their world had revolved inside those points of intersection, had showed itself naked and true. That was how happiness installed itself in a person's life, if happiness was their lot. And now, a stranger sitting here, his eyes empty, his expression helpless.

"You misunderstand," Anja said firmly, removing his hand from her knee. "I'm your wife, and this is our home."

His gaze went hazy: a veil fell over the gleam in his eye as if to mark the end of a performance. Forgetting. The curtain of forgetting. His face went in one second from engaged to baffled, bewildered.

"Home?" he said hesitantly. "I want to go home," he said, his voice hoarse and quiet, like a child whispering to his mother when the adults' visit was lasting too long.

"This is your home," Anja said again.

"The other home. The place where I can get some good soup, or fruit pudding," he said. "The pudding place."

The maple tree still blazed outside. The brilliant ivy glowed where it peeped around the edges of the window. Anja took his hand in hers and they stood up, hand in hand. She noticed he leaned his weight on her, trusted her. At the living-room door he turned around one more time and let his gaze wander over the room, as if to impress on his mind the angles and arches of the place, the bend of the light, the shadows on the wall from the maple leaves moving in the silent wind.

"I was just thinking," he said, almost in a whisper. "Were we happy?"

Anja pressed her finger over his open mouth, rubbing his temple with her other hand. There was desperation in his eyes.

"Let's go now," she said. "Let's go home."

BACK IN HIS BED at the nursing home, he sighed with relief and smacked his lips. He had squeezed her hand uneasily the whole way there in the taxi, the blue veins tight under his paper-thin, creased skin. Anja stroked his head and sat silently beside his bed. Time became meaningless, the seconds and minutes disappearing into nothingness.

It wasn't until she roused herself and got up to leave that she noticed the milky softness of dusk flowing into the corners and realized that hours had passed.

She got up and walked out of the room, closing the door behind her.

"It's like a kaleidoscope, isn't it?"

She was startled, thought at first that one of the nursing-home residents was talking to her. She turned and saw the same man that had greeted her earlier that day.

"I'm sorry," she said coolly. "I don't quite understand."

"A mind with dementia," he said, smiling warily. "It's like a kaleidoscope."

"Yeah," Anja said, noncommittal. She didn't want to get caught up in a conversation with a stranger about the peculiar-ities of dementia. "I never thought of it that way."

"But it is," the man persisted, surprisingly bold. "The way we analyze reality doesn't really apply at all when a person starts to forget. Other rules apply, fragile rules that are hard to describe to outsiders. But there is a kind of hazy logic to them, some sense to what's remembered and what sinks away into the dark. Kaleidoscope logic. Reality is fragmented and the pieces come together in a new way."

Anja's interest was beginning to awaken. The man seemed sincere.

"Is she your mother?" she asked, gesturing toward the old woman's room.

He nodded.

"My husband," she said in answer to the question in his eyes. "Seven years. That's how long he's been ... sick."

"He loved you a lot," the man said, taking her aback. "You can see it in the way he trusts you."

Anja wasn't sure whether she wanted to continue this conversation. She took a few steps forward. He walked with her. The past tense he had used echoed in her mind: *he loved you.* An indicator of time past: love, loved, has loved.

They stepped into the fresh air outside. Maple leaves danced across the asphalt pathway in furious miniature tornadoes. The man looked at the sky, turned up his coat collar. Clouds moving north-west. Dark, majestic shadows.

"Well, see you later," he said awkwardly.

"Goodbye," Anja said.

From the bicycle rack he took a mountain bike — the kind you usually saw young boys riding — jumped onto it, nodded goodbye, and rode away.

As he turned the corner and disappeared from sight, it started to rain. Large drops poured onto the asphalt, angled by the wind, and she realized that she hadn't introduced herself or asked his name.

# Mari

"MARI, CAN YOU stay behind for a minute?" Kanerva says.

Class is over, and Mari is standing at her desk, gathering up her things deliberately slowly. The rest of the students clatter off to lunch. Tinka looks at Mari in amazement and then at the teacher. Mari's embarrassed.

"I have those books for you," Kanerva says, without seeming to sense Tinka's surprise or Mari's embarrassment.

"Oh, yeah," Mari says.

"I'll wait for you at the cafeteria entrance," Tinka says, and leaves, looking behind her once more as she goes out the door.

Kanerva smiles at Mari. That smile again — curious, open. Mari feels like a mystery woman under her teacher's gaze: he looks as if he wants to find out her secrets. The October afternoon is spilling its soft light into the quiet classroom and two people stand facing each other. A bridge between their eyes. Mari wants to reach outside herself and dive into those eyes. She knows there's no turning back.

"I brought you a few of the classics. It never hurts to know the thoughts of those who came before us," he says, playful.

He hands her two books: Tolstoy's *Anna Karenina* and

Dumas's *Camille*. The books have a stale smell, the smell of the thoughts of the past.

"Yeah," Mari manages to say, hanging her head to hide her embarrassment.

She turns to leave and the teacher says bye and Mari says bye. Bye, they say. It's the fifteenth of October, Mari thinks as she walks down the hallway to the cafeteria. The trees outside are shedding their leaves and the sap is flowing through the hollows of her warm body. In the cafeteria, she squeezes her thighs together. The wet between her legs feels slippery, pulsing, and she feels like she's been named, a woman, whole.

"Did you screw right there, or what?" Tinka asks teasingly, but there's a bruised tone to her words.

"Idiot. Of course not," Mari says, but she's unable to conceal her pleasure.

Mari eats her frankfurt gravy and potatoes but she doesn't taste her food — she just keeps thinking about Kanerva, the dimples when he smiles, his clear gaze.

"Hey!" Tinka says. "You could start going out and then you could tell me all the filthy bits. Tell me what kind of a dick he has."

"Stop it." Mari giggles, blushing.

Tinka's fork stops mid-motion. She gives Mari an appraising look. "So, what does he want from you?"

"Well, we talked about philosophy and literature," Mari says, smiling mysteriously.

"And bullshit," Tinka says, biting into her rye crisp and crunching it loudly. She picks up a paper napkin with a roguish grin and dips it in her water glass. "How about a demonstration, so you'll be ready when the time comes. Watch closely: here goes Mari's virginity."

"Stop it." Mari giggles again.

Tinka stretches the wet napkin over the water glass.

"This is the hymen," Tinka mutters. "And here comes Kanerva's throbbing cock," she roars, picking up a knife and pointing it at the glass. "Oh! I want you inside me! Oh!" she continues, piercing the napkin-hymen with the knife and babbling theatrically. "Oh, yes! Thank you! Now I am a woman."

Mari is blushing. The cafeteria cook approaches with the drinks cart and shoots a poisonous glance at Tinka, who continues her tomfoolery.

"Girls, if you're finished eating, go outside. You should be ashamed of yourselves, playing with your food like that. Big girls like you."

"Yeah, yeah." Tinka sighs and puts down her knife.

"The old hag's just jealous. She's such a dried-up old pine cone that she doesn't have any market value anymore," Tinka whispers once the cook has passed. "By the way," she continues, "how'd it go on Saturday night, with that guy I set you up with?"

Mari gives Tinka a sly look. Tinka smiles. Mari has already learned; she knows how this game is played. You have to smile. A lot. And never reveal failure.

"Well?" Tinka presses.

"Well, of course, I put it in my mouth. And then ..."

"And then?"

Mari remembers the *Cosmopolitan* article on sex positions: "Give Your Man Pleasure Beyond His Wildest Dreams." From behind? Definitely too ordinary for Tinka. Standing up against the wall?

"And then we screwed standing up, leaning against the wall," Mari says, looking her straight in the eye.

"You didn't!"

"Yes, we did."

Admiration shines in Tinka's eyes. Mari is startled by the power of her own lie, the ease with which it slipped out of her mouth, and the impression it makes on Tinka. A thing that came out of nowhere and somehow became part of reality. She plucks nervously at her napkin and hopes that Tinka won't ask for any details.

# Julian

JULIAN KANERVA let his gaze wander over the rows of students. They always looked the same, younger every year, self-sufficient, flawlessly beautiful, looking perfect by virtue of their youth, like young sprouts, shamelessly certain that their futures would open up in front of them complete and give them all the best things that they could imagine. That's how it felt to be sixteen, in the first year of high school: no fear, no hesitation. Nothing but possibilities.

Julian enjoyed teaching the first-year course. Some of the students didn't bother to hide their lack of interest, but most of them were cautiously eager to think. And there were also those whose eyes saw the world opening up little by little: at the end of every lesson their eyes shone with a budding insight into that incomprehensibility at the core of reality, all the possibilities that literature and philosophy had to offer. Julian saw it in a few students every year; something almost like dread, a combination of impatience to understand and a powerful realization of something unspeakable. These realizers — that's what Julian called these special students, to himself — were usually girls. Sometimes there were a few boys, too: tormented, misunderstood, artsy wretches. But usually the realizers were girls: girls with serious gazes, ennobled by an inner melancholy, sensitive, touchingly childish and innocent.

The realizers were the reason Julian was a teacher. That dread and impatience and excitement and the flickering threshold of understanding in their eyes.

There was one realizer in this class. A girl who sat in the second row, always in the same place, next to her talkative friend. A shy but open look on her face, a timid smile, and a hint of knowledge of the weight of the world behind her eyes. That kind of girl. Her name was Mari. An all-too-ordinary name for a girl like that.

Julian enjoyed being provocative. He often read aloud from something that would spur a heated discussion. The girls' cheeks would redden with fury, the boys would scoff in embarrassment, and then someone would present a counter-argument, and someone would comment on it, and the debate would be over.

He had a particular quote in mind for today. He had cited the passage in previous years, and it always provoked a lively discussion. The quote today was a game. It was a message for the girl, Mari. Not a serious message — just a playful sentence tossed out for her to catch if she wanted to. These were the little joys of teaching, secret meanings that went over the heads of the less perceptive students, went right past most of them, but hung in the air ready to be plucked by those who were on the right wavelength. Julian had been thinking that they could go out for coffee. She had asked him to recommend some books to her, so there wouldn't be anything strange about inviting her out for coffee. They could talk about literature. Maybe he'd buy her some ice cream. All part of the game — nothing serious.

He primed the game with a relaxed, flirtatious introduction: "Love," he began, flashing a small, teasing smile.

The students were quiet, and several girls in the front row smiled back.

"Love and desire," he said with emphasis, pausing deliberately before he continued. "Could there be any subjects more frequently dealt with in literature than these? What new things could a work of literature possibly have to say about these subjects? And what can we learn about love and desire from literature, when all the essential facts are well covered in *Cosmopolitan?*"

A few students laughed, but the effect wasn't quite as hilarious as Julian had hoped. He continued in a slightly more serious tone.

"I submit that it is in this very subject, the subject of love, that literature's greatest dynamism lies. It allows us to hope for the impossible. It allows us to desire. Literature shows us situations in which a statement and its opposite are equally valid. Literature places right and wrong in question. Do they even exist, right and wrong, and if they do, where do you draw the line between them? These are the questions literature presents to us."

He paused again, dramatically this time, glancing at the realizer in the second row, registering her burning, fervent gaze before he turned back to his book and read, "*A woman's beauty does not belong to her alone. It is part of the bounty she brings into the world. She has a duty to share it.*"

The students were shocked into silent seriousness. No one dared to say a word. Some of the boys at the back of the room had nodded off. The girls in the front tittered. A quick girl on the left end of the front row — a budding feminist, one of those humorless girls who had been awakened to the fact of inequality with all the force of youthful sentimentality — finally raised her hand and answered before Julian had a chance to call on her.

"Why should that be?" she demanded. "Obviously a woman's whole being belongs to the woman herself."

Julian was pleased with the answer: it allowed him to present his planned counter-argument. "Right. A woman's body and being, of course, belong to no one but the woman herself. But beauty. Beauty. How can it be anyone's private possession?"

The repetition was for effect. *Beauty.* He laid stress on the word, and as he did, he looked at Mari. She smiled. She understood his meaning.

Now she raised her hand.

Julian nodded — he didn't say her name, just nodded.

"But what does it mean to share beauty?" she said. "If sharing beauty is a duty, you have to define what sharing it means."

"You've hit the nail on the head," Julian said with a smile, looking her straight in the eye. "That is indeed the problem. Beauty — who does it belong to, and what does it require of you? Not an easy question."

She didn't avert her eyes. So she's not shy after all, Julian thought. Sensitive, maybe, but not shy. Bold, in fact; even brazen. She gave him a challenging look. The air between them vibrated. The game was still pleasurable, innocent. Easy, pleasurable, and innocent.

He could ask her to coffee. Why not? Maybe he would.

## Mari

"Would you like to … shall we go get a cup of coffee? This afternoon? We could talk about those books."

Kanerva presents the question so carelessly that it sounds harmless. It's lunchtime again and they're alone in the classroom.

"Oh, after school, you mean?" Mari asks in disbelief. "Somewhere in town?"

"Yeah. The lunch hour's not enough time to go through everything worth discussing in a classic work of literature." He winks.

He's smiling but Mari senses his nervousness.

"OK," she says with a smile.

"Well, how about we meet in the parking lot, a little after two o'clock?"

"OK. See you then."

He looks her in the eye and she sees that his eyes aren't blue but sea green, like a pond. And under the surface of the water, behind his eyes, is something sparking and flickering and making her uneasy.

During geography, Mari watches the clock. A quarter to two. Thirty more minutes. Tinka's squirming in the seat next to her.

"Do you want to go have coffee after school?" Tinka whispers. "No, let's go to Mickey D's at the Forum. I want to show you the boy I made out with last weekend. He works there."

"Oh, no. I mean yeah."

Mari can't get the words out. The geography teacher turns out the lights and puts a video on to play for the last part of the lesson. A computer animation about the big bang. Mari tries feverishly to think of an excuse for why she can't go out with Tinka. Tinka can't see her and Kanerva leave together. No one can. Mari knows that all the classes get out at two-fifteen. She'll have to leave class early or stay behind until all the other students have left. But what about Tinka? She has to think of an excuse. And then she does.

"Oh no, I can't!" she says. "I have to be at the guidance counselor's office at ten past two. I still have time to make it. See you at McDonald's around four, maybe? I have to go home first. OK?"

"OK, but be there at four o'clock sharp. Don't leave me sitting there waiting for you, or he'll think I'm stalking him."

"Yeah, yeah. I'll see you then."

Mari packs up her books and pens, whispers to the teacher that she's going to see the counselor, and dashes out of the room. From the window in the hallway she can see the parking lot, and Kanerva, leaning on his car, waiting. When she steps out the door his face breaks into a smile. A smile like a crescent moon.

KANERVA DRINKS the rest of his coffee and looks at Mari and smiles. Mari doesn't avert her eyes anymore. She smiles back.

"Why did you want to have coffee with me?" she asks, wondering at her own boldness and calm.

"Why?" he says with a laugh. "Well, can't teachers have favorite students?" He winks.

"Oh, am I your favorite student?"

Kanerva turns serious. She feels his gaze like a knife cutting her loose from the randomness of reality.

"There's poetry in you," Kanerva says. "That's a rare and wonderful thing in a person. You can't just pass it by. The muses demand that it not be ignored." He's not smiling now, and Mari doesn't know if he's serious or joking with her.

"Did you read *Anna Karenina?*" he continues, unperturbed. "What do you think of Anna's lover, Vronsky? If anyone has poetry in him, he does, don't you think?"

"Really?" Mari says, challenging him. "You think that's poetry? Driving someone to their death?"

Kanerva isn't ruffled by her answer. "But does he really drive Anna to her death? Does any character in a tragedy really have the chance to choose their fate? What if all the outcomes are already there at the beginning of the story and the events just come full circle, lead to an inevitable conclusion?"

Mari takes a breath. She's having trouble understanding. The subject is strangely personal to him: Mari can see it in how he leans over the table toward her. His eyes are blazing. It's enthusiasm, but there's something else there, something that makes her feel confused, frightened. Something that's not connected to this reality but to another reality, unknown to her.

"But that's not how life works," she says warily. "What happens isn't decided ahead of time. I can choose what I'm going to do."

"But what if you only *experience* it as free will? What if that's your *perception*, but in reality, all the outcomes of your life already exist, determined by your way of being, and all you're doing is choosing what's been true for you from the very beginning?"

Mari shakes her head hesitantly. "Things can't be like that."

"That's exactly how things are in tragedy. Think of Sophocles's *Oedipus*. Oedipus's parents send their child away to prevent the fate predicted by the oracle, that Oedipus will kill his father and marry his mother. But later on — without knowing it, of course — he does just that, he marries his mother. And then when he's king, he investigates the murder of the former ruler of the city — who was actually his own father — and realises that through this ostensible freedom of his he has sealed his own inevitable fate. In a tragedy, freedom is always an illusion."

He always has the same calm expression, gentle and smiling, an expression that makes everything more real, that makes everything right.

"But what's your opinion?" he continues. "I'm interested in what you think."

With self-conscious movements, Mari stirs her coffee and cream with a long spoon. It feels grown up and important to have someone listen to her and respect her opinions.

"Well," she begins, and pauses solemnly. "I think that you can't rule out free will, not even in art. Responsibility and freedom are inherent in every person."

She's quiet for a moment, searching for the right words. Kanerva uses such fine words, sometimes words Mari's never even heard before. It feels like her own words are inadequate.

"Responsibility and freedom are in all of us; they're part of life," she says, and notices how confident she sounds. "And if art isn't just a reflection of life, of this reality, but is life itself, then those things would have to be a part of art, too."

Kanerva smiles, adversarial. "Responsibility is part of life, the domain of everyday life. It's not a motivation in art. Passion, mania, fate, desire: those are the forces behind art movements. That's where tragedy comes from."

Now Mari knows how to frame her answer. "But isn't that what I was just trying to say? Who says art and life have to be separate?"

Kanerva laughs and looks at her with admiration. "You're too smart for me to teach you anything about life and art."

He's interrupted by the ring of his cell phone. He looks at the display, hesitates an instant, but answers it.

"Yeah. I'm busy right now, in the middle of something. Yeah. You mean now, right now? OK. I'll pick her up. Yeah. OK. Bye."

"What was that?" Mari asks, curious.

"I have to pick my daughter up from kindergarten," he says, getting up. "I can give you a ride home on the way."

"Oh," Mari manages to say. She can sense the flash of disappointment on her face.

She thinks about Kanerva's family. The whole picture comes to her: how he reads the kids bedtime stories and gives them a goodnight kiss and curls up next to his wife in the double bed they share. There they lie, spooning, not letting go of each other all night long. And Mari thinks about Kanerva's wife: she's sure his wife's a beauty, one of those women with intelligent, sparkling personalities and white teeth and perfect skin.

A LITTLE GIRL runs toward them across the kindergarten playground. She has light-blue pants and bouncing brown hair. She looks Mari up and down from under her bangs.

"Who are you?" she demands.

Mari looks at Kanerva, flustered. He laughs.

"This is Mari. She's one of Daddy's students. And this is Anni, my daughter," he says to Mari.

Mari tries to smile but she realizes that Anni's friendship can't be bought with a smile. Anni takes her father's hand with a proprietary air as they walk to the car. Mari lags behind. She feels like an intruder.

In the car, Anni cheerfully tells her father about her day at school and Mari sits quietly in the front seat. Mari berates herself: how could she have let herself fantasize about Kanerva? He obviously couldn't have any interest in her. Stupid, stupid girl.

She watches the stone pavement passing and wishes the trip were quicker. A sick feeling surges in her gut. Suddenly she remembers Tinka: Tinka's waiting for her at the mall.

"Hey, I just remembered that I'm supposed to go ... that I'm supposed to be downtown at four," she says, relieved at the opportunity to escape.

Kanerva pulls over at a bus stop and Mari opens the door without saying anything.

"See you at school, then," he says.

"Yeah, see you," Mari says, and turns to go.

She glances back once more. Kanerva's daughter is sitting in the back seat looking at her intently, and Mari has the feeling that the little girl knows everything, knows more than anyone else. That look, so grave, and Mari can see that she knows — knows the movement of the stars and the direction of the wind, and what's going to happen. And the little girl doesn't retreat from what she knows; Mari can see that, too. She bears its weight silently, clear-eyed.

As she passes the bus stop, Mari sees her own reflection in the glass of the bus shelter: an odd young woman, a complete stranger. She seems to have a hidden power of a kind Mari herself has no knowledge of. She'll have to keep an eye out for that, for everything — she can't let up for even a minute.

# Anni

Anni is walking home from school. She stops to poke at an anthill along the road. You shouldn't poke, Anni thinks, but I'll just poke it a little, just enough to make the ants swarm out.

Anni is six years old, and she's not in nursery school anymore, she's in preschool. Fallen, rain-soaked leaves stink in the ditch. The smell is nice and sickening at the same time. I'm already quite a big girl, Anni thinks and throws a stick into the woods. She'd like to be even bigger; she'd like to walk home from school by herself. But nursery-schoolers aren't big enough to walk home alone and neither are preschoolers. So her neighbor Silja, who goes to middle school, walks with her. Silja waits for Anni outside the school on Anni's half days, twice a week. Silja always holds Anni's hand when they cross the street. Silja has the sweetest eyes, her hand is soft. Anni wants to be big like Silja. Now Silja is talking on her phone, walking a few steps ahead, glancing back now and then at Anni.

Half days are fun. Anni doesn't have to stay at school all afternoon waiting for her mother or father to come, she doesn't have to take an afternoon nap with babies that are still in diapers. Anni slows down and falls behind, pretends she's a runaway. She imagines she's a princess who's been mistreated and has run away from her cruel stepmother at the castle. She drops pebbles that she's gathered along the path so that her sisters can find the way at nightfall, when they can get away from the wicked stepmother.

They come to their own street, Silja in front and Anni behind. Anni slows down again, scratching a rough line in the gravel road with a stick. (It's a marker, Anni will use it to find her way home from the wicked stepmother's prison.) Silja turns to look at Anni, smiles, waves. Anni waves back. Silja disappears around the corner.

Home is a low brick rowhouse surrounding a courtyard that has a sandbox and two swings. Anni walks to the swings and sits down. She doesn't feel like going inside yet. She looks in the windows at the Kuuselas' house. Sanna's mother is home in the afternoons. Anni doesn't want to go to the Kuuselas' until Sanna gets home.

Sanna isn't home from school yet. She goes to grade school. Anni feels a rush of envy. She wishes she went to grade school. Sanna is Anni's best friend. Sanna has told her about the exciting things they do at school: learning letters and times tables, and handicraft class where they knit their own stuffed animals. Anni has already decided that she's going to make a cat in her first year of grade school. Sanna's making a worm. A cat is much harder than a worm.

Anni sees Sanna come in the gate. Sanna has a purple backpack, and pink ribbons on her braids.

"Hi, Anni!" Sanna shouts, waving.

"Hii-ii!"

"Are you coming to our house?" Sanna asks.

"Have you got sweet rolls?"

"Yeah, in the freezer. And cocoa."

Sanna is silent for a minute, sizing Anni up.

"But you have to come to our house anyway," she says knowingly.

"I don't have to," Anni says, although she knows she does. "Besides," she adds carelessly, looking elsewhere, "I have homework."

It isn't true. Anni doesn't have homework, because they don't give homework at preschool. But she wishes she had some.

"You can have Emerald Barbie if you come," Sanna says.

"OK."

"I mean, not to keep," Sanna clarifies. "But you can play with it."

"Yeah."

THEY OFTEN PLAY PRINCESS at Sanna's house. Sanna has nice hair that smells like cinnamon and is easy to put in princess curls. And she has a princess dress. Anni just has a light-blue gymnastics outfit with a thick frill at the bottom, it doesn't have gauze like Sanna's dress. But the gymnastics outfit is the fanciest thing Anni has. If you put a lace curtain on for a train and a foil crown on your head, it's almost like a princess. Or you can close your eyes and imagine princess curls and a ruffly dress. Princess Strawberry, daughter of King Balkur.

But sometimes nothing works. Sometimes Anni squints her eyes and nothing happens. That's because Sanna's standing next to her. Sanna in her frilly dress. Sanna's mother takes her braids out and — oh! Sanna has real princess curls. Shall I give you some curls, too? Sanna's mother asks Anni. No, Anni says. Because she knows she has the wrong kind of hair. Wild, troll's hair.

"I'm the princess," Sanna gushes. "And you're her servant and the prince comes and they get married and the servant holds up her train and they dance and dance."

When Sanna's hair is in princess curls and she has a real plastic princess crown on her head, she twirls in front of the mirror and looks as much like a princess as she possibly could look. Anni holds up her train. Sanna's eyes shine with all the joy in the world. She looks beautiful in the mirror. Anni doesn't. Anni feels like she's all wrong somehow. She covers the mustard stain on the front of her gymnastics suit with her hand and looks at perfect Sanna. It's difficult. She wishes Sanna would fall in the mud, that her dress would get dirty and her hair would go flat. She wishes Sanna was ugly and she was beautiful.

A bad thought. Go away, bad thought.

Finally Sanna gets tired of twirling.

"This is a poopie game," Sanna says, deflated, and stops.

"Yeah. Really poopie."

Anni looks at her watch with an air of importance. She knows how to tell the big hand from the little hand.

"Ah," she says. "It's getting so late. I have to go do my homework now."

A thrilling thought: to be home alone before Mom and Dad get home. Maybe she can make some food for the whole family and when they come home they'll all be surprised to see dinner ready.

"You can't go home yet," Sanna says bossily. "You have to wait here until your mom and dad come home."

"No I don't," Anni says. "I can go home if I want to."

"Aren't you scared? The Masked Murderer might come."

Anni thinks about the Masked Murderer. They secretly

watched a movie about the Masked Murderer in Sanna's big brother's room. The Masked Murderer has big gaping holes where his eyes should be and a scary voice. Anni drives the thought of him from her mind.

"Hmph. Babies are scared, not me," she says.

ANNI OPENS the front door with the key that hangs around her neck. An empty house. Immediately it feels scary. It's quiet but there are weird noises now and then, rustlings and knockings. Anni goes to the living room and rocks for a little while on Mustang, her rocking horse. Mustang's fur has a safe smell, musty and tangy. Soon Dad and Mom will be home. Soon. They'll be home soon.

Anni listens to her stomach. Hungry. She hops off Mustang's back and goes into the kitchen. She looks in the refrigerator. Potatoes and ready-made spinach crepes. She hears a rustle somewhere again. She freezes: the Masked Murderer. She doesn't dare look behind her. Should she hide in the cupboard until Mom and Dad come home? No, not in the cupboard. She could lock herself in the kitchen. Go get her cassette player first, just in case. If she runs fast and doesn't look, the Masked Murderer can't get her.

Anni runs to her room without looking left or right, picks up the cassette player, and dashes back to the kitchen. She presses the button and safe songs begin to play. She picks up My Little Pony and the Emerald Barbie that Sanna let her borrow and puts them on the table to watch over the cooking. "Hoppity hop, cloppity clop," Anni sings, and washes the potatoes and puts them in a pot of water on the stove. This is the kitchen in the castle of the royal kingdom of Azarnafar and the prince and princess are going to be married this evening.

The potatoes and spinach crepes are for the celebration dinner and Anni is the poor scullery maid who cooks the feast and lives on crab shells — that sounds fancy, crab shells, the thing wicked stepmothers feed to scullery maids in fairy tales. But Anni isn't really a poor scullery maid, she's really the king's daughter who disappeared when she was a little girl.

Anni opens up the package of spinach crepes and puts them on a plate and into the microwave. Hoppity hop, cloppity clop, making a wedding feast, and this evening the prince will come and rescue the poor scullery maid.

Hoppity hop, cloppity clop, Mom and Dad will be home soon.

The cassette ends, the button on the tape player clicks. It turns quiet. Anni listens.

There's a rustling somewhere. Anni's scared.

She walks to the kitchen door. She doesn't see anyone. She looks in the entryway — no one. She goes into the living room. Mustang rocks quietly when the wind from the open window hits him. Anni goes over to Mustang and gets on his back.

She rocks fast on Mustang's back. It's OK, she thinks. Dad's at work. Mom's at work. I'll just rock here. They'll be here soon. I'll just rock here. It feels strange between her legs — a nice feeling, forbidden, unusual. Anni rocks herself against the red hide on Mustang's back. Soon they'll be here soon. The familiar smell down in the horse's hairs. Mom and Dad will be home soon.

# Julian

JULIAN GATHERED UP the books and photocopies from his desk, put them in his bag, and walked out of the classroom. In the afternoon, the school was quiet. The light from the window at the end of the hall shone down the long, dim corridor, and he could hear the distant sounds of play from the gymnasium.

Julian glanced out the large window instinctively — was she still in the schoolyard? He didn't see her. He tore his mind away from thoughts of the girl. It was a trivial thing, he assured himself. Just lighthearted fun, completely without significance, a little amusement to brighten up the dullness of his working day. Actually, it would be best to put a damper on the whole thing, act like it never happened. Or maybe not — that would be too obvious, as if it were more important than it was. The easiest thing would be to just be friendly, like he was before, but without showing any partiality. No discussions over coffee in town, no moments alone in the classroom. Teacher and student, that's what they were, nothing more. He wouldn't think any more of it — but he did glance again toward the door that led outside.

As he pulled out of the parking lot, Julian thought about his evening. One of his daughters was at the neighbors' and

Jannika was picking the younger one up from daycare on her way home from work. First they would make some dinner, maybe roasted chicken breast and rice, and then they would go outside and build a fort, or maybe go to the swimming hall.

Anni had learned to swim over the summer and she was proud of it, and Julian had thought about putting her in the class for younger swimmers at the swim club. As he stopped at a traffic light, he sank into thoughts of what joining the swim club would entail for Anni. Whoops of pleasure in the pool. Sewing the round swimming master's patch made of rough chamois onto her swimsuit, beaming with pride. Julian remembered the patch he got for swimming as a child. It felt for a long time like the greatest achievement in his life. Then the unavoidable disappointments would come. A demanding coach who barked at her and told her she was fat when she got a little plump as a teenager. And the men who would watch her fifteen-year-old ass at the swimming competitions, as she bent forward before pushing off into the water at the starting gun. Narrow second-place finishes, injuries, dieting, no longer getting her period. Maybe they should just build a fort after dinner.

Julian opened the front door and put the grocery bags down in the entryway. A pair of frightened eyes was looking at him from behind the living-room doorframe. Anni.

"Daddy," she said in a strangled voice, on the verge of tears, and ran into his arms.

"There's my pumpkin. What are you doing here by yourself?"

He picked Anni up in his arms and rocked her. The flood of tenderness and love felt almost unbearable, tightening his throat and puckering his brow. Being a father was strangely painful somehow. It had been that way ever since Anni was born. He remembered how her birth had made some dam burst inside him, how for several days afterward he had broken into tears at all sorts of inappropriate times. When he held Anni in his arms for the first time, it gave him an almost nauseous feeling, such an absolute responsibility rolling over him. He'd had to run to the hospital restroom, lock the door, and lean his head against the cool, white tiles. He also remembered with embarrassment the sobs echoing through the restroom, grunts almost, like a retching howl. And gradually, there in the restroom in a fetal position, the sick feeling and panic started to fade, replaced by this ache that still represented the essence of fatherhood for him: it was an inescapable responsibility, the knowledge that he was essential to the survival of this little life.

When Ada was born a year and a half later he already knew that there was no going back to the way it was before, and the shameful flood of feeling never came. It was easier with Ada in other ways, too. Ada was an energetic five-year-old, rebellious, but somehow unremarkable. The main feeling he had with Anni, on the other hand, was a hesitancy. Often, a sudden distance would shine from her eyes, something peculiar and adult, and he felt uncomfortable under her gaze.

They had a habit of lying around and playing on the double bed in Julian and Jannika's room after dinner, the whole family together, before the girls went to bed. Those were Ada's moments of glory: she prattled and jabbered and scurried about with all the strength in her little body before it came time for them to go to their own beds in their own room. But Anni might suddenly get up and walk to the door and stand there looking at her family. "What are you doing over there, Anni? Come over here with us, sweetheart," they would coax her. But she had that look on her face, clear and serious and somehow knowing. "No, I'll just stay here." Why? they would ask her. "I'm keeping watch," she answered, and again Julian saw that look on her face that made her foreign, a stranger.

But now, in the bright light of a fall afternoon, in the tick of the kitchen clock, Anni had run frightened into his arms and sniffled against his shoulder, just a little girl. Nothing strange about her, no secret information. Just his daughter.

"Did something frighten you?" he asked, putting her down softly and crouching to her level.

Anni pouted and looked at her toes. Julian gently tweaked one of them. Her leotard had gone sausagey.

"The Masked Murderer," Anni mumbled. "I thought the Masked Murderer was coming."

"Honey, there's no such thing. There's no boogeyman and no Masked Murderer."

"I know," she said feebly.

"Did you have a fight with Sanna?"

"Sanna's stupid."

"Everybody's stupid sometimes."

"Sanna bosses people," Anni said, curling her toes.

"Maybe that's just her way of being your friend."

"No, it's not. She's mean."

"Sweetie pie," Julian said, stroking her hair. "Little girls aren't mean."

A key turned in the lock and Ada's eager face peeped in the door. She yelled and ran to Julian and grabbed him around the legs.

Jannika followed her inside, looking tired. Julian tried to

deduce from her expression whether she was still angry with him from their fight that morning. It seemed like she was.

"Oh, you went to the store, too," she said, without looking at him, and went into the kitchen still wearing her shoes. "If there was a little more communication in this family, we wouldn't always be buying the same groceries twice."

"Well, we can put it in the freezer," Julian answered absent-mindedly and patted the still-clinging Ada on the head.

He thought about the morning — they'd argued about trivialities until Jannika finally left for work, slamming the door behind her. It was always like that with her — she'd always been moody and cryptic. In the beginning it had seemed exotic and marvelous, always finding new, hidden corners of another person. Jannika had been a shifting current that he'd let himself be pulled along with, that carried him away to new lands.

It had happened quickly, Jannika coming into his life. A stranger who loaned him some money in the university cafeteria when he'd forgotten his wallet, a girl studying art history, wearing green eyeshadow, a smudge of thick, dark hair carelessly perched in a tuft on the top of her head, seamed stockings, and a short skirt although it was November. The day after she loaned him the money they saw each other by chance on Unioninkatu and they'd been together ever since.

In bed that first night she'd been like a fierce little animal, scratching his back and holding him in a tight grip between her thin, white legs. But when it was all over and they were lying quietly side by side, and all that separated them from a final and eternal merging together was the damp surface of their two skins, she had turned melancholy and aloof. Julian had felt hurt and at the same time ashamed of his childish feelings. At such an intimate moment, she ought to be thinking only of him. Jannika had turned her head, taken his face between her hands. There was an endless, almost inconsolable, melancholy sea in her eyes. "We'll get married," she said. "We'll end up getting married." Julian had never quite known how to interpret this: whether it was the announcement of a coming dawn of happiness spoken by a person in love, or the calm, imperturbable acceptance of the banality of life. But that's what had happened — they got engaged and a few years later they were married.

She still had that quality after ten years together, a riddle that couldn't be put into words, a melancholy that Julian never could figure out. It just wasn't exotic or fascinating anymore. When it was some random Thursday and there were the children and the rounds of everyday life, spaghetti and taking turns with the dishes, Jannika's moodiness was trying and tedious.

"I bought chicken," Julian said, and clapped Ada in his arms. "Shall we make that for dinner? Or what did you buy?"

Ada's sticky hands touched Julian's neck. Anni came to the kitchen door with a plastic pony and a Barbie doll in her arms, her eyes shining.

"No, I have a surprise for you. You don't have to make dinner, because I already made it!"

Jannika lifted the lid of the pot on the stove, surprised.

The stove seemed to be on, set to low. Julian looked into the pot — it contained some muddy-looking potatoes.

"And there's spinach crepes in the microwave," Anni said proudly, going to the cupboard to get out some plates.

"Were you here by yourself?" Jannika demanded, pouring the potato water into the sink. "Weren't you at the Kuuselas' this afternoon like we planned?"

Julian could see the little wrinkle on Anni's forehead tighten, breaking her satisfaction in two. She looked at her toes again, as she did in all the uncertain moments of her little life. Jannika poured the potatoes into the sink, turned on the tap, and started to rewash them.

"We've talked about this," Jannika said, annoyed, in a sudden gust of parental authority. "You're not allowed to stay home alone, or to turn on the stove or the oven. You could start a fire."

"But I thought," Anni began, "I thought that ..." The explanation got stuck in the expression of guilt on her face.

"Now, now. Nothing bad happened," Julian said, trying to make peace. "And Anni, Mommy is right. You're not allowed to be here by yourself."

"Don't make light of it and don't tell me how to raise my daughter!" Jannika snapped. "What makes you think I'm some kind of weakling who's incapable of handling differences of opinion with my own daughter?"

"Anyway, I want spinach crepes!" Ada announced, wriggling out of Julian's arms onto the floor and sitting down at the table.

Jannika wrenched the utensil drawer open and started to set the table. Julian sighed and began to put the groceries in the refrigerator. Anni went to the table and played quietly with her plastic pony. The pony galloped on the meadow of the oilcloth, clomping its purple hooves.

Silence reigned as they ate dinner. Jannika clinked her cutlery wearily and pretended to eat. Ada put the little round spinach crepes up to her eyes, made holes in the middle and peeped out at them, chuckling at her own cleverness.

"Don't play with your food, Ada," Jannika said, and took a sip of water, watching for the slightest glance from Julian.

Ada put the whole crepe in her mouth, took her sister's plastic pony and walked it along the tablecloth to drink from her milk glass. The pony drank long and enthusiastically. Ada made drinking noises.

"How do horses drink, Daddy?" she asked. "Do they use their tongue like a cat, or do they drink through their nose, like an elephant?"

"I don't know," Julian said thoughtfully. "With their tongues, probably."

He looked at Anni, quiet and serious, watching everything, especially her mother. She seemed to feel somehow responsible for her mother's bad mood.

"Girls, how would you like to build a fort after dinner?" Julian suggested.

"Yeah!" Ada said.

"I will if Mama comes, too," Anni said, looking warily at her mother.

"No, Mommy has something she has to write for work," Jannika said, already softening. "You all go ahead."

"I'll stay here with her, then," Anni said.

"No, let your mom work in peace and quiet," Julian began, but got another frosty look from Jannika that said, Don't tell me when I want to hear the sound of my child and when I don't.

He continued diplomatically. "Won't you come with us, Anni? We need three tough soldiers to get the roof on the fort. Mine and Ada's four hands aren't enough."

Anni smiled a little. "Well, all right then."

THAT EVENING, when the girls had already gone to bed, Julian unbuttoned Jannika's shirt in the moonlight and uncovered the silvery arc of her shoulders. Jannika was thin — skinny, in fact. Julian found himself wondering if she ate enough — was she watching her weight, exercising compulsively? Her eyes were shut and she leaned her head against his caresses, like a cat giving in to his touch, showing that she does, in fact, care about the creatures around her.

"Let's not fight anymore," Julian whispered.

"Mmmm ..." Jannika said, guiding his hand along the ridge of her collarbone to her breasts.

Julian laid her on her back and pulled at the waistband of her skirt.

At first there was passion, even strong passion. He kissed her breasts and spread her legs. On the spur of the moment he tore off her white cotton underpants — they tore surprisingly easily, with a ripping sound like in a movie — and it made Jannika let out an involuntary moan of excitement from deep in her throat, which excited Julian more.

Then he thought about the girl for the first time. She forced herself into his thoughts. What would it sound like if the girl moaned like that at his touch? Exciting — unbearably, incredibly erotic. Julian closed his eyes as he pushed inside Jannika. He thought of the girl's pale breasts. They were small, perfect — he knew that's what they were like, although he hadn't seen them. Jannika wrapped her legs around him, pulled him closer, asked him to look at her. Julian opened his eyes, looked at his wife, came closer, deeper, thinking about the girl, her hips that had never brought a baby into the world, her cunt, how it would feel, thinking about her while he made love to his wife.

Jannika lifted her hips closer to him, surrendering to his thrusts, and he was overtaken by guilt. His passion died quietly, lingered around his hips like a reflexive impulse, and faded. Jannika stopped her movements and took his head between her hands. "What is it?"

"Sorry, I … I don't know what happened," Julian said, and rolled off her.

Jannika turned on her side, her back to him, and reached one arm to caress him conciliatorily.

"It doesn't matter. It's all right," she whispered. "It's all right."

Julian moved closer to her, curled up against her back and stroked the arch of her waist and hip. Her skin shone in the light of the moon, pale and sleek. She was trembling a little. Julian was ashamed. Her breathing soon grew steady, turned heavier and deeper. He waited for a long time before he let go of her and turned to his own side of the bed.

He lay there on his back in the moonlight and thought about when they had made love the first few times after Anni was born. They had waited a long time before they tried. It hurt her the first time, and she bled. They'd kept going to the end, though, and Julian had felt like he was desecrating something. It was like crossing a line between the sacred and profane in other ways, too: milk had flowed from Jannika's heavy, slippery breasts. He was sucking her breast and got some milk in his mouth and felt like he might vomit. It had been so long since the last time that his erection was painfully hard. Jannika felt different, softer and slicker. He came almost immediately and since she hadn't yet, he thrust a finger inside her and soon she whimpered in her familiar way. Then she had cried, cried and curled herself around him, her hair hanging in wet clumps around her face, her breasts heavy and slippery. The crying didn't stop.

He hadn't been able to sleep that night. He lay awake, alone, listening to the sounds of Jannika and Anni, who was six months old, as they slept, and thought, This is how happiness comes to you, when you find your own place in the world. In this room, with nothing but the thinnest of surfaces separating you from the ones you love.

That was light years away now, Julian thought. Jannika had been at her most exposed then, completely open. Now she'd changed, turned in on herself, become more secretive.

He found himself thinking of the girl again.

Was there something in the girl herself that had caught his attention, something he couldn't ignore? Or was it just the nature of the situation, an opportunity presented to him that he couldn't pass up? Life was like that sometimes; it offered itself like a work of art waiting to be created. Were feelings any less real because they were conjured forth by the laws of art?

Suddenly he thought of Schubert's *Death and the Maiden*. That's what it was, he thought, inspired by the clarity that comes at night. The intensity of the Allegro, the incredible opening beats, muffled, dramatic. But especially the Andante movement. The slow beginning, almost crooning, tender and lingering, like the shy gaze of the girl. The bouncing, playful melody — and then the dramatic strings wedging its way into the sweetness, the minor key rising stealthily, imperceptibly to the final major. Like reality itself: light, almost imperceptibly light, until it turned heavy. It wasn't the poetry of the situation that made him think of her again and again, it was the girl herself. Her rhythm was music, a Schubertian drama, a sense of the painful lightness of life.

Julian sat up in bed and looked at the moon glowing in the sky. It was gigantic, yellow at the edges, friendly. Schubert boomed in his head and his blood seemed to rush faster in his veins. He had to do something. It was decided now — and justified. He couldn't let that kind of rhythm and poetry pass him by.

# Anja

ANJA PRESSED THE BUTTON on the copier and waited for something to happen. The machine was mute. The display showed the brusque pronouncement: *Section two is jammed. Open door two and remove paper.* Anja sighed. She glanced around her — the hallway was empty. The students were in class, the department staff at their lectures or who knows where. She would have to solve the jam herself.

She opened the copier door. Now the machine told her to move some gizmo so that she could reach the paper jam. She rattled something that looked like an ink cartridge deep in the bowels of the machine. She could see the paper that had caused the fatal jam distantly in the copier's innards.

Anja sighed again.

There was always some obstacle. Just when she thought her existence was turning lighter, when it was getting easier to breathe, some reminder of the weight of the world would arrive: the copy machine wouldn't work, the computer would crash, the plumbing would spring a leak and spray water over the floorboards, wet the rugs — with dirty water if your luck was particularly bad, dirty water reaching as far as the clothes closet and staining the carefully crocheted lace along the edge of your sheets, your floral-print summer dress. It was to remind you that things weren't working. The world was reminding you how difficult life was, how you shouldn't start thinking life was going to be easy. You had to call the repair service or someplace, the IT department or the building superintendent, and help always came. Some man — a plumber, an electrician; in any case, a man — would come, and he would see the trivial mediocrity that your life had become through the years, when you weren't watching. Piles of newspapers on the kitchen table, half-eaten cheese sandwiches. The lotion and soap stuck to the shelf in the sauna, last summer's birch whisks. Sheets left to languish on the clothesline. The repairman would see all of it when he came to fix the machine or the pipe — the row of coffee cups on Anja's desk, the dust on her computer screen. And her face. See it completely, although she tried to hide it with a smile. Those moments left her with a wrung-out feeling; a repairman coming to fix a machine but becoming an inadvertent witness to the futility of the passing days, the weight of existence.

She looked at the copier and the jammed paper peeking out of it and felt exhausted. What if she just left it there and went downstairs to use the library copy machine? Somebody else could call the repairman. Anybody else.

"Isn't it working?"

Anja gave a start and turned to see who was speaking. It was the man from the nursing home. The kaleidoscope man. The mountain-bike man.

"There was a time when I was considering quitting the university entirely because of copy-machine problems," he said good-naturedly. "Whenever you have course material you have to copy you can't find a single machine in the building that works."

"Uh-huh."

"But I stayed on."

"Good."

"Nowadays I've gotten pretty good at figuring out what's wrong with them."

"Ah."

"Paper jam or some other malfunction, ma'am? Leave it to me," he said.

"Better you than me."

Anja couldn't tell if he was kidding. He bent over the machine and removed a part hidden under the jammed paper. The sheet of paper slid out easily. He closed the hatch and flashed Anja a bashful smile. His gaze met hers, then turned quickly away. A charmer, she thought. Possibly dangerous. Maybe even a criminal. The handsome ones are always the worst.

"You could have got it loose," he said. "This was one of the easy cases."

His smile was like a little boy's. He looked into her eyes for a second, his gaze angled away, his smile asking for permission before it brightened. His eyes were moss green.

"Thanks," Anja said.

"Johannes Nurmi," he said, extending his hand.

"Anja Aropalo," Anja said, shaking his hand.

"Professor Aropalo?" Johannes said. "Literature?"

"Yes. Literature. Mainly classical literature. And aesthetics — philosophy in general."

"Art history. That's my field, I mean. But I'm not a professor. I've been in England writing my thesis for the past few years."

"Right. So I haven't met you before," Anja said. "Except recently. At the nursing home."

"That's right. That's where we've met before."

He became quiet, perhaps realizing that Anja didn't want to talk about her husband or his illness. Johannes was younger, perhaps forty. A smooth-talker? No. A born charmer. Maybe even unaware of his own attractiveness. He still didn't speak. Just looked at her. Could a man like him be shy? Or maybe it wasn't shyness — he had come up to speak to her at the nursing home.

"So," he said finally.

"So," Anja answered.

"I was thinking, professor, if you'd like to hear more about that kaleidoscope idea, I could show you something. But it's large, so you'd have to come to my house to see it."

Anja was confused. Was he asking her on a date? Or mocking her? No, he seemed sincere.

"Why not? It sounds interesting."

"I live right near here. At my mother's place — temporarily. She's only been in the nursing home for a few months, so I haven't arranged her financial affairs yet."

"I see."

"If you'd like to," he said. "If you would like to come, how about tomorrow evening? I can cook something for you."

"All right. I will."

Johannes smiled. An unusual man.

"See you then, professor," he said, turning to leave.

"You keep calling me professor," Anja said.

"Aha. So I do," he said.

"You can call me Anja."

"Right. Sorry, Anja," he said with a smile.

Anja made a note of how the stubble on his chin and the hair on his arms was a lighter color than on his head. Maybe he dyed his hair. She'd never met a man who dyed his hair. But how would she know? Maybe all sorts of men dyed their hair all the time and she just didn't know it.

"Right, then," Anja said, smiling. "Let's meet tomorrow. Around six o'clock?"

"Six it is. I can send you my address by email."

"Good."

Johannes turned and went out the door. Anja remained standing by the copy machine. Had she just made a date? If she had, it happened by accident.

*

GUSTS OF WIND threw discarded wrappers and pieces of news-paper into the air. The market square was emptying out as the last vendors loaded their goods into trucks. Anja was early. It made her nervous. The sea rose and fell, rough, blue-black, threatening, like the breathing of an animal asleep. Anja and the sea had always maintained a formal distance. The sea frightened her. She felt its endless vastness mocking her somehow. Years ago she had made the mistake of going out on the water with a friend who was an avid sailor. It was a miserable day — unending vertigo and nausea in the tiny cabin of the boat; the sloping, slippery deck leading straight into the chilly arms of the sea. And all around them the blue wall of water that approached and withdrew with the rhythm of waves high as mountains. Since then she'd had the good sense to acknowledge her smallness and stay on land.

And now — autumn and Helsinki. It was a peculiar city.

It had a separate identity for each season. There'd been surprisingly little rain in October. Even now the sky was a shining, open vault, like a prayer. And the black trunks of the trees in Esplanadi Park were stark against the sky — the contrast was fantastical, almost sinister. Now that the trees had shed their leaves, sounds were harder, the tram's rattle more like a hacking. Ripples of wind reached in and touched her skin. Soon the snow would come and everything would go quiet again, the world would sink down and Helsinki would doze in winter's pocket, at least on those days when there was no wind and the traffic sounds disappeared into white, freshly fallen snow.

She walked along the edge of the market square, crossed in front of the church, lingered for a while in its stark environs to kill time, and then continued to the shore at Pohjoisranta.

This is where she and her husband were the first time they spent more than an hour looking for the car.

A SUNNY DAY IN JUNE. Seagulls flying around the market square, shrieking. The car has disappeared.

"Damn it," her husband says. "It must have been moved. They've come and moved it."

Anja tries to reassure him. He doesn't believe her.

"The damn thing's been towed. There's nothing we can do about it. If it's towed it's towed."

"Stop it," Anja says with a laugh. "When did you start blaming everything on other people? You've just forgotten where you parked it."

It's ridiculous. How did they get this way? Always looking for something. Half of their time spent searching. Socks, glasses, wallet. The car — how can a person make a car disappear?

Here they are, after twenty years, looking for the car at the market square, bickering.

He doesn't find it funny, she thinks. He's serious. Is he serious? Can't he see that it's funny?

"I don't know why you always have to start in on who's to blame," he bellows.

"You were just blaming the authorities." Anja snorts. "Towed? Why would anyone come and tow your car away?"

"They might have," he says. "The police or somebody. Inspectors. Anybody."

Now Anja's getting angry, too. "Listen to yourself! Inspectors? For heaven's sake! You find the car — I'm going to get some coffee."

She turns and takes a few angry steps toward the market café. He comes and shoves her. Just a little shove, but still a shove. It occurs to her that he's serious. This isn't a joke to him.

"It's damned difficult to live with you sometimes," he shouts, to back up the shove. "Sometimes I think ... I think you're an evil woman."

"Are you going to threaten to divorce me again?"

Stupid fights, she thinks. He never used to threaten divorce. Now everything turns into a fight and all the fights end this way. Maybe they'd be better off if they were apart. That's what he said: it would be better. He could do what he liked, in peace.

"I don't have much choice when you act like this," he shouts.

Anja doesn't intend to listen to any more of this. "What about how you're acting? I'm going to get some damn coffee."

She walks to the market café and orders coffee and a donut. The donut is safe, sweet. She gulps the coffee. He strides along the market square and disappears around a corner.

He means it, she thinks. How did he completely lose his sense of humor? Does he even love her anymore? Or maybe she's the one who's tired of it. Maybe they should go to couples therapy or a relationship retreat. Why would a person make such a fuss about losing their car?

Half an hour goes by, forty-five minutes.

Anja drinks another coffee and eats another donut. It's not as good as the first one.

Where is he?

She gets up and walks along the edge of the market, crosses the street. A seagull caws and the market vendors gather up their unsold goods and put them in their trucks.

Worry starts to weigh on her. This isn't normal. You can't just lose a car like that. The car you parked yourself — how long could it take to look for it? A thought enters her mind. The same thought she's had before: What's the matter with him?

Then she sees him. He drives slowly through the traffic until he's next to her. He found the car after all. She glances at him. He's sulking, doesn't even look at her. Anja doesn't look, either. She continues walking, quickens her steps. He drives along beside her, following the movement of traffic. Then he speeds up with the rest of the cars and leaves Anja behind. I'm going to divorce him, she thinks. Move away. He's so mule-headed. Who would want to live with a person like that?

Her husband stops at a traffic light and opens the car door. Anja runs to the car and gets in.

"Where did you find it?"

"Over there," he mutters. "A few blocks away."

"Oh, you mean where you parked it?"

"Of course," he grunts. "Where else would it be?"

They don't say anything more. He grips the steering wheel and stares straight ahead.

Anja gives up eventually, makes a conciliatory gesture. She stretches her hand out and squeezes his arm.

"Just think what it would be like if we had children," she says. "We'd be forgetting them all over the place. The store, the playground."

He relents a little, smiles.

"You weren't really angry, were you?" Anja asks.

"What about?"

"About losing the car."

"We didn't lose the car," he says, looking her in the eye. "It's right here."

Anja looks at him and an uneasy feeling runs down her spine.

He smiles.

"Just teasing you," he says, and winks.

Anja smiles. The smile is a little forced.

There's anxiety underneath it.

JOHANNES LIVED IN the most expensive building on the street. Or rather, his mother did. I'm going to meet a man at his mother's house, Anja thought, and felt a vague uneasiness. Maybe this is a date, she thought, as she rang the buzzer.

Johannes was waiting at the top of the stairs. The lights in the stairwell turned off as she climbed up to him. A wedge of bright light stretched from the apartment into the hallway.

They said their hellos in the dimness and Anja could see that he was getting a proper look at her for the first time. It was a stolen glance: she felt his eyes scan her profile against the cool shadows on the corridor wall. He was trying to take her measure, and it made her uncomfortable.

He led the way into the apartment. A long-haired, stiff-eared dog trotted up to meet them, wagging its tail. It sniffed her eagerly and she gave it a pat. A memory of Terri unfurled in her mind. She was a member of their family for many years. When Anja's husband got sick, Terri got depressed — first she stopped wagging her tail, then she slept all day in the same spot next to the kitchen stove. Then she died. That's how animals know they've come to the end of their days. When her master let go of his life, she knew her time was up and decided to die. Maybe she'd had cancer. Or maybe she just wanted to stop living, wanted to stop wanting. That's how an animal dies; when she stops wanting anything anymore.

Anja glanced surreptitiously into the living room: shining floorboards, pale walls covered with rows of bookshelves.

Johannes led her to the kitchen and poured red wine into glasses that waited on the table. Anja tried to refuse it with an uncertain movement of her hand.

"I already opened the bottle," he insisted. "You have to drink at least one glass, just out of politeness. I can't throw out wine this good."

Anja took a sip from her glass. The wine was velvety and aromatic. Johannes took a dish of potatoes — already baked, apparently — out of the refrigerator and put it in the oven. Then he gave her a head of lettuce to cut up and busied himself with the meat. She watched him with interest as he cooked. The meat had been marinating on the kitchen table.

He cut the meat into steaks on the chopping board. He pressed the steaks flat, didn't season them, put them straight in the pan that had been heating on the stove. He browned them quickly, transferred them to a large iron pot, and sprinkled them with salt and white pepper from large grinders. Anja wasn't a very knowledgeable cook herself. Her husband had cooked their better meals, when he still had his memory.

Anja examined Johannes furtively. His posture was straight, his build surprisingly perfect. He had broad shoulders, athletic in a fit, muscular way that Anja wasn't used to. She'd only seen bodies like that in movies and advertisements. At first glance he looked bigger than he actually was. When you looked closer, you saw that he was slim, almost wiry, like a triple jumper or a hurdler. Maybe he did sports as well as research, played floor hockey or intramural football.

He was one of those men who retained a certain boyishness into middle age. You could look at him and see what he had been like when he was sixteen, sitting on a window ledge in a school classroom. One of those boys with an honest gaze that wandered around, stopped for a second on a girl, a quick glance that immediately moved away. A boy who came into a room, said something about the weather, didn't look you in the eye at first, then did, smiled, told you about something he was reading about the curvature of space or black holes. A boy who talked about the curvature of space and didn't have the courage to ask a girl to the movies.

Anja straightened her hem. This was dangerous ground. She should be on her guard.

Johannes opened the french doors off the kitchen and Anja noticed for the first time that there was a sort of terrace outside. She saw her own face reflected in the glass of the doors: she looked startled, strange, oddly distorted, like a stranger. She got up and walked to the doorway to avoid looking at her own reflection. There was a summer kitchen on the terrace — a stovetop and an oven, already heated. Johannes put the meat in the oven.

"There. Now we just have to wait."

THEY ATE AT THE TABLE in the living room. Johannes put some piano music on the stereo, something Anja didn't recognize.

Then he looked her in the eye, closely, challengingly. His eyes were brown. Yesterday they had looked moss green. When you saw them up close, in daylight perhaps, they were moss green. Maybe his eyes changed color with his mood. Worry, affection, anger, love, lust. Maybe only someone who was close to him could see all the hues in his eyes. Anja realized that she was imagining what his lust was like. The thought was inappropriate, and she had to rinse it away with a generous swallow of wine.

By the end of the meal she'd drunk three glasses and started to have a feeling of unreality.

She felt like talking, telling him about her husband, about their life and how it had changed with the forgetting.

"You know," she began warily, "when my husband started to forget, the most painful part of it wasn't that he didn't remember certain things. What did it matter if he didn't remember everything? Forgetting is freedom; sometimes it's a mercy. If only he could have drawn the line at forgetting things. But he started to lose his purpose. That hurt more, the fact that he stopped wanting to do anything."

Johannes nodded.

"That's the most hopeless thing about it," she continued. "It's something you don't even think about until someone close to you starts forgetting. It's only when the memories start to fade, when they're already lost, when they only come out at random, that you realize that their plans have disappeared, too. There are no more possibilities. It's like the human mind gives up its possibilities when there are no more memories to serve as a horizon for the future. My husband doesn't have any hopes for the years to come. He has no plans."

"None?"

"Well, he has one. The ultimate plan."

"What's that?"

"He has death. He plans to die."

Anja swallowed her wine hurriedly. Now she'd said too much. It would be inappropriate to say anything more. Johannes seemed to realize the sensitivity of the situation, got up from the table, and stretched out his hand.

"Come on, I think we're ready for what I planned to show you."

She wiped her mouth on her napkin and got up. Johannes led her out of the living room into the hallway and to a sturdy, closed door. Before he opened it, he turned and took her hand again. His eyes were questioning: Are you ready? Anja didn't know what to expect. She steadied herself for the worst: some kind of perverted sight that might even make her feel sick. She instinctively turned to look for an escape route as he opened the door.

The room was dark. It took a second for her eyes to adjust. It wasn't just a room, it was a large salon. There was no furniture in it — just the parquet floor and three tall windows that let in the pale light of the sliver of moon. Finally she saw what was there: all of the walls were covered in photographs. Even the ceiling was full of them. They were large, letter-sized, and they didn't seem to have any common theme.

A day on Mannerheimintie in the seventies, a laughing child

with a beach ball, a mysterious woman from the nineteen-twenties looking sternly into the camera. Some of the pictures were of two images juxtaposed: the twenties woman's seductive smile in front of the Three Smiths Statue among twenty-first-century rush-hour traffic. If you turned your head and looked at it from one side, you could see another face take shape over the woman's face.

Anja looked at the profusion of photos, confused.

"Are these pictures you took?"

"No. My mother took them. I don't know exactly when. Maybe she was already starting to forget. I think they've been here for years. When I came to Finland last summer to arrange things here, I found this room like this. My sister wanted to take down all the pictures right away, but I wouldn't let her. I thought they might have some meaning."

Anja nodded, not knowing what to say.

"Do you understand now?" Johannes asked. "Kaleidoscope logic. Something just bubbles to the surface, rises to significance without any intent. But for the one experiencing it, it has tremendous meaning whenever it happens."

Anja knew exactly what he was talking about. "Chronology is the first thing to break down when a person starts to forget."

"Yes," Johannes said.

Anja continued, unrestrained, suddenly feeling that she could talk about anything. "But if the forgetting continues, time disappears entirely. Experiences flatten out. Plans and memories disappear."

She could feel her heart pounding. All of a sudden she felt like telling him everything, all of it, saving the biggest for last. She couldn't say it. She breathed quietly as the silver light of the moon brushed the walls of the room.

They stood there a little longer, not speaking, listening to the silence rise from the corners of the room and wrap itself around them.

When they went back to the living room and closed the door behind them, reality seemed to settle back into place and Anja thought she ought to leave. Johannes helped her with her coat in the entryway.

"I'd like to see you again," he said without hesitation.

It felt hard to say no, but criminal to say yes. She was married and her husband was alive — in a different reality, but alive, nevertheless.

Johannes seemed sincere. Maybe it was because of his way of talking: lingering over the first words of every sentence, the first syllable of every word. His S's were soft — caressing, in fact. Perhaps it was a remnant of some accent. Maybe he'd lived somewhere in the north as a child.

"Well, we'll see," she said.

She opened the apartment door, thanked him for the meal, and was turning to leave. But something made her turn back; she took a few steps toward him, reached out her hand fervently, and took hold of his sleeve, as if begging for mercy. She could hear a strange breathlessness in her voice, almost like a whisper.

"I promised him. I promised ... promised to ... kill him."

The words came out in a jumble. Johannes looked calmly into her eyes. She said it again, slowly and clearly this time, as if explaining the nature of the situation to herself:

"I promised my husband that I would kill him when he couldn't remember anything anymore."

Johannes didn't take his eyes off her; he just nodded.

"These things happen," he said quietly. "People promise

things to each other. They make promises that are hard to keep."

Anja felt her knees shaking. Tears pressed against the back of her eyes.

"I can't. I can't do it," she whispered. "I already feel guilty. Would it change anything? It would only make the guilt more real. It would only complete what's already there. I've already done it by thinking that I could."

"Who are you asking for forgiveness?"

"I don't know. I don't know if forgiveness is possible."

They stood facing each other. A minute passed, perhaps two.

"Are you going to tell anyone about this?" Anja asked. "Are you going to go and tell someone?"

"Who would I tell?"

"I don't know. The police or somebody."

"No," he said. "I won't tell."

"Why not?"

"Sometimes we promise things to the ones we love. Even criminal things. It's not my place to judge that."

Anja opened the door at last, but then turned back again. "What is it that you want from me?"

Johannes shrugged.

"I want to get to know you," he said.

Anja looked at his feet. For some reason he wasn't wearing any socks — she hadn't noticed before. Bare, surprisingly brown toes with perfect toenails. The toes seemed to burst with humanity, painfully innocent, as if their precise forms were secretly etching themselves in her memory and the thought of them would come back to her when she woke up in the middle of the night, their complete helplessness. Uncomplicated, fulfilling their purpose, not asking anyone's permission, just instinctively reaching out in all their perfection, with all their small details.

It would be so easy to stay here, with him, in this strange, familiar man's foyer, to go into the living room, sit on the sofa, rest in his arms with her head against him, close her eyes. It would be so easy to justify it to herself, to give in.

She brushed her hair from her face, for something to do.

Now it was really time to leave.

She looked at Johannes.

"All I have is the past. Memories, and meaning through them."

OUTSIDE, THE WEATHER was starting to freeze. Anja walked slowly downtown, breathing deep. It was completely still. The shock made her walking unsteady. She looked at her hands in the moonlight: they were trembling.

She stopped under the soothing shelter of the trees in the park. She felt like crying. She tried to cry but the tears wouldn't come. She crossed the esplanade. The black trunks of the trees had started to turn shiny; a frozen, night-time storybook forest. She turned at Kämp Galleria and headed toward Aleksanterinkatu. She stopped in front of the Fazer café to look in the window at the gingerbread village. It was built for the coming Christmas. She remembered the excitement of waiting for the gingerbread village to appear in the window when she was a child. She had to go and look every day to see if it was there yet, and then one day it was: perfect little windows and doors, sugar-coated rooftops, and gingerbread men and elves dancing along a candy-covered road. She'd looked at it for hours, certain that its miniature perfection was real and alive, at least at night, when no one was looking.

She walked to Railway Square. She was beginning to feel calmer, no longer on the brink of tears. She almost felt like smiling.

She got on the bus at half-past nine and, in its stuffy warmth, peace finally returned to her.

The bus passed Kaisaniemi and picked up speed, stopped only once on Hämeentie, and then sped onto the highway and into the dark of evening. In the warm, comforting vibration her breathing started to level out and her hands stopped trembling.

SHE WOKE UP at four-thirty in the morning. Snow had begun to fall during the night. An awareness of a change had filtered through her sleep: something strange had settled into the house — maybe it was fear, or maybe hope; she couldn't tell the difference anymore. Once she was awake, she couldn't get back to sleep. She watched the flakes drifting lazily against the window, miniature, eight-cornered lace, and she remembered the feeling of the first snow from her childhood.

She made some coffee and went to get the newspaper, walking in her husband's large rubber boots over the still-untouched snow. The boots left enormous tracks in the snowy white. At the mailbox, as flakes drifted down onto her hair, she glanced around her, then lifted her arms and twirled silently, like a child.

# Mari

Tinka has got fake IDs from somewhere. According to the card, Mari is twenty-one years old. Tinka is twenty-two.

They start getting ready for graduation night at five, in Mari's room. Tinka is putting streaks in her hair and looking at a map of Helsinki while the color takes hold, planning their route: Iso Roobertinkatu, Fredrikinkatu, Uudenmaankatu, Erottaja, Kamppi.

"It'd be best to pick up some men right away so they can pay for us the rest of the night," Tinka muses. "Maybe suck them off in the bathroom, so they'll be obliged to pay."

"No," Mari says. "My mom can give us some money. I, for one, am not gonna suck anybody off."

Tinka looks at Mari from under her hair-color foils, amused. "Listen, that's how things work in the real world," she says, doodling hearts on the map with a pink felt pen. "A girl has to be ready to make sacrifices."

"No," Mari answers, her voice drawing a decisive line. "I want to make my own rules."

Tinka's expression changes from knowing to pitying. Mari knows what that look means. Big sister instructing the ignorant child.

"Oh, you," Tinka says, puckering up her mouth. "You'll be Miss Virgin for the rest of your life, that way." She laughs and colors the nail on her left big toe pink.

Mari looks at Tinka in confusion and realizes she never bought her story of wild sex in the rec room, not for a minute.

"But I …" Mari stammers, trying to get control of the situation.

"Oh, honey — did you think I believed that? I saw that the two of you were in there together for about five minutes. But we can fix that tonight. Even for you!"

Mari looks at the floor, embarrassed. Stupid. A pitiful, inexperienced little girl. And that's when she decides: it's going to happen tonight.

Tinka gets up and goes into the bathroom to rinse the dye out of her hair. Mari steps in front of the mirror, looks at her reflection, and considers a plan of action. Virginity, and how to escape it. There are two things that worry her: kissing and blow jobs. Her kissing skills were judged to be negligible as early as seventh grade: a boy from the class above her, a school party, a first kiss in the fluorescent reality of the girls' toilet. The kiss — her tongue groping clumsily along a row of teeth — then a peevish suggestion: "Don't poke with your tongue like that, it makes me feel like I'm gonna puke." Ever since then Mari has had the gnawing conviction that she is completely inept at matters involving the tongue. This certainty hangs over her head like a flashing neon sign: Cow tongue. Suffocatrix. This certainty stands between her and her becoming a woman. And now she's certain of something else: she doesn't know how to suck a man off like a woman should.

"I wish I had a drink already," Tinka says impatiently. "Is there anything in the liquor cabinet here?"

"Yeah, but I've never taken anything out of it. I know my mom would notice."

"She won't notice," Tinka says, tossing her head. "Take something that's clear and replace it with water."

Tinka hops to her feet and is already out the door. Mari follows behind her, obedient. When they get to the living room, Tinka heads for the glass-doored cabinet.

"What should we have?" she says in a high, excited voice as she opens it.

Mari glances at the door. Her mother might come in at any moment. Tinka ignores her warnings, opening bottles and smelling their contents. She takes a big swig from a bottle of vodka. The taste makes her nose wrinkle. "Ugh. Awful. But it'll do." She takes out her pink water bottle and fills it up. Vodka spills on the table next to Mari's confirmation portrait. Tinka bends over and licks it up.

"Hurry up," Mari urges. "My mom'll kill me if she —"

"Calm down. We're fine — and your mom is quite easy to get around. I've chatted to her. She likes me."

"Huh? When did you talk to her?"

"On the phone. I called and she answered. I said I was your 'girlfriend'. I know how adults think. You have to talk to them a certain way. Believe me, your mom likes me."

"Uh, I'm sure she does."

They still have to sneak into the kitchen and fill the vodka bottle with water to cover their tracks. Tinka goes first, holding the bottle, and Mari tiptoes behind her. Tinka's already in the kitchen when Mari hears the key turning in the front door. Mom.

"What are you standing there for?" her mother asks in surprise, putting her shopping bags down on the floor.

"I'm not, I mean ..."

Mari can hear Tinka clattering in the kitchen and realizes that Tinka hasn't heard her mother come in. She can picture the chain of events if her mother sees the bottle: first a deep silence, then a sit-down at the table, more deep silence, heavy, accusing. An interrogation and a lecture on alcohol. And polite disapproval directed at Tinka, the instigator, the little pusher who lured Mari into ruination.

Mari's mother takes off her shoes and picks up her shopping. Mari panics. She can't let her mother go into the kitchen.

"What's the matter?" her mother asks. "Don't just stand there. How about some tea?" She walks past her and opens the kitchen door, in spite of Mari's vague attempt to stop her.

Mari lets out a yelp at the desperate moment of discovery — her mother opens the door and stands on the threshold looking at Tinka. But then Mari sees that the bottle's gone, that Tinka is smiling a triumphant, sunny smile, self-assured, like she owns the world, with the pink water bottle full of vodka in her hand.

"Oh!" Mari's mother says, surprised. "Are you Tinka?"

"Yeah. Hi," Tinka says, shaking hands politely.

Mari watches, mesmerized, as Tinka displays her mastery of yet another game. Her mother is sold immediately.

"It's nice that Mari's got a new friend. You're a very nice girl, Tinka," she says, putting the teakettle on the stove. Tinka winks at Mari over her mother's shoulder and, to Mari's horror, takes a swallow from her water bottle.

As they have tea, Tinka wraps Mari's mother around her little finger, smiling and talking about her plans for the future. Mari's mom nods approvingly. Tinka takes occasional sips of vodka from the plastic bottle and says with clear eyes that girls have to make sure they stay hydrated.

"It's good for your hair and skin," she says, flashing Mari a conspiratorial grin. Mari looks down at the table, silently munching the scones her mother bought and slurping her tea.

Result of this tea party: no catastrophe, no alcohol lecture, no arrests. Instead, her mother hands her forty euros with a smile.

"You can spend it at McDonald's or something," she says happily.

"Yeah. We're going to a movie first, then to Mickey D's," Tinka says, beaming.

Her expression doesn't falter.

AT THE BUS STOP, Tinka stands so close to Mari that she can feel the damp warmth of her breath. Even now, with the vodka fumes, Tinka smells like roses and fall apples as she takes a tube of strawberry lip gloss out of her backpack and glosses her lips.

"Now I'm gonna teach you how to sweep a man off his feet with a kiss," she whispers, pressing up against Mari.

"What? What are you doing?"

Tinka smiles and takes Mari's face between her hands. Her eyes turn serious; she strokes Mari's face with gentle fingers. Mari feels her heart thudding, striking at emptiness.

"You're so pretty," Tinka whispers. "Don't let anybody tell you you're not."

Mari tries to smile, but the smile gets stuck somewhere in the back of her throat. The realization that something new is happening has the smile in its grip and won't let it go. Mari looks at Tinka and tries to figure out just what that something is. Tinka just looks back at her, serious, not speaking. Tinka smooths her lips with her finger and then spreads the lip gloss on Mari's lips, which are stiff from the autumn wind.

Mari opens her mouth to say something but Tinka presses a finger against her lips.

"Shh," she says, bringing her face right up to Mari's face and just breathing there, like she's found her place in the world.

Tinka closes her eyes, and Mari does the same.

"Nice and slow now," Tinka whispers, and carefully touches her lips to Mari's.

The kiss is slow, light, and soft, the kind that makes your knees weak and changes the rhythm of your breathing, the kind that makes the world more beautiful. Tinka flicks her tongue against Mari's tongue and then presses lightly against it. It feels slippery and exciting and Mari sinks deep into the feeling of the kiss. The stiff grass crackles under their feet and the world rotates; the world has become a great spiral of sounds and colors with these two mouths in the middle of it, pressing against each other as if everything were clear since the beginning of time, as if there had never been anything else but the arch of stars in this October night sky and the never-ending swirl of this kiss.

When it's all over, Tinka pulls away from her as if nothing happened, bends over her bag, and takes out the pink water bottle. She swallows the vodka with gusto, like a man, and offers it to Mari. Mari takes a wary sip. Tinka grins.

"This isn't any lesbo shit. It's just something a woman needs to know how to do." She spits on the ground to back up her words.

Mari nods solemnly.

IT ISN'T THAT EASY using the fake IDs. They try three bars before one lets them in. As soon as they get inside, Tinka sizes up the offerings.

"Look at that guy. He's got a gleam in his eye," she whispers in Mari's ear, cocking her head toward a light-haired man. "Hey, he's coming this way! Smile, now. Let's snag him!"

The man approaches them the way Mari's seen men do in movies. Midnight, the smoke, the noise, the bar full of people. She wonders what he'll say first. *Do you come here often?* she thinks, and decides that if he says that, she'll pretend she didn't hear him. The man comes closer and she notices that he's actually a boy. Just a boy. Mari puts on a smile. She can see that he knows, they both know, the whole thing is understood: no commitments, no phone numbers, no promises. Maybe not even names. Tinka flicks her fiery hair and flashes her magic gaze.

"You have nice eyes," the boy says to Mari.

To Mari's surprise and Tinka's bafflement, he pays no attention at all to Tinka, just looks straight into Mari's eyes.

He offers to buy her a drink. Tinka demands a cosmopolitan and he brings a drink for both of them.

"What would you think if we both picked you up, the pair of us?" Tinka asks defiantly.

The boy smiles, amused, and turns back to Mari. "Is your friend always so direct, or just tonight?"

Mari smiles. Tinka snorts in disgust and gets up from the table, leaving Mari and the boy alone. Mari turns her head and tries to keep Tinka in her field of vision among the crowd, but the boy turns Mari's face back himself.

"Don't worry about her. I'm sure a person as blunt as she is can manage on her own."

"Yeah."

"But what about you? Who are you?"

"Uh, Mari. Just me, I mean. I'm just me."

The boy smiles and leans toward her. She can smell the alcohol on his breath and it occurs to her that she doesn't want to kiss him the way Tinka has taught her.

"I think you should come home with me tonight," the boy whispers.

Mari smiles. This game is working. It's progressing just like it's supposed to. And Mari knows how the game ends, she knows it with certainty: it's going to happen tonight.

They get up from the table and he puts his arm around her shoulders. They walk toward the cloakroom and Mari sees Tinka one last time. She's watching them from far away, through the smoke, the cosmopolitan still in her hand, and her eyes look glassy, serious. For a fleeting second Mari sees sadness in her eyes, but then someone comes between them, and Tinka's eyes disappear from view. Mari turns and walks out the door.

ON THE WAY HOME, on the way to a stranger's home, Mari listens to the boy talking. He talks the whole way. There are silent spaces to fill; the truth can't be given any chance to intrude. This must be what people talk about. Work or school, anything at all. Mari listens. The boy confesses in a quiet voice that sometimes he feels really low. Really low, Mari thinks. Me too.

And once they've closed the door behind them, he comes close to her — a hard erection, hoarse breathing. Mari's heart is throbbing. He kisses her. He tastes like cigarettes and beer, she thinks. There's something meaty about the combination of flavors, something that brings to mind some kind of Karelian stew she was forced to eat in kindergarten. She starts to feel vaguely nauseated. The boy takes off his pants. The tip of his penis pokes out of his underwear, moist and shining, and Mari finds herself thinking how much it looks like the ones men have in porn movies. Just a little smaller, and with more hair around it. Are they all the same, then?

Mari settles onto the bed and lies down. She takes off her underwear and lets him come to her. He fucks in an inexperienced, careless way, going too deep, and Mari thinks that maybe she ought to rock along with him. The pain changes at a certain point from stabbing to white, floating, dim, as she rocks along with him. At the moment of discharge, a viscous yelp, Mari's gaze falls on the lamp on the night table and it occurs to her that there's a lamp like that at her grandma's house, pieces of colored glass soldered together with metal. The lamp and the curtains must have been chosen by his mother, she thinks, or maybe his girlfriend.

The boy turns his back to her and falls asleep. Mari lays awake. She looks at the red numbers on the digital alarm clock. Three-twelve. Three-thirteen. Three-fourteen. His breathing deepens, turns snuffly. Three twenty-one.

When you sleep next to a stranger, you may accidentally get too close. People are at their most helpless when they're asleep — vulnerable, childlike. Sleep removes all the masks, and all that remain are intimate gestures: the clicking sound of a tongue, a sigh, a muffled rustle. The one who's awake in this sudden intimacy, the one who witnesses all the stranger's movements of his extremities as he sleeps, the changes in the rhythm of his breathing, is the one with the power. And that power doesn't feel good. It feels alarming, bizarre — dangerous, in fact. It's like suddenly becoming initiated into secrets that you'd prefer not to know about.

Mari watches the boy as he sighs, scratches his leg, moves

his head on his pillow. Three-forty. Only an hour until the newspaper carriers are out. She feels a throbbing pain between her legs. The musty smell of the condom still lingers in the air. The boy starts to snore. Through the window, Mari sees that it's started to snow outside. One more hour and she can leave, walk out the door and through the falling snow, leaving tracks in the new, cottony-light drifts.

But she doesn't wait until the morning. She goes out into the snow in the middle of the night. It's hard to walk, it hurts between her legs, she's bleeding.

She's overcome with unexpected amusement. So that's what it's like? Not exactly what she expected. Not at all what she expected, in fact. Not particularly enjoyable, or even entertaining. But definitely new, certainly strange. New and strange. Adult.

MARI GETS HOME, goes into the bathroom, lets the blood flow, takes out the razor she uses to shave her legs, breaks off the blade guard, and cuts slashes in her thigh. One, two three.

She can hear herself moan. It comes so easily, so unforced. A moan with a strange tone in it. It's more real than any of the half-forced sounds she's just been letting out, in a strange bed with a strange boy. The blood rinses away, down the drain with the water. Water pulse-blood cunt-blood, all mixed together. Mari lets the blood flow. Just lets it flow.

★

THE NEXT MORNING in the kitchen, as her mother is pouring her ever-present herbal tea, Mari makes a fateful mistake: she reaches for a roll from the basket, leans carelessly on the table, and presses her pajama-covered thigh against the table's edge. Her pajama-covered thigh and five layers of bandages. The bandages that cover her three lovely cuts. The wounds gape open, flowing like the very life of the one who cut them.

But this is a mistake. A mistake with consequences: as the thigh presses against the table, Mari gasps in pain, sinks back into her chair. Her mother's expression becomes alert.

"What? What's wrong? Are you sick?" she says.

"Oh, my back's just sore," Mari mumbles, surreptitiously putting her hand over her thigh.

That's when her hand feels something damp and she realizes with horror what's happened: the blood has soaked through. She tries desperately to spread her hand to cover the flood. But it doesn't work: her mother's eyes fix on her hand, and her flannel pajamas with the jumping lambs on them gradually turn from white to bright red as the fresh blood soaks through.

"What's happened to you? My God, what the hell happened to you?" her mother says, angry, horrified.

"Get off it, Mom. I'm sure it's just, you know, my period," Mari sputters, turning her face away. "Don't look. Don't look, Mom." She can't cry, not now, not right now.

"Mari. Look at me and tell me. What's going on? What the hell is going on?"

"Nothing. Nothing at all."

"Did someone hurt you?"

The question is a sob. For the first time, Mari is able to grasp her mother's fear: the fear is the sob reaching through the air between them. Her mother asks again.

"Did someone do something bad to you?"

And then the next, inevitable question:

"Or did you do it yourself?"

"Fuck off," Mari groans, and gets up from the table.

Her mother grabs the sleeve of her sweater and holds on tight, not letting her go. Mari wrenches herself away. That's a mistake, too, she realizes. The sweater slips down and shows her upper arm, the wounds piercing her baby-white skin like a row of exclamation marks. The sweater hangs in her mother's hands for a moment and her face is frozen, gaping, the sweater falling in a strangled clump on the floor, the plastic buttons clanking against the wood, and Mari can't stop looking at her eyes: an empty look, completely expressionless.

"What exactly is this?"

Her mother's voice has shrunk to a whisper. Something inside Mari shifts, something closes up, turns her expression to glass. She sees herself just looking at her mother, motionless, speechless. Her mother takes her by both shoulders and shakes her. Mari stands there, like she's turned to stone.

Something outside her, a distant voice, registers the brittle emotion that the moment brings, etches it on her memory. *So now you're caught, and you don't feel anything. Maybe a little bit happy, a little bubble of joy under the surface, because you've been up to something secret, something of your very own.* It's like a pleasant little game, like a didactic play in grade school about what happens when daughters keep secrets from their mothers. Mari feels the blood flowing from the wounds on her thigh and down her leg and dripping silently onto the floor. If the blood has time to soak into the wood, into its porous cracks, it will be stuck there and never come clean, no matter what soap you use. Human blood is like that — it leaves a stain.

Mari's mother slaps her cheek with an open hand.

Mari pulls away and repositions herself, steps from outside

back into her own space. She sees her mother flinch at what she's just done. She's never hit Mari before. The blow was light, to wake her up, just a slap, and it didn't leave any perceptible trace except a little warmth on the curve of her cheek. But something else has shifted, something that doesn't reach the level of perception. Something in motion that can't be stopped now.

Her mother is shocked at what she's done.

"I'm sorry, I'm sorry, I'm sorry," she says.

Her voice is mechanical, toneless.

"What exactly happened? What happened really?" she whispers.

She slumps into a chair, lifts her teacup to her lips with a trembling hand as if it can wipe her hand's crime away, obliterate it. The teacup won't stay in her grasp; it falls back into its saucer with a clatter and breaks into shards. Tea splashes on the table.

Her mother's question slices through the air, which has turned heavy, impossible to breathe. The question rises to the peak of the roof and hangs there, waiting for an answer.

*What exactly happened? What happened really?*

No answer comes, and Mari turns, walks out of the kitchen, climbs the stairs, and closes her bedroom door behind her.

A dense silence falls around her.

Two minutes pass. Mari watches the door. Her mother will follow her, of course. She sits on the bed, presses her hand against her thigh, prays for the bleeding to stop.

Her mother pushes the door open. Mari turns slowly to look at her. Her mother glances around the room. She needs evidence, incriminating evidence, anything to lay Mari's secret life bare, to make it clear. She could hug Mari. She could do that so easily, take a few steps toward her, take her in her arms. Mari might even let her do it. But right now all Mari's mother has is this desire to know.

She starts randomly, rummaging through Mari's things in sheer panic. The desk drawers, the clothes closet, the back of the bookshelf. Finally she comes to the dresser, the one that has the knife and bandages in the top drawer, all of Mari's hidden equipment for making her existence easier, clearer.

Mari thinks about this equipment. The horror at the thought of its discovery is a distant lurch inside her. And, as if she can read Mari's mind, her mother opens the top drawer, stares at its contents, and takes out the knife. Mari doesn't try to stop her. It doesn't matter — her secret's out, completely out. She makes a note of her own dull reaction. Of how meaningless it all is, how trivial. A feeling of panic bounces dully behind her indifference. Soon it will spill out, at any moment, slowed down, like shouts at an accident.

Her mother's reaction is slowed, too.

A second passes, then another. She doesn't say anything, just holds the knife in her hand, the blood dried to a sticky stain on its blade.

A number of empty, unconvincing explanations zip through Mari's mind, none of them good enough to say out loud.

"What are you doing to yourself?" her mother finally says.

The question is a desperate whisper. Mari can see that as much as her mother fears someone doing something to hurt her, someone else, some stranger harming her, she is just as fearful of the alternative: that Mari did this to herself.

She strides a few steps to where Mari is sitting, takes hold of her arm.

"Damn it, tell me. You're going to explain this to me."

Her mother pulls her up and hustles her out of the room, rushing behind her down the stairs. For the first time Mari thinks that the game has gone too far. Up to now it's just been a game. She had thought she might be that kind of girl, the kind filled with longing, the kind who draws herself into the moment in little, sharp cuts. She liked the game. She enjoyed it. But now her mother is angry. Now it's gone too far.

Mari's mother takes her to the kitchen, sits her down at the table. She gets antiseptic and sterile swabs from the first aid kit, makes Mari sit where she is, orders her to take off her stained pajama pants, and cleans the wounds on her thigh. She bandages them again and looks up at Mari. Fear huddles behind her anger. The look demands an explanation.

"Spit it out, damn it. You're going to tell me exactly what's going on. Are you using drugs?"

"No!"

"You've lost weight, too. Have you been eating properly? Have you been throwing up?"

"What? No. Honest, I don't throw up." Mari is in a trance.

"It's been a long time since I've seen you eat a proper meal," her mother says, not taking her eyes off her.

"Fucking hell," Mari says, turning her face to the window.

Her mother goes to the fridge and gets out the butter and cheese. She takes a roll from the bread box, splits it in two with a furious slice of the knife, and butters both halves angrily. She slices cheese on top and slaps the sandwich down in front of Mari.

"Eat it. I want to see you eat it, right here in front of me."

Mari looks at her mother in disbelief. She's serious. Mari carefully picks up the sandwich and bites off a piece. Her mother tells her to hold out her arm and starts cleaning the cuts on it.

Mari eats, her arm stinging, the sharp jab of the antiseptic sinking through her skin into her flesh, and her mother watches her eat, like a hawk. Mari's mouth twists into a sob. She swallows the dry sandwich. She just has to eat it.

She begs for mercy with her eyes. Her mother's mouth is a tight line. She's still holding the wad of cotton in her hand. The only gesture that softens the edge of her control is a hint of a tremble in her right thumb and forefinger.

"I'm going to keep an eye on you," she says. Her voice is shaking. "This kind of thing cannot happen. You are my daughter. You can't hide things like this from me."

"Can I go now? Let me go now," Mari whispers, her voice strangled.

Her mother nods and looks away. Mari can almost see a flicker of regret in her face, around her mouth. It might be fear. Maybe it's fear. But Mari refuses to believe it. All she sees is this: the power that briefly slipped out of her mother's grasp has stabilized again, returned to where it belongs.

# Anja

HER HUSBAND'S been working too much lately. Even into the night. He sits in his office under the bright light and draws. Anja tries to get him to make something to eat, to rake the yard, to go to the store, the theatre, the movies. He refuses.

"I'm working, can't you see that?"

"I see," Anja answers.

"This has to be done very soon," he says, bending over his drawing again. "I have a deadline. Next week."

A deadline. He always has a deadline. Every week. This is how it happens, Anja thinks. This is how couples grow distant from each other, how they sit at the same breakfast table — if they even do that anymore — and don't speak. Share a newspaper and sip their coffee, mutter a few words about the weather and the headlines and then hurry off to work. If only they had a child. Then they would talk more, about the child's school and piano lessons and summer vacations and allowance. As it is, all they have is this stale twosome, silence at meals, turning away from each other in bed at night.

Anja tries to peek over his shoulder at what's on his desk: what exactly has he been up to all these evenings?

"What is it?" she asks.

"Stop it. You're bothering me," he answers.

Anja doesn't give up. "What are you drawing?"

"This is a confidential project."

Anja's suspicions are aroused. Confidential? Since when did the architecture firm's projects become confidential? He covers his work with a large tablecloth and glares at her. Where did he get a tablecloth — from the linen closet? Why? She looks at her husband, not knowing what to say. Something is troubling him, an annoyance, or some sudden worry, she can't tell which.

"I'm sure you can show it to your wife," she coaxes. "No project is that confidential."

He resists, pushing the cloth to the edges of the table to ensure that nothing shows. The whole idea of the tablecloth seems ridiculous, melodramatic.

"Show it to me," she insists.

"No," he says.

"Come on, show me."

"Well, if you don't tell anyone else about it. You can't blab."

"Who would I blab to?"

"This is top secret," he says again.

"I understand," Anja answers.

He takes hold of the edge of the tablecloth and pulls it away with a magician's flourish. Anja looks at the drawings. Her first reaction is an involuntary laugh. Is he teasing her? He pouts like a child and looks at her expectantly, holding the white tablecloth in front of him like an apron. Anja's laugh fades. She looks at the drawings again. Sketches. Rough, arching lines that form something like a building. It resembles a child's drawing, the kind of thing a child would draw on a long, rainy day. It's carefully done, though, detailed, clever even. But childish, helplessly infantile. It can't really be a commission.

Anja looks at her husband, aghast.

"Well?" he says.

"Well, what?"

"What do you think of it?"

"Are you serious?"

"Serious?"

"Yes. Are you serious, or is it some sort of joke?"

"Are you calling my work a joke?"

"Honey ..."

"What?"

Anja starts to cry. The tears flow silently. He looks at her in shock, then down at his drawing. Doubt shows on his face, surprise and a shadow of fear: like a child who's been caught misbehaving.

He sits helplessly in his chair.

Anja goes to him and kisses his forehead, smooths his hair. He wads the tablecloth in his hands.

"I think they've been talking at work. Saying that I'm not doing well."

"Have they?"

"I've been having trouble with my lines lately. My strokes. That's what old age does. I can't draw a straight line anymore. I'm losing my grip somehow. I can't design anymore. I don't know how."

Anja takes him in her arms and holds him tight. Sometimes it feels like she can't get close enough to him, her beloved, like she ought to be able to get inside him, into his inner space, and even that wouldn't be close enough. Her husband extricates himself from her embrace and looks her in the eye.

"I couldn't remember a client's name last week. An important customer, a big design contract. I had completely forgotten about the project. How could I forget something like that? Is that normal? The client asked me about the designs, and I didn't know what to say. I didn't know what he was talking about — I didn't remember."

"You're absentminded. You've always been absentminded. I'm sure it's nothing."

How long will she lie to herself, deny what she sees, just to be protected a little longer? The drawings lie on the desk like a silent shout. She's careful not to look at them, not to say anything more about them.

Just so they can be here together a little longer.

THE CRIME THAT her sense of responsibility told her must be committed had to be planned precisely. It was important that her plan have a backup plan, and that her backup plan have a second, emergency backup plan.

Anja had made a list of various ways of dying when she was planning her own exit. Now she opened the locked drawer of her desk and took the list out again. The first choices — hanging, slitting your wrists, throwing yourself under a train — were out of the question, of course. She crossed them out.

She had read somewhere in a detective novel about an insulin overdose. It was fourth on the list. It was a good idea, and even gentle, according to Anja's understanding of the physiology of dying, but acquiring the necessary materials was problematic. Insulin wasn't available without a prescription. Anja tried to think up a story to get her sister to write her a prescription for it, but rejected the idea quickly. Marita was too curious: she would demand to know what she wanted the insulin for.

Of course she could always break into the nursing-home drug supply. But that wouldn't be wise: they would keep an exact account of all the drugs. Anja put a question mark after insulin overdose.

An air embolism was a possibility. She remembered reading a crime novel where that was the murder method. The simplicity of the idea seemed brilliant. Air in the bloodstream was usually an accidental cause of death, the result of carelessness. A person on an intravenous drip would get air in their veins from the IV for one reason or another, and the air would move through their veins and end up in their heart or brain.

It was important that the death be peaceful and painless, gentle, as only a considered, deliberate death could be. It was also important that her own role in the death be a passive one. It would be less like a crime somehow if she just sat by and watched the life slowly drift out of her husband's body, the slim frame of flesh and bone that had already started to dissolve along with his memories.

An embolism seemed smart for practical reasons, too. Because of his medication, her husband regularly suffered dehydration, which was treated with an IV drip. He was given intravenous antibiotics for various infections. An air embolism was a genuine risk with these treatments. If it happened it might not arouse as many questions among the staff as some other indeterminate cause of death.

But then Anja started thinking about the air moving through his veins. How could you steer it? And what if it moved through them in some disastrous way that wasn't fatal but caused unbearable pain, pain that would make him scream in anguish and bring the nursing-home staff running? She couldn't take that risk. She rejected the idea of an embolism.

She thought about his regular medication. He'd been prescribed Ebixa. It affected the chemical transmitters in the brain and had been used to treat Alzheimer's for a long time. What were Ebixa's effects in combination with other drugs? Was there a drug that wasn't recommended for those taking Ebixa because the two drugs were dangerous when taken together?

ANJA TOOK the Fennica pharmaceutical guide from the drawer and laid it on the desk. Her sister hadn't noticed it was missing; Anja had taken it from her office the last time she visited. It was last year's guide — her sister might happen to need this year's, and Anja couldn't risk having her notice it was gone.

She glanced at the door. She'd locked it, just in case. She opened the book and started flipping through the pages. She was trying to stay calm, but her breathing was shaky.

Ebixa. She searched for the section where they talked about drug interactions. Ebixa had strong interactions with some drugs that affected the central nervous system. There were other warnings as well, but nothing that was fatal. It warned about changes in plasma levels. Anja wasn't sure what that meant.

She looked up from the book and sighed. She would have to know a lot more about pharmacology to be able to develop a discreet method, something that couldn't be connected to her.

She leafed aimlessly through the pages. A drug catalogue is of no use if you don't understand the vocabulary of the profession. What kind of drug was she looking for exactly? Something with an effect that was potent and quick, something that would work when combined with other drugs, and be eliminated from the body quickly, without leaving a trace.

She turned another page. Suddenly there it was, quite by accident. *Dormicum.* The name had an ominously placid rhythm, fateful, and Anja held her breath, shocked that she'd found what she was looking for. She scanned the rest of the entry:

> *A short-acting sleep medication, with midazolam as its active ingredient. Should not be used in combination with drugs containing erythromycin. Reported interactions with some antifungals (Nizoral). Maximum recommended prescription 20 tablets.*

There were also warnings about the use of Dormicum when pregnant or breastfeeding and in cases of organ failure, but she didn't need to read those. She knew enough already. This was it. She knew that erythromycin was an active ingredient in antibiotics. Her husband had frequent infections. Did they treat him with drugs containing erythromycin?

The most important thing, though, was that the drug was "short-acting." That meant that it would take effect quickly and disappear from his system quickly. Just like she wanted: untraceable.

She looked up from the book again and stared out the window at the bustle of people on Aleksanterinkatu. Drops of sleet were falling. The day folded into evening, the sleet fell, Anja breathed silently there before her discovery and felt the triumph of it breaking through the thin thread of her sadness. Now she had to carry out her plan. There was no excuse for backing away now. All she had to do was make up a story to get some from the pharmacy.

★

"AH," THE DOCTOR at the health clinic said, glancing at Anja over his glasses. "So you're having trouble sleeping."

"Yes," Anja said humbly.

She was ashamed. It felt even more as if fate were mocking her. It was the same doctor she'd had when she came for the Doxal in the summer. For one horrified instant she thought of her patient information. Would he be able to see her psychiatric consultation and the fact that she was referred because of "suicidal behavior" in her medical record? But the doctor just smiled amiably. Maybe psychiatric information was in a different file, she thought, relieved.

"And what about your depression? Was it helped at all by the antidepressants?"

The doctor tapped his pen on his knee and tilted his head to give her a kindly look.

"Well, I took them," Anja mumbled.

"That's good. And what was the result?" he asked, glancing at his papers. "Was it what you'd hoped?"

"Pretty much," she said, gazing out the window.

He looked at her patient information, then back at her.

It occurred to her that he might refuse to prescribe any medication for her. She had to be careful. She had to lie, if the situation demanded it.

The doctor glanced at his computer monitor again.

"I'll prescribe Tenox for you," he said. "It's a common sleeping medication, effective and reliable."

Anja shook her head tensely and made a noise of protest. The doctor raised his eyebrows.

"I don't think it'll work," she said. She could hear the nervousness in her voice.

She needed an explanation. In a split second, she thought of a brilliant excuse, held together by a careless lie.

"I've tried them. They didn't work for me."

The doctor sighed, turned in his chair and looked at her. There was a little bit of doubt in his eyes already. Or maybe it was just weariness.

"What drug were you thinking of, then?" he asked. "Did you have a specific medication in mind?"

Anja fiddled with the hem of her skirt.

"Yes," she began warily. "My sister is a doctor and she recommended ... Dormicum. She said it was ... fast-acting. I'd like to take Dormicum, if that's all right." Anja could feel the sweat on her hand against the smooth fabric of her skirt.

"Dormicum is an old product," the doctor said. "It has numerous side effects."

His doubt was apparent now, and gave his voice an authoritative tone.

Anja strove to sound nonchalant. "I've used it before. I'm used to it."

He peered at her, evaluating.

She lied some more. "I haven't had any problems with Dormicum. It works for me."

The doctor pondered a moment. "All right," he said finally. "If that's what you want. I'll prescribe Dormicum."

He turned to write the prescription.

Anja interjected: "Could you possibly write me a double prescription?"

He glanced up in surprise. She quickly thought up another lie.

"I'm going out of town at the end of the month, to a conference in the United States."

His hesitance seemed to strengthen again.

She continued in a light, melodious voice. "The time difference and everything. I have an important presentation to give, and it would be miserable if I ran out and couldn't sleep before my talk."

The lie glimmered through her explanation. Or maybe only she could hear it, the hint of a tremble in her voice.

The doctor picked up his pen, tapped it on the desk, and looked her sharply in the eye.

"I've been in similar situations myself," he said, speaking slowly and deliberately.

Anja's heart thumped. "What situations?"

Silence. The lie floated in the air, and the doctor was just about to reach out and grab it. At any moment he might realize it, call the police, report a crime. Anja looked at the door. There was still time to escape if she got up right now and ran.

But a sympathetic smile spread across the doctor's face. "Conference presentations. Sleepless nights. Anxiety."

"Oh," Anja said with relief. "Right."

"I suppose I can write you a double prescription," he said kindly. "For the advancement of knowledge, since you're giving a presentation."

"For the advancement of knowledge," Anja said, camouflaging her deception with a forced smile.

The doctor typed the prescription, printed it, and handed it to her with a smile on his lips.

Anja thanked him and said goodbye, gazing at the floor.

AT FIRST SHE THOUGHT she would wait until there was some kind of infection. She quietly conferred with the nursing home about the details of her husband's medications. She couldn't ask about it directly, of course — that would arouse suspicion — but it was clear that they were very strict about their treatments for infections; patients with dementia were never given any drugs containing erythromycin. In any case, if she wanted the cause of death to be untraceable it was best not to have a plan that relied on the drug interacting with other medications. The sleeping pills would be eliminated from the body more slowly if they were combined with erythromycin. They would leave traces and suspicion would be directed at her. So she shouldn't wait for an infection to occur, at least not because of the erythromycin, anyway. But if her husband did contract some virus, or even pneumonia, his death wouldn't seem as unexpected.

She mulled over the alternatives for two weeks. On the sixteenth of November, her husband contracted a case of the common flu. It had begun as a cough over the previous weekend, and progressed as a mild fever. No antibiotics were prescribed. Anja thought the flu would have to do.

There was nothing unusual about the day itself. She just knew it was the right day. A clear sky, temperatures just above freezing, the puddles iced over and the ground covered with frost. It was a Tuesday.

Anja went swimming in the morning. She swam a kilometer and a half and then floated for another fifteen minutes, drifting on the slanting blue water, wishing she'd sink to the bottom but remaining afloat, her hair like sea algae, caressed by the water. When she lowered her head under the water, it was wonderfully quiet. Under the water she felt wonderfully light. Under the water she could forget.

But she got out of the pool and walked across the cold tiles to the sauna and sat down on a bench. A fat woman with breasts that hung to her waist threw half a ladle of water on the sauna stove. In the hiss of steam, Anja could have cried; her sniffles would have been concealed by the sigh of the vapor. But she just sat and watched the steam filling the air, the angles of the benches, and the way the fat water-thrower gradually disappeared into the arms of the mist.

THE DAY WAS CLEAR. The sun shone at a slant and made the frosty bricks of the Stockmann department store sparkle. A workman was unloading a moving truck on the corner, his breath steaming in the sharp air as he laughingly yelled to a partner deep in the cab of the truck. How lucky to be a man unloading a truck on a morning like this, Anja thought.

She caught the bus at Railway Square. Once she was on the bus, numerous reasons to give up her plan came to mind. The day was too beautiful, much too beautiful. On a day like this she ought to be riding her bike along the Vantaa River, stopping now and then to sit on a bench and have a snack, hot coffee from a thermos and a ham-and-cheese sandwich wrapped in waxed paper. She could still do that, she thought. She could still do it if she got off, changed buses, went home and got her bike, packed a picnic. The river with its little inlets, a thin layer of slush on them that had formed during the night, the fresh air and the bicycle tires rasping against the frozen gravel path. There was still time, she thought. She put her hand in her purse and fumbled for the bottle of pills, its small, innocent shape. Dormicum.

The bus slowed, pulled over at a bus stop. Anja was already getting up, pressing her heels against the floor, laying her left hand on the back of the seat in front of her. But just as she was about to stand, she found that her legs didn't have the strength. Her motion was left half-complete, stalled, and died. She had to carry this out to the end now.

They came to the nursing-home stop and Anja got off. During the short walk, a surprising calm at the fact of it descended on her. She opened the door and walked across the lobby, greeting the receptionist as she always did.

Her husband was sitting in the day room, his head turned to look at something out the window. A bird fluttered from the bird feeder to the branch of a nearby tree, as if it knew it was being watched. It soon flew back, pecked at something in the feeder, turned its head, and flew away again. Her husband coughed.

Anja put her hand on his. He turned his head and looked at her, or past her.

"Wet hair," he said hoarsely, and tried to lift his hand to touch her hair.

"Yes, it is," Anja said with a smile. "I've been swimming. That's why my hair's wet."

She listened to the sound of her own voice. It sounded strangely ordinary, but like it was coming from someplace far away, from behind a closed door, from another time, an entirely different reality.

"Fish swim and birds fly," he said with a sigh, and lowered his hand, turning back toward the window. "People don't have wings," he said wearily.

Anja helped him stand up, let him lean on her. They walked slowly to his room. When they got there he sat down on the bed, looking away. Anja helped him lie down and sat next to him on the bed.

She waited a moment, then took the pill bottle out of her purse. She'd poured the contents of one bottle into the other, doubling its contents. She realized that it would have been better to grind the tablets up at home: he might not be able to swallow dozens of tablets, since even swallowing one was hard for him.

She thought that this was another, final reason to turn back — the fact that she hadn't thought to grind up the tablets at home. Perhaps she should go home to do it, wait for a better time. If she ground them up with the mortar, they'd take on a peppery flavor. Wouldn't that be a good way to leave this world, with the taste of pepper in your mouth?

No. That was no excuse. She had to act now.

She picked up a spoon left on the table from some untouched meal, folded a piece of paper she found in her purse, and poured the tablets into the folded corner. Her hand shook a little as she crushed the tablets against the table with the spoon.

Dormicum. The word itself was like a lullaby. *Dormi* — it meant "sleep", of course. And *cum* — "with" or "together." *Sleep together.* The name was a direct invitation to sink into slumber. To lay down your head, close your eyes, and drift away from reality. *Let us sleep, and never wake again.*

Anja looked at the folded paper full of powder. Her husband had turned away from the window and was looking into her eyes now, not past her or through her but straight into her fear and uncertainty. And, in his eyes, Anja couldn't see the request that she was here to fulfill. She saw a completely different request, the request you usually see when you encounter someone weaker than yourself, when you raise your hand against the weak. It shone from his face, naked, demanding, and suddenly all the power was in that request. It was the same power that shines from the eyes of an animal caught in a trap — not the power to blame or to act, but the power to assign responsibility; and that carried all the power in the world.

Anja didn't know what happened. She didn't know how long she stood there, her husband's naked request there with all its power, but she saw her right hand pick up the folded paper with the powder inside and pour it back into the pill bottle. Her hand shook: the powder fell on the sheet next to her husband's hand. She brushed it onto the floor. It stood out against the blue linoleum like a streak of ash. She scratched it away with her foot.

She couldn't look at him now. She hung her head and quickly said goodbye, squeezing his hand hesitantly and taking a few panicked steps toward the door. In the doorway the pill bottle fell to the floor with a clatter and she picked it up and put it in her purse, then opened the door and hurried, half running, down the hall to the lobby and out of the building.

Outside, a wall of cold air met her. It reached into her lungs so suddenly that she felt like she couldn't get her breath. She felt like throwing up. She wandered toward the wall of the nursing home, stumbled around the corner, and sank to her knees in the snow. It was fresh, still soft, and without thinking she pressed her bare hands into it. The cold was a distant sting. The cold felt good. Tears finally came. She sobbed, there on her knees, with her hands stuck in the snow.

A waxwing was sitting in a rowan tree. Just like the one along her street, she thought. The waxwing watched her from the branch, not judging, not consoling. Just looking at her, watching over the emptiness of the snow.

IT WAS ALREADY EVENING when Anja walked across the market square and past the front of the church and turned onto Pohjoisranta. She wanted to take the same route, although she could have got there faster. Even in the dark, she found the street, as if she'd always been on her way to this place.

Johannes was home, answered the buzzer right away, waited at the top of the stairs.

"Come in," he said. "Let's go inside."

AFTERWARD ANJA THOUGHT that in a strange way it was familiar. One understanding look as he gingerly stroked her neck and ran his fingers through her hair.

He pulled his shirt over his head in one movement. Anja took off her shirt and her skirt, unhooked her bra. Now they were both naked, looking at each other without making a sound. Anja felt the combined weight of sadness and comfort on her shoulders. And, as if he sensed her feelings, Johannes reached out and stroked her shoulders, his thumbs touching her collarbone, the little hollow where her collarbone touched the base of her neck.

Anja sat down on the bed and Johannes stood in front of her. He opened her thighs and brushed his fingers along their inner surface. In a completely natural, eloquent motion, he put his hands on her breasts. It didn't feel particularly pleasurable yet, but it didn't feel bad either, just familiar somehow.

He kissed her breasts and had a full erection now. She looked at his penis. It was different from the one she was used to, slenderer somehow. She noticed a funny little birthmark on its lower surface. She reached out and took it in her hand, like she was greeting it. Her thumb touched the birthmark and pressed softly against it, covered it, then she moved her hand so that it was visible again.

Johannes started to get more aroused, and Anja felt something awaken in herself, too. The desire came from a distance, in the shadow of her other emotions. It came to her easily:

she could invite it in like an old acquaintance that she hadn't seen in years. Old and yet new. Strange and not strange. That's what the desire felt like.

Johannes gently pushed her onto her back and entered her and they made love in silence, with the snow falling outside the window, to the steady rhythm of each other's breathing.

# Anni

THE TOYS HAVE TO BE in the right order. A row of stuffed toys on the shelves, each one with its own name. The big bear, her oldest toy, first, and a seal that's missing one eye last. There are thirty-three of them altogether. There isn't room for all of them to sleep with her at once — she tried it, but they filled the whole space and she had to sleep at the foot of the bed. That's why she has a list of their names. Each one gets to spend one night with her in turn. So no one gets hurt feelings. So they don't fight with one another. A terrible thought: what if they don't even look forward to their turn to sleep with her? What if they'd rather stay on the shelf? What if they hate Anni and don't want to be near her?

Last night was the one-eyed seal's turn. During the night, the seal fell on the floor. Anni felt guilty as soon as she saw it. He was cold. Now he's mad at her. She has to do something to make him feel better. Maybe she'll let him sleep in the best place, right on her pillow, all next week to make up for letting him fall on the floor. But not too close to her, in case he doesn't actually enjoy sleeping next to her. It would be awful if he fell on the floor and then she made it worse by having him sleep too close to her. So the seal will sleep on her pillow for a week, but not too close.

Anni jumps out of bed and sees that Ada's already up. She can hear Ada's voice from the kitchen. And Dad's. Maybe Mom has already gone to work.

Anni looks at the story calendar. It's the thirteenth of November. She squeezes her eyes shut and makes a wish before she dares to look out the window. Her wish: that the snow hasn't melted. She and Sanna have been wishing for snow for several weeks. They had a deal that as soon as it snowed they would play in the fort in the woods every day. Today will be a good fort day, Anni decides. Maybe the best fort day ever.

There's a good smell from the kitchen. Dad made pancakes. Right away Anni thinks that something's wrong because he's making pancakes on a school day, a work day. But when she goes into the kitchen he says cheerfully that he has no work this morning and that's why it's a pancake morning. He makes the best pancakes in the world — Pippi Longstocking pancakes, Swedish pancakes like in the book.

Anni sits down at the table and Dad fills her glass with milk. She takes the largest pancake from the stack. Ada has spread both jam and sugar on her pancake. Anni does the same. She takes a big bite. The sugar scratches in her mouth on top of the sweet jam taste. She rolls the pancake into a tube and takes a bigger bite.

The morning show is on the television. They might even get to watch cartoons this morning if Dad takes them to school in the car, she thinks. Dad has sugar at the corners of his mouth. On the television they're saying that there's a war somewhere.

"Daddy?" Ada says.

"Yes?"

"Will the war come here?"

"No. No, it won't."

"Good."

Anni's mouth tastes sweet. She takes an even bigger bite. The scratch of the sugar. No war is coming, no war. She reaches for her glass of milk and thinks that if she can drink all her milk before the music is over at the end of the news, then everything will be all right and nothing bad will ever happen to anyone in her family. If she can just drink all her milk, she thinks.

IN THE AFTERNOON, Anni and Sanna play in the fort for hours. Their favorite game is Poopies and Propers. The Poopies live in a broken-down house. Everything in their life goes wrong: their house used to be nice but it got all broken-down because the dad drinks and the mom went crazy. It's a game Sanna made up. The Propers' house is always tiptop. Dad helped them build the Propers' house — it has walls made of real wood nailed to a tree and it's very homey and the Propers' mom makes sweet rolls and they have a nice tablecloth and the children are good.

The Poopie children are naughty. And dirty. Sanna and Anni put their dolls into the snow and the mud and then they look like the Poopie children. The Poopie children don't have any toys or even any shoes and they have to go to the bank to get food because their dad drinks all the food money.

Sometimes at night, when she's alone under the covers, Anni cries about the Poopie children.

"You whore, you crazy whore," Sanna sings, swishing the Poopie children in the snow.

"What's a whore?" Anni asks.

"Stupid. It's just … that kind of woman. She has pretty earrings and a skirt and she just goes to hotels all the time. She gets paid to go to hotels."

"Oh."

Anni thinks about the trip they took to Greece. It was hot and there was a little refrigerator in the hotel room with lovely chocolate bars and little cans of cold soda. Anni imagines a whore going to a hotel with pretty shoes and a skirt and sitting on the sofa drinking Coca-Cola out of a little can. It must be nice to be a whore.

"The Poopie mom maybe used to be a whore, but then she just went crazy and she goes around naked everywhere," Sanna suggests.

Sanna wants to be the Propers' mom and the Poopies' mom, too, because she thinks Anni doesn't know how to be a crazy whore. Nobody needs to be the Poopies' dad because he just drinks all the time. Anni can be the Propers' dad. He has a piece of bark for a cell phone. Anni talks into it and pretends to carry a briefcase because he's a boss and he's rich and important and friendly. "Hello, this is Mr. Proper," Anni says into the cell phone. Mr. Proper. That sounds right. That's what adults say. Anni tries to think of fine words. Mr. Proper talks about "the exchange," in an important voice. That sounds perfect. Anni thinks of more perfect words. Mr. Proper buys some shares. They're like money but more valuable. "One Exchange, please," Mr. Proper says into the bark cell phone, slurping imaginary coffee from an imaginary cup. Mr. Proper is a boss. He rules the world.

Then Sanna's big brother Samuli comes and ruins the whole game. He comes by fast on his bike and runs into the Poopies' fort, and the wall made of branches falls down.

Oh no! Everything goes wrong for the Poopies. The dad drinks and the mom is crazy and now their house has fallen down, too. They have nothing left!

Samuli rides away on his bike and doesn't care when Sanna yells and swears at him.

"Lucky it wasn't the Propers' house," Anni says, but Sanna is mad at her, too, and pushes her down.

Snow goes in her mouth and nose.

"Sissy baby," Sanna says. "You're a sissy baby shithead." Then she turns around and runs away.

"I am not," Anni says.

She gets up, tears pressing against the back of her eyes. Sanna is already a long way down the road. Anni stands there in the snow. She's afraid to be alone in the woods, but she doesn't go after Sanna. She knows that it will be days before Sanna wants to play with her again.

It'll be dark soon. Anni looks at her wristwatch. Having a watch, flourishing her arm when she looks at it, still makes her just as happy as always. The watch has a pink band and a picture of a cat on the face. She went to buy it with her mom before she started preschool. There are a lot of things about the watch that are hard to understand. If she accidentally puts it on the wrong wrist, will it run backward? Of course not, she decides. The real world will continue forward no matter which wrist it's on.

The watch says it's a quarter past five.

Anni starts to walk home. She decides that Sanna can come and apologize. She often doesn't come, even if she started the fight. Anni often ends up apologizing first. But Sanna has to apologize this time.

AT SIX THAT EVENING they eat meatballs and mashed potatoes and the whole family is there. Mom smiles at Dad over the table. Anni smiles, too. This isn't an argument day.

"Did you have a nice day at school?" Mom asks.

"Yes," Anni says, popping a whole meatball in her mouth.

Ada rolls a meatball over the tablecloth.

"Don't play with your food, Ada. Put the meatball in your mouth."

Ada wrinkles her nose. "But it rolls. What's the point of making balls that you can't roll?"

Mom smiles, and so does Dad. Everybody's smiling. Anni sighs with relief. For a little while they can be happy and don't have to worry.

BEFORE BEDTIME, Mom reads them a story. Anni snuggles against her on the left and Ada on the right. Anni presses her head against Mom's chest and listens to the story, lets all the other thoughts out of her mind.

Sometimes you have to wrap your hard thoughts up in paper in your mind and close the package tight so that the thoughts can't get out, so you can have a little peace. The Hard Thoughts Package. Anni thinks about her argument with Sanna, throws it to the bottom of the package, Sanna's angry look and the mean thing she said; that word that Sanna yelled at her goes on the very bottom, an ugly word that kids aren't supposed to say. Then Anni thinks about Daddy and that girl in the car, the look on the girl's face, and she throws that in the package with the other thoughts. Last of all she thinks of Mom's bad mood and scolding, and she separates Mom's bad mood from her good mood and she puts the bad mood in the package on top of the other thoughts, and she closes it up in her mind. It's in the corner of the room and she won't look at it again for the rest of the night.

Ada's already asleep. Anni starts to feel herself slipping into sleep, too. Right now everything is good, she thinks, on the threshold of sleep. Right now everything is maybe the best it's been all day.

"Anni," her mother whispers, and strokes her hair. "Can you tell Mommy a secret?"

"What secret?" Anni says, becoming alert.

"A secret that we can't tell Daddy."

"Well, maybe," she says doubtfully.

Usually Anni thinks it's fun sharing secrets with Mom. She and Mom go under the quilt and turn on the flashlight and take turns shining the light on their faces and they tell each other secrets. About those things, *those things*, like Mom says. Ada can't come under the quilt with them when they do that. *It's just for big girls*, that's what Mom said to Ada. Anni feels important at those times. But now she senses something unpleasant in Mom's question, something that belongs in the Hard Thoughts Package in the corner. And she notices that the package in the corner isn't sitting quietly in its place anymore — it's starting to rustle and open itself up.

"Do you know," Mom begins, and Anni can already tell from the way she begins that she should make her words into a truth that Mom wants to hear now. "Do you know if Daddy has been with some stranger, some girl for instance? Or have you ever been with Daddy when there was a person like that there — someone you don't know?"

Anni knows this: there are truths that are true, and truths that are built from your words and from the spaces between your words — the silences, the part that you're not telling.

It's not the same thing as lying. It's not the same thing at all. It's more like protecting. And Anni knows that now is a time to speak that kind of truth, to speak in a way that Mom *can* hear the whole truth if she just *wants to*, if she just pays attention to the places between the words and behind them — the empty spaces. And Anni says, "No. No strangers — just his work friends when we went to his work after daycare — and students, from where he works."

Anni quickly thinks of the brown-haired girl with the pretty coat and the lovely eyes again. She wants to have eyes like that when she grows up. She quickly thinks about the fact that the girl was in the car, and Dad was looking at her and talking with her. A quick thought that Mom can take hold of, if she wants to.

But she doesn't take hold of it, and Anni thinks that maybe she doesn't want to know, not enough. Mom gives her a goodnight kiss and turns out the light.

The My Little Pony light is left on. The ponies are bouncing through a meadow of flowers. It's good to have that light on, so the Masked Murderer won't come. So Ada is safe. So Anni doesn't have to watch over Ada all night. So she can close her eyes. The narrow, warm wedge of light from the My Little Pony lamp will watch over Ada as she snuffles in her sleep. The wedge of light reaches to the corner of the room where the Hard Thoughts Package is, and Anni can see that it's not closed anymore, it's opened up and the Hard Thoughts have jumped out, and they're coming toward her.

She lets them come.

First she thinks about Sanna when she's angry. *Sissy baby shithead* — that's what Sanna said. She didn't mean it. She was just being bossy because she wanted Anni to be her friend. That's what it was.

Anni sighs. She decides to tell Sanna she's sorry. First thing tomorrow. She'll say she's sorry and promise to let Sanna borrow her watch. Sanna will probably ask her to give it to her to keep. And maybe Anni will give it to her to keep.

Then Anni thinks about Mom and Dad and the girl with the beautiful eyes, and she decides that Dad must be protected and so must Mom, and she must never tell her the whole truth, the truth about what was happening or what was going to happen.

Last of all Anni thinks about everything together, and she crosses her fingers under her Moomin blanket and prays that everything will be all right and nothing bad will happen to anyone. Then she shuts her eyes and leaves the My Little Pony light to watch over Ada's sleep and the Hard Thoughts Package through the night.

## Julian

JULIAN WATCHED HER while the class wrote their essays.
Sometimes he had to look away so no one would notice. But
she was so beautiful, especially now that he'd realized how
fascinating she was. He couldn't seem to stop looking at her.

She lifted her head and looked back at him. She didn't smile,
just looked at him, straight-faced. Julian smiled a little. Then
she smiled, too. Her smile was so bright, the kind of smile that
made the world settle into its proper place when you looked at
it. She had been quite a bit more serious lately. Had something
happened? The seriousness made her seem nobler somehow,
unique. During class she would sometimes be looking out the
window, lost in thought, and suddenly turn to him, with all the
seriousness and all the joy of the world in her eyes. Then Julian
would stumble over his words, falter, lose his rhythm, and have
to give the students a group project so he could sit down and
collect himself. She had all the power. He felt helpless before
her, not responsible for what might happen.

He'd thought about the first move, when to make it and
how. He'd thought about suggesting they go to coffee again,
maybe even to dinner. But it felt like they'd already passed that
phase. There was a sense of something between them that was

so clear that perhaps there was no need to do anything but approach her, directly and straightforwardly.

There would be one possibility next week: the school was holding its monthly dance. The themes were usually something amusing — the Wild West, the eighties, *Saturday Night Fever*. The dances were arranged by the student activities committee, which was made up of the kind of loud, glittery, blonde girls who wore tight jeans and pink shirts and always had something to say. In the past, these events had made Julian smile — their purpose seemed to be to give the girls a chance to be seen in less clothing than they wore during the day, faces made up, hair coifed. Dancing would always begin at some point in the festivities and the girls would keep him dancing all evening, without a break. He always slipped away as soon as he'd fulfilled his obligatory duties.

But this time it was different. The party would be the perfect opportunity to approach the girl. They would be thrown together by circumstances and their paths could cross as if by accident. And half the classrooms in the school would be dark and unused during the dance, just waiting for someone to step inside, waiting for deeds not meant for others' eyes.

Julian thought about what it would feel like to touch her. Her soft, smooth skin and the incredible pale tenderness of her breasts. No man had ever touched them. If he did touch her, it would have to be from behind at first, caressing the delicate fuzz on the back of her neck. From there he would move his hand between her shoulder blades, press her vertebrae, gently, like marking a path to lead him back once he'd entered the land of forgetting that her tender, untouched skin offered.

He thought about her inner thighs and the pleasure that waited between them. Then he realized he was getting an erection, which was entirely inappropriate. He had to think of something un-erotic, quick. He conjured a mental picture of his workmate, Tanskanen, who taught English. Tanskanen was handsome, a big talker, the kind of man who had more women than he could count on his fingers. The girls in the school nicknamed him Tush. It may have had something to do with his well-toned ass. Julian thought about Tanskanen's ass. They sometimes went to the gym together. He thought about Tanskanen's muscular ass after a few deep squats, sweaty with exercise. Sometimes Julian happened to be behind Tanskanen when he did his squats, and he couldn't help but see the outline of his balls hanging below his shorts at the deepest point of the squat. He thought about the sight of them and his budding erection went away immediately.

The fastest writers were already handing in their essays. Mari was always among the last to turn hers in and Julian hoped that she would be the last one today, so that they could have a moment alone together.

He found himself thinking about touching her again. To make love to her would mean forgetting, complete escape. He remembered reading somewhere that in a moment of complete presence, no memory is created. Remembering requires distance — your consciousness has to be reflective, has to make its way across a distance to reach the event in order for you to be able to bring a memory of it to mind later on. But the moments that you dive deeply into, the moments that are so powerful that they determine the entire meaning of life, have a veil of oblivion over them, precisely because that consciousness is shattered by the pressure of their intensity. Moments like that hurtle out of the chaos into the reality of the person experiencing them, then curl up inside him and leave no trace. They're deserted islands in the river of consciousness, open country where the reigning melody is silence. That's how it would be with her, he thought. No trace of memory. A moment of absolute presence, and in that moment pure being.

The open country of forgetting.

Julian roused himself from his thoughts as the last student but her came to the front of the class. He tried to look at her, to find out if she noticed that they were left alone. She continued to concentrate on her writing.

"Hey, Mari," Julian said with a smile. "Finish up now, class is almost over."

She lifted her head and smiled. Julian felt the excitement rising up again. There was nothing he could do about it: she had all the power.

"I'm almost finished," she said, and bent over her work again.

He walked over and stood beside her and felt an irresistible urge to reach out and touch her. He brushed her shoulder, as if by accident.

"I'll give you a perfect score, anyway," he whispered. "You write so well that you don't really leave me any alternative."

She lifted her head and smiled again.

"Well, I guess it's finished," she said, standing up and handing the essay to him.

"Right," he said slowly.

He wanted to prolong the moment between them, to just be quiet, to be there under the power of her delicate presence.

"Are you planning to come to the dance next week?" he asked. "I suppose you must be, since it's compulsory."

Julian could feel his heart racing. It was embarrassing,

really. He was afraid she would notice how flustered she made him. But she just smiled.

"My essay may not meet your expectations this time," she said with nervousness in her voice. "I couldn't concentrate for some reason, didn't have any ideas."

He took the notebook from her. "Really? Is there anything you're worried about, anything you want to talk about?"

She looked away. Julian thought he'd happened upon a sensitive subject. Maybe everything wasn't as it should be in her life. Without thinking, he stretched out his hand and touched the edge of her face, moving a wisp of hair from in front of her eyes. She trembled a little, but didn't pull away. He grew bolder and stroked the outline of her face with the back of his hand, felt the light moisture of her breath when his wrist passed near her mouth. She stared into his eyes with an almost horrified look. His consciousness, too, was pierced by a lucid feeling mixed with horror. The open country of forgetting — this was the gate that led to it.

"You're ... you're unusual," he heard himself say, hoarsely, far away.

She backed away then, and the magic was shattered. She gathered up her things, breathing quickly. Avoiding his gaze, she mumbled bye and hurried out of the room.

Julian stood where he was for a long time, the clock on the wall ticking in the grayness of the afternoon, and felt the excitement subside. His erection was still throbbing, demanding, tying all of his thoughts to the feel of her skin, the warm promise in her breath of what was to come.

JULIAN GOT HOME AT FIVE. Jannika was in the kitchen making dinner. He took off his coat and shoes and stood in the kitchen doorway trying to interpret the tone of the day from her body language: should he relax and chat to her about this and that or should he be on his guard? He was tired of it. Always having to read her, always sensitive to her moods, approaching her like a puzzle whose answer was always just out of sight. He picked up her mood from little hints, in the way she moved.

Jannika had her back to him — she hadn't heard him come in. He came closer, trying to get a glimpse of her face. A strange feeling came over him: as if he were afraid of his own wife. She lifted her head and smiled. Julian was relieved.

"Where are the girls?" he asked, and brushed his lips against her cheek.

"They're both at the neighbors'."

"Ah. What are you cooking?"

"Chicken. There's wine, too." She smiled and turned to look at him.

Julian smiled, too. Everything would go smoothly today. Somewhere under the surface there was a hint of a strange feeling, as if he were betraying the girl's trust by smiling at someone else, touching someone else. He recognized that it was a ridiculous thought, and he realized for the first time that it was his wife he was betraying. Deliberately, without any qualms. But Jannika had been difficult for a long time. She was well aware that things between them were not as they should be. She knew that her moody behavior created a distance between them. And although that distance didn't give him a right to have another relationship, it was, in a way, a mitigating circumstance.

They set the table and poured wine into their glasses. They ate by candlelight and enjoyed the silence. One of them would say something and the other would nod, talking about trivial things, welcoming the quiet as if by agreement.

It started with the second glass of wine. Julian forgot to be wary — the wine relaxed him and he forgot to be on his guard.

"I was thinking I might start working on my dissertation again," he said. "There are some good lectures going at the university. I thought I might go when I'm not working and get a bit of a feel for the project."

He'd been planning his doctoral dissertation for years, had even started writing a couple of sections. But something had always gotten in the way — Ada's birth, Jannika taking a steady job. But now it felt as if he could find time for it.

He got excited talking about his plans and at first he didn't notice Jannika's silence. He had a brilliant topic in mind: freedom and the tragic hero. He'd made a bit of a start on it in his master's thesis, but he'd have to really apply himself to write a dissertation. Jannika had been enthusiastic about his dissertation plans when they were first dating. He remembered her intensity, the look on her face, leaning forward as he breathlessly explained the scope of the philosophy of tragedy in the wee hours of the morning, the wine feeding his inspiration. She was different then. She used to store away every word he said.

Now she was sitting in front of him with a distant expression, looking out the window, which reflected the depressing, star-shaped paper Christmas lantern in endless repetition. He stopped mid-sentence.

Their fights always began from the most ridiculously insignificant comments. Jannika's general aloofness annoyed Julian. When she was in a bad mood, she had a way of answering him with mere grunts when he tried to talk to her. She was doing it now, without warning, when the subject of the dissertation came up. She looked away, withdrew, disappeared into a different reality.

"What is it?" Julian asked.

"Hmm."

He was immediately irritated.

"I see," he said, in a tone of surrender. "So you're not interested?"

She grunted again, not turning her gaze from the window.

"Write your dissertation, if that's how you want to spend your time," she said, and took a sip of wine through thin lips.

There it was. *If that's how you want to spend your time.* An unconcealed jab. It was a challenge to fight, and it was all that was needed. Julian instantly felt rage bubble up inside him. He was also aware of a fleeting ray of pleasure flashing through the anger, but he didn't give it any thought.

"What's that supposed to mean? I suppose you think I've been neglecting things at home? I think my use of time is pretty well prioritized for the good of the family."

Jannika grunted again. "I wouldn't say that."

"What would you say, then?"

"A career is a career, that's all. If you want to do research you're going to have to make some choices about your career and your family life."

"Why are you the only one here who's allowed to have a damn career?"

Jannika was the one who had been working the most the past few years. Julian had spent half a year at home when Ada was a year old — after her maternity leave Jannika had received an unexpectedly good job offer from the National Gallery. He'd thought that he would have time for his dissertation later.

"Whatever," Jannika said. Her expression changed from defensive to harsh. "But I'm not going to stay home and wash your socks because you decide to play the scholar. Do what you want, though; write your dissertation, write two goddamn dissertations if you like."

"Maybe I will. At least then I wouldn't have to sit around this goddamn house watching these little performances of yours."

Jannika slammed her wineglass down on the table. The stem broke cleanly in two, right in the middle. Wine splashed onto the tablecloth. Now she was staring at him with angry black eyes. Fury shone out of them, then was extinguished as quickly as it had come. She closed back up into herself. The wine dribbled across the tablecloth in a dark puddle, silently soaking into the dry fabric. She looked through him. Her face showed no expression. He was left alone with his rage.

Jannika got up from the table with slow, stiff movements, went to the cupboard, and got out the canister of salt. She came back just as slowly, walking as if in a dream, and sprinkled salt over the wine stain.

Julian's anger grew with her indifference. He stood up and grabbed her arm. She turned to look out the window again. She looked almost bored, as if family life with all its problems were tedious to her. Fighting was impossible, but Julian's fury was boiling so insistently that he couldn't leave the situation as it was. He squeezed her arm, knowing that his grip was too tight already — it was going to leave a bruise. She seemed to become even more distant. The situation was a variation on their idiotic, ritual fights.

"Say something, damn it," Julian hissed, tightening his hold.

Jannika turned her head. She still had the same stupid, bored look on her face.

"Whatever. Do what you like," she said. "It doesn't matter to me."

Julian could almost hear something snap inside him. A humming, whistling sound floated somewhere in the back of his head and the whole scene became like a photograph with blurred edges — the cloudy wine stain on the tablecloth covered in salt, the broken wineglass like an absurd exclamation point poking up from the stain. The tight expression on Jannika's face and the Christmas star in the window. His own hand raised to strike, himself ready to take a step down a path from which there was no return. Time stood still and wrapped itself around that gesture — a raised hand. Now she was looking him straight in the eye. There was no fear or confusion in her eyes. No surprise, no disappointment. Just a calm, matter-of-fact look.

"Daddy?"

Anni and Ada were standing in the doorway, shocked. Anni looked at Julian questioningly. Jannika glanced at her daughters. Her expression still hadn't changed. Julian loosened his grip and lowered his hand. Jannika picked up the salt from the table absentmindedly and put it back in the cupboard. The little girls still stood in the doorway. They had heart-shaped gingerbread cookies in their hands. They were holding them up with both hands, like shields. Julian sat back down at the table. He suddenly felt ill, drained of all energy. The Christmas star in the window swayed in a current of air and reflected its soft red glow into the kitchen.

# Anja

Anja gathered her lecture notes from her desk. She should organize her papers better in the future. The lecture was starting in fifteen minutes and she still didn't have all of the copies she planned to hand out to the students. She opened her desk drawer. There was a black notebook in it. Not the notebook that had caused that painful realization years earlier, but the same kind of notebook: small, black, smooth, innocent. So innocent that you wouldn't think it could have the capacity to change anything.

Anja is cleaning her husband's office. The desk is covered with papers. There are always all kinds of papers on it — drawings, lecture transparencies, meeting notes. The vacuum hits the leg of the chair. The chair sways and knocks over one of the stacks of paper. One of the notebooks opens as it falls on the floor and Anja can see what's written in it.

Why does she look? There's something in people that's so curious, that always has to be looking, even when they know that they don't necessarily want to see, don't want to know.

And that's exactly why Anja looks at the notebook's contents, which seem innocent enough at first. She knows that she doesn't want to know, but she looks anyway. It seems to be a diary. Under the date are brief comments, names Anja recognizes as her husband's colleagues', site locations, detailed directions for driving home.

That's when she realizes the obvious:

It isn't a diary.

It's a book of reminders.

Her heart thuds for two heavy beats. She's stupefied, almost amused, and the thought comes to her: life is going to change, completely. Life is finally going to change, right now, because of this innocent-looking black notebook.

She picks up the book with shaking hands.

She can't resist leafing through it.

*Wife,* it says on one page. Written underneath are Anja's full name, date of birth, field of work, dissertation subject, job title, how long they've been married, details of when they first met. Her favorite foods and movies, her favorite books. All the things a person should carry in their mind, things you shouldn't need to remind yourself of.

She holds the notebook in her hand for a long time, waiting for tears that don't come, looking at the summer outside the window, the birds in the trees and the climbing roses next to the porch. The roses are exasperatingly red — they almost stab the eyes when you look at them. Terror is trying to burst out of her but if she concentrates on the roses, their aching brilliance, the truth can etch itself in her mind gradually, without panic.

WHEN HER HUSBAND comes home she's sitting on the living-room sofa. He takes off his shoes and coat and says something about the ripeness of the summer light. Is it heavy, the July light? he says, half to himself. No, it's not heavy yet. Just strong the way light can be. A knowing light. And as much as Anja would like to talk about the light and nothing more, just the strong light of July and the peonies and the squashes ripening in the garden, not making a sound, sure of their goal — as much as she'd like to talk about all of this, she says something else instead.

"You don't remember anymore," she says.

"What?" he asks.

"You've started to forget."

"Yes," he admits. "I'm beginning to think maybe I have."

He comes to her, sits on the sofa, reaches a hand toward her, lost. The fact trembles there between them, desolate, big as life. Now they've said it, they've made it real. He takes Anja in his arms and they sit holding each other in a corner of the sofa, the way they always do, and Anja thinks that they still have this, at least, being in each other's arms.

He breaks the silence by saying what they're both thinking.

"I have to go in for an exam," he says, holding her tighter. "I have to get an exam right away."

"I'll come with you," Anja says. "We'll go together."

They don't say anything more. They sit there and look at the strong July light, sharing the knowledge that there are small moments that can change your life completely, irrevocably. This is one of those moments. Their life has completely, irrevocably changed. The change happened even though the July light is as strong and knowing as it was in summers past and the squash still grows in the garden without making a sound.

ANJA PUT THE NOTEBOOK back in the desk drawer. She would just have to manage without the handouts. She closed the door behind her.

The lecture hall was almost full. Anja put on her professorial expression — a friendly, open gaze, a self-assured half-smile, the look of a woman who knew her place in the world — and walked to the front of the room.

A quick glance at the audience. Hello. Hello everyone. The students definitely thought she was old; maybe they talked about her with ridicule, maybe with admiration. But she knew how to do this. Anywhere else she might be uncertain. But not here, standing at the front of a lecture hall.

There was someone new in the second row. Anja had a distant memory of him from the graduate seminar. Intense, older than the other students but still ludicrously young. He used to lean forward to hear what she had to say. A look on his face like a predator, or a rescuer.

AFTER THE LECTURE the man came up to talk to her. The boy, she thought as he came closer.

"Julian Kanerva," he said, reaching out and shaking her hand.

Anja noticed an engagement ring on his left hand. Or maybe it was a wedding ring. Not such a boy, then.

"Anja Aropalo. Nice to meet you."

He hesitated a moment. "I'm planning to start research for my dissertation," he said. "The topic might be in your area of speciality. I was wondering if I could meet with you and discuss my plans."

"Certainly," Anja said. "My office hours are Wednesdays from two to three. You can make an appointment by email if you like."

"Thanks," he said. "I'll do that. I'll see you then."

"Yes," Anja said with a smile.

# Julian

JULIAN SAT IN HIS CAR in the school parking lot and looked straight ahead. Snowflakes were falling on the windshield. She would have some in her hair when she got here. They hadn't spoken to each other since that surprising episode a week ago. But she had smiled at him in the lunchroom on Monday. The smile had turned him on. It was an invitation. Permission.

He got out of the car and locked the door. There were students in the schoolyard. He glanced quickly at all the faces; she wasn't there. He went inside.

Tanskanen met him at the door to the teachers' lounge and winked.

"Dude, what a dude," Tanskanen said.

They always greeted each other the same way. Tanksanen would say, "Dude, what a dude," and Julian was supposed to answer simply "Dude." It was stupid, but for some reason it had become a habit. Maybe because at school, at least, it always made the girls laugh when they heard it.

"Dude," Julian said.

Tanskanen had relationships with students. It was suspected, but never spoken of aloud. And he'd never been caught. He was clever — he never met them in public places, never prolonged a relationship that threatened to become serious, never got involved with girls who might turn bitter and threaten to expose him. Tanskanen liked the kind of noisy, giggly, glittery girls whom Julian was slightly afraid of. But the most important thing was that they were loyal. No confessions to their classmates. No gossip.

It was Tanskanen's influence that made Julian dare to think about a relationship with the girl. It wasn't really all that wrong when you thought about it. High-school students were, to all intents and purposes, adults. If both people desired it, you could see it as two adults doing what they felt like doing, of their own free will. Entirely natural, when you thought about it. As long as both people wanted it. And in this case, both people seemed to want it.

"I've been assigned to chaperone the jelly-roll competition," Tanskanen said with a grin. "I would have preferred the yoga group."

Julian took up his bantering tone. "You ought to uphold your nickname by doing your yoga in the front row of the class."

"I only do yoga for a select audience, behind closed doors, at night," Tanskanen said.

"I don't doubt it. And what might my role at this shindig be?"

"If the stars are still aligned and the portents still hold true, you're to make the women laugh all evening."

Julian stiffened. Tanskanen smiled all the more.

"There's a list on the wall in the teacher's lounge. It has you marked down as a dance instructor." Tanskanen laughed.

"Aha," Julian said with relief. "That suits me."

"Keep your hands where they belong, now. A light touch on the waist. Leave the asses be."

"Excellent advice," Julian said.

HE SAW HER walk into the gym at 8.37 p.m. He was looking absentmindedly at the clock above the door and noting the time when he saw her standing under it. A beam of light shone from the clock and she was standing in its glow, the doorway framing her clear outline, the whirling spotlights installed for the evening caressing her silhouette and then turning away again. It was just like he'd imagined it: she had snowflakes in her hair.

Julian walked over to her. He felt nervously aware of his own body. Like he'd felt in confirmation class or in middle school. She had snow on the toes of her boots. An object dangled from one of her hands. It was a pair of dancing shoes. Red, with thin straps to be tied around the ankle. The thought of her with them on her feet made his breath quicken with desire.

"I'm late," she said with a smile.

Julian tried to collect himself. "You haven't missed anything yet."

She took off her coat and bent over to change her shoes. As she bent over, her skirt lifted ten centimeters higher and Julian could see a sweet little birthmark on her inner thigh, just under the hem. A faint spot barely visible under her thin stockings. It was mind-blowingly sexy. It was disconcerting to know it was there, on the intimate inner surface of her thigh, a place no stranger's hand had ever been, untouched, white, open. He impressed it in his mind, sketched its outline in his memory, as if it were a landmark along an unfamiliar road.

She straightened up and was noticeably taller than before. Her gaze found his — a brief look that turned away self-consciously. He noticed himself staring too long at her and turned and walked quickly away.

THE STUDENT COUNCIL had hired a dance instructor, a loose-limbed man. Julian guessed that the next hour would be an embarrassing one. He didn't particularly enjoy dancing.

He glanced at the girl once more before the lesson began. Her friend had asked her to dance. They chatted and laughed. He could pick out her laughter from among the other voices. It floated above the hum of conversation, significant, slicing through the air and forcing its way into his consciousness, throbbing, urgent. Her laugh was delightful: it bubbled up, husky and cooing, from someplace deep, then floated into a bright falsetto. He wanted to hear her laugh again and again. He felt jealous that it was someone else who had made her laugh. He decided not to watch her anymore. He should keep his distance. The game was a welcome one; to delay the moment, postpone it until the climax was inevitable. And it wouldn't do to have her notice him staring.

The dance instructor called everyone together and started to explain the evening's program. Julian smiled at one of the senior girls, and she came and asked him to dance. He agreed, embarrassed; he wasn't going to come out of this with his dignity intact.

He took his partner by the hand and glanced across the gymnasium again. A secretive, guarded look: the girl had taken her friend's hand. Now she was looking at him. He couldn't interpret her expression. Her gaze cut through the air like an electric current. He felt his heart beat faster.

There followed some embarrassing samba steps and movements that Julian couldn't master. The instructor noticed his difficulties and made him an object lesson, correcting his steps in a teasing tone. Julian tried to keep his sense of humor. He watched the girl out of the corner of his eye the whole time. She looked as if she'd mastered the movements — she was smiling, laughing, radiant. Every movement of her arm was poetry.

The compulsory lesson lasted an hour. His humiliation was at its peak when the dance instructor finally released them from their agony. The music changed from a Latin rhythm to a waltz. Julian smiled at the senior-class girl he'd been dancing with and slipped hurriedly to the edge of the room.

It was a tradition at these events that everyone would gather at the end for a party. The tables were set with food made in a student workshop. Julian picked up a few large olives from the salad dish and stepped to the side. He located the girl: she and her friend had taken a position on the opposite wall of the gym. Her knee was bent in a delicious way, one leg resting against the other, like a colt. The image of an untamed, half-wild, colt-like girl, and of himself as the one who would tame her, aroused him again. He shifted the game to the next stage; he looked at her for such a long time that she turned her head. Their gazes met and she quickly looked away. He stared at her again. A moment went by. She tried to behave as if she didn't notice. She smiled at her friend. Her friend looked at Julian and whispered something in her ear. She looked at him again, this time for a long time. She smiled. The smile was achingly bright, a smile that could make the mountains move east and the clouds move west and north-west across the sky. But he might have seen a hint of terror opening up behind that bright smile. The situation was moving inexorably toward its exciting conclusion.

# Mari

Mari is standing in the gymnasium entrance, just outside the door. Before she opens the door, Tinka gives her an approving look: they've spent the whole evening getting ready, and judging by Tinka's expression, their efforts have paid off. They've been planning their outfits for weeks, imagining combinations that would be glamorous enough to make the girls on the student council jealous and to provoke flummoxed looks from the boys.

"See what I mean?" Tinka whispered. "The point is to look glamorous but casual. Like we haven't gone to any special trouble."

"Yes," Mari said.

Tinka smiled. "Now all we have to do is dazzle them," she said.

Tinka's tools for bedazzling are a fuzzy pink sweater and a short denim skirt. She paid fifteen euros for the stockings. They're made of smooth, spidery stitches, and Tinka's legs have never looked better. They show off her high heels, which are impossible to walk in, let alone dance in. But blistered toes are a small price to pay for being admired by dozens of boys.

Mari looks at herself in the mirror, and she likes what

she sees. She's wearing a black skirt — exactly the right one, Tinka picked it out — and her hair is arranged in waves around her face. Tinka did her hair, too, and made up her eyes. Mari can admit it now: she is pretty. Tinka has made her pretty.

"You're Cinderella," Tinka says, winding her arm around Mari's waist.

Mari knows that. She's Tinka's Cinderella project. She's clay in Tinka's hands, molded into beauty. This is the night when Cinderella will step into the ballroom, the moment when a nobody becomes a fairy-tale creature of beauty, when every head turns with sighs of sheer delight and no one can take their eyes off her.

Mari looks at Tinka in the mirror, and for the first time she sees something in Tinka's eyes that makes her uneasy. Is Tinka jealous? She didn't want Mari to be the prettiest — Mari knows that wasn't what she planned. They stand side by side in front of the mirror and Mari is afraid she might be prettier than Tinka.

Tinka's smile grows vague. She tries to keep it taut.

"Maybe I won't put on these red shoes," Mari suggests.

They've chosen perfect dancing shoes for Mari, irresistible, red Cinderella shoes, but now she feels like they might be too much. They're still in the box; she's still wearing her usual winter shoes.

Tinka finds her smile again. "Don't be silly. Of course you should put them on."

"They'll make me taller than you."

"So what? That doesn't matter."

Tinka is smiling. Mari has her permission to be beautiful today, the most beautiful of all. For today, at least.

As Mari steps into the ballroom, she only has to glance in Kanerva's direction to know it's working. It's working just like it was supposed to. She looks at Tinka beside her to share her excitement, but Tinka has that look again, the one that might be jealousy, or sadness, or both at the same time.

Tinka pulls Mari onto the dance floor as the lesson begins. Mari turns her head to look at Kanerva. Kanerva looks back, stares. Joy shoots through her.

The dance instructor goes over the steps for more than an hour. Tinka follows his instructions with her mouth in a tight line, focused, a trace of annoyance in her eyes. Mari can't concentrate. She keeps turning her head, and Kanerva is always watching her, watching her the whole time.

The lesson ends and Mari sees Kanerva walking off the dance floor. He leans against the wall and watches them.

"He's staring at us," Tinka whispers, leaning toward her. "Look at him stare."

Mari smiles, doesn't dare to look, looks anyway, for a long time now, smiling. This is what it's like to be an adult, she thinks.

Mari looks at Tinka, unable to hide her happiness. Tinka's smile is stuck, her cheeks tight. She looks tense. Mari doesn't care about that now.

"Wanna dance?" Mari asks.

"Stupid," Tinka answers bluntly. "We can't dance together anymore. We have to wait for someone to come and ask us."

"Oh," Mari says.

Tinka looks away. Maybe the Cinderella game has gone too far. Maybe Mari really is prettier than Tinka. Or maybe Tinka wants Kanerva for herself.

Then Tinka turns back to her and says abruptly, "I guess we might as well."

They dance together until halfway through the song.

Mari sees Kanerva approaching out of the corner of her eye.

Julian.

At the instant when he takes the first step toward her, he's not Kanerva anymore, not her teacher. He's Julian. Nailuj. Julian, and everything that matters is contained in him. She's known all evening that this will happen, that it will happen just like this: Julian walking a few steps, not looking at her at first, looking at something else, like he doesn't care. But then he turns. And neither of them can hide what they know or push it away anymore. This time and this place and nothing else, just these two people, two orbits intersecting. They step toward each other, as inevitable as stars approaching each other in a predetermined trajectory. Mari doesn't see Tinka anymore. It may be that Tinka says something, but Mari doesn't hear her. Later she may be ashamed of this moment, her own brash boldness, her certainty of her right to take her place here in the glow of Julian's gaze. But she's not ashamed now. She's not afraid. Julian's gaze draws a clear boundary around her.

Julian steps in front of her, leans forward a little, and takes hold of her. It's an invitation to dance. Maybe to the other people present it looks like an ordinary gesture. But it is anything but that. As Julian takes hold of Mari, she steps outside her ability to control her own destiny. She knows this: once she steps onto Julian's territory she will live in Julian. It will be her only home, her place in the world.

She feels the weight of his hand against her back, curved around her ribcage. Her fingers are placed between his fingers, and nothing has ever felt more real than his touch. Their shared gaze is like a chasm that she's falling into. It's a chasm of terror, and wonderment, and she sees that they share this knowledge, how this can be so new and yet so utterly familiar.

Julian leans closer and Mari feels his breath on her face. Its warm, damp current is such an intimate sign of his closeness that her knees tremble and she feels herself getting wet. A hot, shivering flood moves through her body and curls up in a ball, warm, waiting, somewhere near her womb.

Julian smiles a little. She hasn't noticed the music that they're dancing to, she hasn't even noticed the movement of her own feet, but now he leans even closer to her face and whispers the words of the song in her ear.

Mari smiles. She wants to kiss him right here.

And it's as if he's read her thoughts. He breathes against her ear — she can't tell if he's just breathing or if he's kissing her earlobe — and then he whispers impatiently, in a soft voice, thick with passion, "Should we go someplace quieter, maybe have a chat?"

Mari nods. A strange feeling surges through her, a mixture of shock at the question, unbounded joy, and paralyzing fear at the inevitability of the thing.

Julian takes a step back, looks around him for the first time to make sure no one is watching. Mari, too, lets her gaze wander over the crowd of people. She remembers Tinka. She sees her standing next to the wall near the table of food. Tinka is looking at her. There's that sadness in her eyes again, Mari can see it. And she sees something else: is it worry? How could she be worried now, when the thing that Mari has prepared for is happening?

She decides not to care. She decides that Tinka doesn't need her right now.

Julian touches her lightly on the back and leads her toward

the door. No one takes any notice of them. They step over the threshold of the gymnasium door, walk out as if it were a harmless matter, this leaving, and no one realizes what their stepping over the threshold means. They're stepping into a shared space, away from the time that other people occupy, into a world that opens up within this one, an unknown expanse. This is their space, the shared wilderness of their skin, where a tongue will linger in the hollow of a navel, search for a resting place along the curve of a pelvic bone. Where the hollow of an eye will find its place against the rise of the cheekbone of the other's face, fit perfectly into it like a piece of an ancient jigsaw puzzle.

The foyer outside the gym is dark. Julian takes hold of her without hesitating. They walk through the dim passageway to the double doors. She is thinking two thoughts. First, she thinks that the gym door separates two different worlds of scent. The smell of the gym foyer is a mix of lemon-scented cleaning solution and the blunt odour of worn rubber exercise equipment. As the door opens, the smell of the foyer dissolves into a gentler aroma, always the smell of coffee, even in the evening, and the safe, electric dust smell of AV equipment. Her second thought: Julian's hand is warm. The warmth of his hand pushes her other thoughts away; the fact of the warmth of his hand wraps around her like a halo and holds her tenderly inside it.

In the dim passageway, Mari feels a slight doubt for the first time. It's just a hint, a thin thread hindering her steps and pulling her back toward the safe lights and cheerful voices of Tinka and the gym. Julian's hand is just as warm against her skin. But still.

No — the decision's already been made. No one is watching

them here, no one can stop them. This is what she's been waiting for, preparing for. Now it's happening.

The hallway is lined on one side with darkened classrooms, their doors open. They walk hand in hand toward Julian's classroom, as if by agreement. Everything in the room is as it is in the daytime; the darkness simply softens the shapes of the objects. Yet nothing is as it usually is. They come to a stop at the windows opposite, in the shadow of a large split-leaf philodendron. Its friendly, dark-green leaves caress Mari's shoulder blades as Julian steps closer to her. He reaches toward her and, as if continuing the journey he began earlier, strokes the line of Mari's cheek with the back of his hand. She feels her heart beat faster. She looks for a sign of doubt in his eyes, but sees only expectant tenderness.

Their faces touch, and Mari closes her eyes and decides to take a step backward, cross this threshold without looking. She feels the roughness of Julian's cheek, and as joy mingled with terror pounds in her belly, against her ribs, she thinks, This is a man, a grown man, and he wants me now more than anything else.

"Should we kiss?" he whispers hoarsely.

Their lips rest against each other for a moment. Mari lets go of all her thoughts and dissolves into him. Their tongues touch shyly, wonderingly. Julian tastes like a person. He tastes like hope and expectation; soft summer nights; a lake lying like a great, bright mirror reflecting a flutter of waterbirds flying above; a feeling of not wanting to be anywhere else; a happiness that is right nearby, almost already here. The warm feeling bound up in a knot in her lower abdomen, somewhere near her womb, begins to slowly open. It pours out its sap and she becomes quite wet, feels her clitoris throb in rhythm with her heartbeat. All of her thoughts drain away from consciousness, shift into her fingertips, and drip out of her, meaningless.

The kiss deepens and they become one breath, one sigh, one moist being, their boundaries melting into the gentle darkness of the classroom. She can feel him growing harder, and an overwhelming, triumphant joy streaks through her mind. She feels like a woman.

Without meaning to, out of pure reflex, her hands find their way between his legs, feel the incredible reaction aroused by the pressure of her body against his. He tilts his head back and gasps under her touch. She quickly looks at him — has she gone too far? — but he has closed his eyes and is holding on to her with both hands. Emboldened, she starts to rub him now, his penis already insistently hard inside his pants. Should she unzip them? Should she suck? Suddenly his penis is frightening. She doesn't know how long she can suck it before he climaxes, lets loose that musky fluid. She doesn't want it in her mouth.

He opens his eyes and slowly slips his hand under her shirt, feeling around the edges of her bra. He lifts the bra gently, revealing Mari's smooth, small breasts and hard, tightened nipples. He pulls her shirt over her head, lets it drop to the floor. She feels a sudden shyness. She feels exposed and helpless. But Julian doesn't notice her hesitation. His eyes are locked on her breasts, gazing at them as if enchanted, and she feels a vague embarrassment. He presses his right hand lightly against her left breast and strokes the rosy bud of her nipple with his palm. She tries to breathe. Her breath comes out in a broken, trembling mist.

Julian seems to interpret her sighs as excitement, because now he comes closer, right next to her so that she can feel his rock-hard penis against her stomach. He bends over and takes her nipple in his mouth. She looks on in horror as he sucks, not knowing how to enjoy it — it feels so coarse and strange and overdone. Maybe it's not too late to back out, she thinks, glancing at the door as he sucks. But then he lifts his head higher, breathes hotly in her face and pushes his entire tongue in her mouth. There's nothing I can do, she thinks. I have to stay here.

She remembers a swimming competition when she was eight years old. Her father had got it into his head that she should try competing and started taking her to swimming classes. The first competition was a shock to her. Suddenly everybody wanted to win: even the kids she knew were suddenly her opponents, glaring at her. Her father wanted her to win, watching the whole thing from the second row of the stands, a stopwatch in his hand. And Mari stood in a diving position at the edge of the pool before the starting signal and wondered if it was too late to back out. She could say she felt sick. She could pretend to feel faint. She could play dead, anything, just so she wouldn't have to dive. But then, right before the starting signal, there was a dreadful stillness, a sweet indifference. None of this matters, she thought. Nothing at all matters. None of it makes any difference. And she saw herself jump into the cool cradle of water that awaited her like a liberating dream.

She remembers that moment now, and cool disinterest washes over her, a distant, pleasant feeling tied to the absolute insignificance of everything. It's happening now. It doesn't matter. She lets it happen. And with an almost sinking feeling of indifference, as if compelled by the dictates of passion, she unzips his pants, tugs on the waistband of his underwear, and frees his penis. She remembers the instructions the boy at the party gave her, goes over them in her mind before bending over and taking the warm, male-scented organ between her lips. The last thought she has before the jump, before she falls into this fleshy, hairy, moist, eternally elastic moment, is a feeble encouragement. You're not supposed to think, she tells herself. Just let go and let it happen.

# Julian

THE FRENCH WORD *désir*, Julian thought, has its root in the Latin word *desiderare*, whose literal, concrete meaning is *free from the influence of the stars*. For centuries, the philosophical tradition has held that human desire is a weakness, something predestined and inevitable, even animalistic. Something that makes a person less than godlike. For just as long — for always, in fact — the movements of the stars have been thought to have a power that regulates human activity. But based on its etymology — free from the influence of the stars — *desiderare* is actually the opposite of inevitability. Could it mean freedom, a radical break from predestination, from the dictates of fate? What a beautiful thought: that a person doesn't have to be godlike to be free. He just has to desire.

Everything happened just as Julian had dreamed it would. She wanted it, too. No words were needed, just a gaze of shared understanding.

He'd been afraid that she wouldn't be passionate. That if she was in fact untouched, she might freeze up under his touch.

But she was lusty, hot, wanted to suck him off as soon as they were where no one could see them. He let her suck him so long that he almost came. She sucked greedily, her eyes shut as if it were her only food. He stared at her lips as they closed around his erect cock. The sight of it made him even more excited. The greedy little bitch. He felt like saying it out loud. Greedy little bitch.

She stopped sucking and stood up. He wanted to push himself inside her. He brushed away the hair that fell onto her forehead. She was looking past him somehow.

"Do you want to keep going?" he heard himself whisper, inwardly praying that she did.

She nodded, put her head against his chest, and took hold of his penis again.

He turned her around with her back to him and lifted her skirt. He pulled down her tights and her pink underwear. The only moment of doubt was when he saw the tights and underpants bunched around her ankles, over her red dancing shoes. There was something childish about it, and for a second he thought of Anni, who hated it when her tights went all sausagey.

But when he put his hand on her moist crotch, his doubts dissolved. The wonderful little bitch. Completely wet.

He pushed the index finger of his right hand into her tight, wet pussy. She trembled and gasped.

"You're completely wet," he said in a whisper.

He would have to ask, it was unavoidable. She guessed what he was thinking, said it before he could speak.

"I'm on the pill. For my period."

He moved his finger gently, pressing a second finger against her clitoris. What a wonderful, tight cunt she had. She sighed and pushed her rear end toward his cock. He grabbed her hips with both hands, pulled her ass close, and pushed into her.

Fuck, what a cunt, he thought, and then let go of all thought and fell into a roaring moment that stretched into infinity.

# Mari

As she walks home, Mari can feel Julian's semen trickling into her underwear. This is how it works. This is what I want, she thinks. She opens the apartment door. The door's usual click sounds completely different. The dog comes to meet her in the entryway. She pats him absentmindedly.

She doesn't know if she wants to bathe or let Julian be in her, a flowing feeling inside her. It feels strangely disgusting.

No, it's wonderful. Wonderful Julian. Mine.

She gets the domino cookies from the cupboard and mixes cocoa powder into cold milk. There's a familiar tapping from her mother's office. Mari hopes she doesn't come into the kitchen. It feels like her mother would be able to see Julian in her face, to smell his scent on her.

The cocoa bubbles into the milk in powdery pockets. The pockets sink in a spiral, melt into the milk as Mari watches, dazed. She remembers mornings in kindergarten, the same kind of cocoa. Feeling like she couldn't wake up, the film of cocoa sticking to the roof of her mouth. But she had to wake up and put on her mud pants. She still has to wake up and drink her cocoa. There are some things you can never escape.

She starts to pull a domino cookie apart. It's best if the

cream filling stays on one side without breaking. She closes her eyes. Suddenly a perfect circle of filling feels like the most important thing in the world. If this cookie's filling isn't broken, if it's all on one side, she thinks, then everything's all right and Julian loves me and making love is wonderful and adult life is good and right. She opens her eyes. The filling is all on the right side, in one piece.

Mari sighs and licks the cookie. She feels the trickle of Julian's semen. She can feel it even when she sits down. Wonderful Julian. This is definitely a good thing, she thinks. Definitely a good thing.

*

ONCE YOU DIVE IN, you can't come back up again. No matter how much you might think otherwise. If being in someone's thoughts counts as being someplace, Julian is living inside Mari.

December comes, along with exam week. Mari takes her exams, geography and history, works through her math problems. Mercantilism and tectonic plates, derivations and equations. Kanerva is always there at her shoulder as she draws lines on the graphs in her math notebook. Not Kanerva anymore, though — Julian. Julian is in her head, living there behind her nose, his arm wrapped around her ribcage. He's inside her. It feels wonderful and frightening at the same time.

During exam week, Julian monitors the Finnish language and literature test, and Mari sees him watching her the whole time. He comes close to her, bends over her so that it looks to the others like he's helping her with a question. He puts his hand on her hair at the base of her neck. No one notices, everyone's focused on their writing, and he moves his hand down her back. He picks up a pencil and writes six words on the graph paper: *I want you all the time.*

After the test they walk side by side down the long, quiet school corridor to the student council room and he licks her until she has to bite down on the rough fabric of the sofa to keep from yelling.

AT THE CHRISTMAS PARTY, Mari sits in the last row next to Tinka and looks at the back of Julian's neck. She tries to draw his outline in her mind. They haven't talked about the Christmas holidays. They might not see each other at all during the break.

Tinka has been acting strange. She hasn't mentioned Julian at all. Mari wants to tell her everything, no matter how big or small, the shape of his back, his hair wet with snow, the way he sighs when she touches him. But Tinka doesn't ask about it and Mari is afraid to bring it up. Tinka talks about exams and the new year, trips to the cabin and the coat with a fur collar she knows she's getting for Christmas.

"What was your best score?" she asks in a whisper while the choir sings "O Holy Night." "Did you get any tens?"

"In geography and lang and lit."

"Nerd," Tinka says with a smile. "I got eights in everything, except for a seven in French."

Mari smiles back. Maybe Tinka isn't really mad at her.

"Wanna have some drinks tonight?" Tinka asks. "Buy some bubbly and drink it in my room? We could make chocolate tarts and color each other's hair."

"Yeah, let's," Mari says.

"We could make champagne jello. It's good, and you don't

have to eat much before it goes to your head."

For that moment, everything is perfect. Tinka is smiling at Mari again, and Julian turns his head in the front row, seeking out her gaze. He finds her and his smile hides a tenderness meant for only her to see. The music students are singing "O Holy Night" and tonight they're going to make champagne jello.

IN THE SCHOOLYARD, Julian strides past her. She turns to watch him go. He makes a quick gesture with his hand. "I'll call you." Mari nods, straight-faced, and watches him disappear into the building. There are other teachers around. She can't run after him. She looks at her phone's display, its persistent little bear logo. She knows now that the next two weeks will be spent waiting. The letter J in the phone's memory lists Julian. Mari focuses all her thoughts on that letter J. Julian is going to call. Julian wants her and he's going to call her. He wants her all the time.

THAT EVENING, Mari is combing lightener into Tinka's hair. The red dye has already been applied and rinsed out, but there's a separate packet of highlighter. Tinka is spooning wobbly champagne jello into her mouth.

"I've got a thing this weekend with a guy who has a really weird cock."

Mari is no longer shocked by Tinka's conversation-openers.

"Well?" she says after a pause, spreading lightener on the crown of Tinka's head.

"Well," Tinka says, and Mari knows she's in for some exaggeration. "For one thing, it's horribly big. And it's crooked."

Mari can see that Tinka's trying to think of striking details.

"Plus," Tinka continues, prolonging the suspense, "the guy has horrendous staying power. We fucked a bunch of times and he could have kept going who knows how long."

"Ah," Mari says.

"And now he's calling me every day. And sending me tons of texts."

"Uh-huh."

"He's a real man. A total stud. Not at all a pansy."

Mari doesn't say anything. She knows what Tinka means. Or rather, who she means.

"We should find a man like that for you," Tinka says, looking at the highlights in the mirror. "So you'd learn something about these things." She tilts her head nonchalantly.

Mari eats her chocolate tart, says nothing. Tinka doesn't seem to have a clue.

"But what's the deal between you and Kanerva?" Tinka asks suddenly, in a pestering tone. "He fucked you, right? You let him fuck you."

Mari flushes red. Tinka really has no idea.

"Don't use that word," Mari says indignantly.

"Excuse me?" Tinka snorts. "I saw what the two of you were doing. Half the fucking school saw. All the teachers saw. You were screwing each other. I'm sure even his wife knows the two of you have been fucking."

Mari is furious. What right does Tinka have to come between her and Julian? It's nobody else's business. Tinka is standing now, her face red with anger. The thick strands of treated hair slap against her cheeks as she shakes her head. She looks ugly, Mari thinks with satisfaction. How could she have ever thought Tinka was pretty?

"It isn't fucking," she says coldly. "It's not some dirty screw.

It's not the kind of thing you do with your stupid guys."

Mari is silent. Tinka looks at her condescendingly. Her condescension drills a hole between Mari's eyes and drives into her head. Mari hardens her expression. Tinka is a childish, silly girl. She doesn't know anything about real life.

"It isn't fucking," Mari says finally, slowly, frostily. "It's making love. We were making love."

"Fuck off." Tinka sobs, and tears start to run down her blotchy cheeks. "Can't you see that Kanerva's using you?"

"Stop it!" Mari shouts. "I love Julian. And he loves me. Understand? He loves me."

"No, Mari. No."

The tears run down Tinka's cheeks, but she makes no sound. Mari watches, horrified. Tinka means it. It's the first time Mari's ever seen her cry, and she means it.

"I'm going home now," Mari says.

"Kanerva's a shit," Tinka tries once more.

Mari had almost softened because of her tears, but now a new thought occurs to her: Tinka's jealous.

"Why would you say that?" she asks, her voice icy with anger.

The tears still flow fast down Tinka's cheeks and drip onto her sweater.

"I'm your friend," Tinka says.

"Well, don't hassle me, then."

"Kanerva's an adult. He's married."

"Don't start on that," Mari says coldly. "You're jealous."

She picks up her bag and packs her pajamas back into it. Tinka stands beside her, still crying silently. Mari isn't looking at her anymore. She closes the door behind her, goes downstairs, sputters something about a stomachache to Tinka's parents to explain her departure, and walks out the door.

It's frosty out. The heavy snow from earlier in the evening has closed the world in on itself. The spruce trees along the road press their limbs toward the ground. Tinka's jealous, Mari thinks. That's what's going on. Because Mari and Julian love each other. Tinka doesn't know anything about what true love is. She's jealous.

*

MARI'S MOTHER WANTS to have a big Christmas. It's important to her that everything is just so — large glass ornaments bought from a home-decor shop, a perfectly shaped tree. They have to have a great big ham, even though there aren't enough people to eat it. They have to have a French Yule log cake covered in thick frosting although no one wants any. They have to have cheese and wine and a trip to the cemetery on Christmas Eve and a concert of carols at the cathedral. Mari's father's on a business trip — Japan again — and won't be home until the week before Christmas. Mari ends up going shopping with her mother, looking for the perfect red and gold items for the Christmas table: napkins, napkin rings, flower arrangements.

Mari drags herself along behind her mother from Stockmann department store to the home-decor place on the south side of town and back again. Her shoes are soaked through with slush from the frozen cobblestones. The sky hangs like a grey rug above streets strung with Christmas lights.

This is day number three. She hasn't seen Julian in three days. The days are lone continents, broad deserts. Her phone is as mute as a stick of wood. She's written a long text message to him. She has it saved in her own message folder and edits it every evening. But she doesn't dare send it. What if his wife reads his messages? Or his daughter? Children play with their parents' phones. The little girl might read Julian's messages by accident. Mari sinks into hopelessness. She can't call him. He has to call her.

Her mother hurries her to the pedestrian crossing at the corner next to the Swedish Theatre. It's then that Mari sees him. At the crosswalk, on the other side of the street. The tram rattles by and hides him from view for a second.

He's holding a little girl's hand — the same girl who was in the car, the one who looked at Mari for a long time — and she's holding another, smaller girl's hand. The girls are wearing matching coats and knit hats with pom-poms. Mari's breathing stops; her heart skips a beat. She begins to pant with nervousness. Her mother gives her a questioning look. The light has turned green. It's time to move. Halfway across the street, Julian notices her. He recognizes her at once and his gaze is somehow resigned.

"Well, hello!" he says when they're within hearing distance.

Mari tries to smile.

Julian turns to her mother. "You must be Mari's mother," he says, smiling, reaching out his hand. "Julian Kanerva, Mari's language and literature teacher."

Mari can see from the corner of her eye how her mother's expression brightens.

"Oh, hello," she says in a sickly sweet voice, shaking hands. "I am indeed Mari's mother."

Mari looks at Julian's children. The smaller girl worms her way to her father's side. The bigger one tells her to keep still.

Mari looks down. There's slush piled on the toes of her shoes. She can't look at Julian now. How can he actually be talking to her mother? She steals a glance at him. He's looking at her warily. She sees that thing in his eyes that's only for her, and smiles a little.

"Yes, Mari's a really exceptional student. Smart and insightful."

Mari's mother laughs, unnecessarily loudly. "Really? At home she's quite ordinary."

Mari feels anger redden her cheeks. Her mother's flirting. Is she flirting for real?

"No, no," Julian insists. "Mari has poetry in her. That's a rare and wonderful thing in a person."

Her mother stands there, not saying anything, seeming to examine him closely. Mari is shaking, terrified. For a moment everyone is silent. Julian looks Mari's mother calmly in the eye. She manages a smile.

"Well, it's wonderful that things are going so well for her at school. It's great to hear that from a teacher. Mari is so secretive sometimes."

Julian's children are starting to get restless. The younger one has picked up a lump of snow from the sidewalk and is forming it into a snowball. The older one is tugging on Julian's sleeve. Mari can see her watching everything, taking in every word, every nonchalant smile, every change in intonation.

The trams are clattering around them. This is the only time I'll see Julian the whole Christmas break, Mari thinks.

Her mother flashes an even more ravishing smile. "Well, merry Christmas. I'm sure I'll see you on parent–teacher night."

"Yes. Merry Christmas," Julian says.

He leaves with his children. Mari turns to watch him go. He turns once more and gives her that look. She takes hold of it. Wraps it around herself.

"Why haven't you mentioned your language and literature teacher?" her mother asks later, when they're sitting in Café Esplanadi, Mari tearing pieces off her Christmas cake.

"Oh, he's just trying to be nice. I'm not his favorite student or anything."

"Nonsense. He's absolutely thrilled with you. What was his name again?"

"Julian."

"Julian," her mother says, tasting the name slowly.

Mari feels stripped, like her mother can see everything. Julian's name is hers. Only she can say it, taste it.

"Well, you did get a ten in lang and lit, after all, didn't you?"

Mari doesn't bother to answer; she just turns to look out the window. Her mother doesn't seem to notice her discomfort at all.

"Well," her mother says carelessly. "I'll meet him again on parent–teacher night, I suppose."

The fluffy bits of Christmas cake stick in Mari's throat. She mixes her coffee with her spoon. She looks at her mother on the sly. Does she know? Is she sharp-eyed enough to notice? Suddenly the scarf around Mari's neck feels tight. Like she can't breathe. She feels like crying. Maybe she will try to call Julian. Maybe she'll do it today. Just to hear his voice.

# *Anja*

THE DECEMBER LIGHT leaned low; the mornings reddened and moved slowly toward day. Then a brief interval of brightness, the sun reaching out red, level with the branches of the pine trees in the yard, never managing to turn yellow before it set again, sinking back into darkness. She was going to her sister's house on Christmas Eve. Johannes had invited her for Christmas, but she still felt like a traitor when she thought about what they had been doing. She wanted to spend Christmas with her husband at the nursing home. First, dinner at her sister's, then the nursing home, where she would light four bright candles in the window. She thought about the Christmas they'd had two years ago. They'd already decided he would go to a nursing home, but the realization hadn't yet hit them.

They'd fed the sparrows and made mulled wine. In the evening they just lay side by side after their sauna. He was breathing in her ear. It was their shared ritual of tenderness. Maybe he was making himself more real that way, his breath heavy, whispering a word or two. My love, he might say. My wife. My girl. Whether or not he remembered was irrelevant. It didn't matter if he'd completely forgotten everything.

They were close to each other and he could name her as someone who belonged to him, a part of himself. Their limbs belonged to each other, they'd become one over the years they'd been together.

ANJA KEPT GOING to the university over the Christmas week. It felt good to just lock herself in her office and write. She didn't run into anyone in the department hallway; everyone was already on vacation.

She had arranged by email to meet with one of the doctoral students on the Wednesday before Christmas. The man she'd met at the lecture, Julian Kanerva. He had a name like a character in a novel.

Julian Kanerva arrived at two o'clock on the dot, as agreed, and stood in the doorway, stood there for perhaps a minute before Anja looked up. He seemed unsure of himself. The doorway framed his insecurity, making it more apparent than before.

"Excuse me," he said. "I had an appointment to see you."

"Yes," Anja said, and smiled. "We've already met." She stood up to shake his hand. "Although I haven't seen you lately at the lecture."

He stretched out his hand. "I earn my living as a teacher. High school — Finnish language and literature. It keeps me busy. I don't make it to lectures as often as I'd like."

Anja searched her desk for the email he'd sent to outline his planned thesis. She'd printed it out for their meeting, made some comments in red.

Julian Kanerva was definitely ambitious — arrogant, in fact. The email contained a breathless exposition of the philosophy of tragedy. *The biggest challenge will be limiting the scope of your thesis*, Anja had reminded him diplomatically in her reply.

Julian sat down in the chair across from her and looked at her.

"Well," she said.

"Well," he replied.

"What is it that you actually want to argue in your dissertation?"

"Actually?"

He gathered up all his energy to explain his ideas. A boy, Anja thought. He's like a little boy brought to the front of the class to show that he has the right answers on his homework.

"I was thinking ..." he began, hesitant. "I was thinking I would start with an analysis of the structure of tragedy. As a tragedy unfolds, some break in the plot has to occur that makes the events progress rapidly toward the resolution. Some pivotal event occurs, and it's as if time stops. The turning point is a decisive change that makes all the events of the story relate to one another. The change is inevitable — there's no going back."

He was picking up speed. There were always plenty of students like him: young scholars who lived for theory, whose research had a personal significance. You had to be careful how you supported them: praise them a little, but make sure that they didn't overreach.

"The thing that I'm most interested in is the type of textual analysis you plan to use to define the problem," she said, attempting to dampen his enthusiasm.

"Well," Julian continued, "in my view, the pivotal event in a tragedy is often connected with death."

"Do you plan to analyze a classical tragedy, then?"

"Yes. I intend to examine Sophocles' *Antigone* from a particular point of view."

*Antigone.* Of course. "What would it be — your point of view?"

"I want to look at the character of Antigone. Above all, her desire for death — the fact that she desires death."

"What do you base that on?" Anja said.

She could see that Julian Kanerva craved opposition. He wanted to present his argument. He leaned eagerly toward her.

"Right. Antigone's defiance of King Creon's command not to bury her brother, who has conspired against him, leads in the end to Antigone choosing death. She would rather choose death than obey an unjust law, the prohibition of the burial. She says, *how sweet to die in such employ.*"

"Why do you feel that the refusal to obey the law necessarily implies a desire for death?"

"Because Antigone's desire is excessive. She sacrifices her life for her brother's burial. It's an unreasonable, inordinate desire that is, in the end, directed toward death."

Anja didn't give up. "So how can such a desire be justified?"

Julian said slowly, relishing the words, "It's about meaning. Without desire, everything would be empty and meaningless. Without desire there's nothing."

Anja had to smile. This fellow was no slouch. She changed the direction of the discussion: "Do you think Antigone's death is unavoidable, that she has no other alternative?"

Julian seemed to consider this. "She has the weight of her family's fate within her. It's a kind of inevitability. I think when you look at the catharsis in tragedy, her death is unavoidable. It's a function of the tragedy."

"Is death always inevitable in tragedy?" Anja asked.

"Yes," Julian answered without hesitation. "In a tragedy, death is inevitable."

He paused, looked into her eyes intently, and smiled. She shifted her position in her chair.

"So," she said, temporizing. She wanted to be moderately supportive, not overly enthusiastic. "This all sounds basically promising. But I would encourage you to pay particular attention to restricting the scope of your theme."

"Agreed," Julian said. "Shall I send you an email once I have my outline sketched?"

"Yes, do."

Anja stood up to indicate that the discussion was over. Julian Kanerva stood up, too. He turned, ready to leave.

Anja couldn't resist the temptation to add, "Do you think this theory is adaptable to life, to our reality? I mean, the theory that desire reveals life's meaning?"

Julian Kanerva turned and looked at her, surprised. He seemed unsure how to respond. Then the surprise changed to a teasing smile. "Who says tragedy and real life have to be separate? Or to put it more generally: who says art and life have to be separate?"

Anja laughed. "Nobody," she said. "But it could be dangerous, mixing life and art."

"What if it's more like the two spreading into each other, overlapping, melting together, each expanding across the other's boundaries?" he said.

Anja didn't back down. "But maybe desires are always subordinate to what others ask of you — in real life, I mean."

He continued smiling. "That's what I used to think, too."

"But not anymore?"

"Something changed my mind. Maybe it's possible for art and life to blend into each other. To bring passion, desire, and fire into life, the way it is in art."

Anja looked at him defiantly. "And what about death? Does that attitude toward life need a tragic death to define it?"

He laughed. "Yeah, that could constitute a problem."

"I should say it would be a problem," Anja said with a smile. "If change in your life can only be achieved through death."

Julian Kanerva was silent for a moment.

"You and I may have a difference of opinion on this subject," he said.

Anja laughed. "That's a good thing. It's healthy to disagree. To have a proper basis of mutual misunderstanding."

He caught the reference and grinned.

"Goodbye."

"Goodbye."

# Mari

CHRISTMAS EVE IS a long, languishing day, creeping toward its demise. In the morning Mari decorates the tree. Her father drinks his first cognac at ten. Her mother sets the table for Christmas dinner, Villeroy & Boch dishes in their correct places, to the millimeter.

Mari is in her room, putting on a wine-red velvet sheath dress and shiny stockings. She looks at herself in the mirror and thinks about the sweet blade of a knife; its clear, liberating cuts. She could easily get a knife from the kitchen. She could give herself two or three cuts in her thigh, or in her arm, if she wanted to. It's a small, consoling thought. An island of her own in this interminable day.

The guests are coming at four. Her mother's sister Anja and her father's younger brother Heikki and his family. Mari's cousins immediately take over the house with noisy, boyish commotion. Her mother makes her keep them company. They could play Monopoly or Hotel, just so Mari keeps them quiet, even if it's only for a minute, she says. Mari submits to her role as babysitter and tricks her cousins into buying hotels on Erottaja and Mannerheimintie. She establishes a hotel complex on Liisankatu and Esplanadi and rapidly acquires a monopoly.

As the game progresses, Mari's mind keeps wandering to her telephone. I won't look at it yet, she thinks. I'll check it in an hour. She concentrates all her thoughts on one hope. The hope that Julian has called. Or at least sent a text message.

After an hour of playing Hotel, a scuffle over the largest hotel breaks out between her cousins. Mari stretches her leg out beside her on the floor. The carpet has left a vivid waffle pattern on her stocking-covered leg. Mari looks on in boredom as her father and Heikki sip their wine. Heikki is looking at her with new eyes. She knows what the look means: she's a woman now. She turns her head and tries not to think about that look.

Her phone displays two missed calls and the envelope icon. Mari's heart leaps with hope. The calls are from Tinka. Disappointment seeps through her like a slow animal. The message is from Tinka, too. *Merry Christmas. Sorry I was so schizo. Still friends?* Mari answers with a flat *Yeah* and wishes her a merry Christmas.

DINNER TAKES FOREVER. The rutabaga casserole sticks to the roof of her mouth and the red wine turns her lips purple. Heikki starts up a heated discussion with Anja. It's his favorite subject, with the same basic outline at all their family dinners. As soon as he gets a little drunk, he demands that Anja discuss the relative importance of various areas of study. He begins with good-natured swagger.

"Well, Anja, have you found out the fundamental nature of reality yet?"

Anja meets the challenge calmly, sips her wine and looks him brightly in the eye. "Not yet, but any minute now. Rest assured that if I do, you'll be the first to know."

She winks. Her sarcasm hangs over the table.

Mari's mother looks at Heikki with a patient expression. Her father is content to eat in silence. It's all too familiar to everyone. Anja's quip just gets Heikki more worked up.

"What is it you study again? The plight of the modern human?"

"The tragedy," Anja corrects him. There's a touch of coolness in her voice.

Heikki snorts to indicate that nothing could be more of a waste of time. "So what's the crux of your research? What is the tragedy of modern man? What's weighing us down with sorrow?"

"This ham is excellent. Very tender," Heikki's wife says, trying to change the subject.

"Yes," Mari's mother says, grateful for a new topic of conversation. "It's actually pre-roasted."

Heikki laughs good-naturedly. "Right. Exactly. Plenty of food and fun for us. And yet humanity's plight is nothing but sorrow. Right, Anja?"

"Let it go," Heikki's wife says, a hint of annoyance behind her smile.

"Now, now," Heikki says with artificial good humor. "I'm just discussing humanism with Anja. Exceedingly important stuff. Really it is. So, Anja, tell us what's troubling humanity at the moment, generally speaking."

Mari's mother starts pointedly jangling the serving utensils. Mari can see her annoyance. Desperation, in fact. Anja isn't bothered by the tension in the air. She's not smiling anymore, but she meets Heikki's gaze with her head raised.

"Well, generally speaking," she says, managing another smile, "the thing that usually troubles us is death. Our own and others'."

"Right, right. And this is the monumental idea you plan to prove in your scholarly publications. You give lectures on this stupendous insight."

"Precisely," Anja says.

Heikki ponders this, taking a sip of wine.

"Well, tell us what death means to us. What's the meaning of death?" He speaks heatedly, not waiting for an answer.

"It's the final possibility," Anja says.

"Possibility?" Heikki says, feigning bafflement. "Isn't it more like something everybody has to face? I wouldn't call my own death a possibility."

"True," Anja says. "That's why it's the final one, but it's a possibility nonetheless. Awaiting all of us. Inevitable."

"So why call it a possibility, then? How is it the final possibility?"

"It has to do with the perception of time, when it comes down to it. The sense of time."

Heikki laughs openly.

"Damn," he says in disbelief. "The sense of time. And can you tell us what that is?"

"Not me, but other thinkers can. I'm just talking about what other people have thought about."

"Well, tell us what it is, this sense of time."

Anja tastes her wine, looks at him, and says with bright eyes, "The sense of time is memory and intention. Memory and intention delineate the perception of time."

Heikki shakes his head, grinning sarcastically. "And here I was, thinking time was a continuum of present moments. Isn't that indisputable? One moment following another? It's not that complicated."

Anja smiles as she answers. "Chronology is misleading.

Every moment gets its meaning from elsewhere: from the past, or from what's to come. A person is always dislocated."

"A revolutionary idea, I must say. But have you thought that messing around with the idea of death might just be a compulsion of yours?" He pauses briefly, then continues. "Since someone you love is lying in the hospital? Certainly much smaller things can become" — he considers what word to use — "obsessions."

Now Mari's mother is looking at him in horror, not even able to object to what he said, just staring, at a loss for words. Anja's expression doesn't falter.

"I certainly can think of this at a personal level, too," she says frostily. "You can think of someone else's death as a kind of final possibility. Maybe even more final, since it isn't my possibility. There may be a request, for instance. A demand to be allowed to die." She pauses. "Or a request for help dying."

She seals off her words with a sip of wine. Her gaze still doesn't falter.

No one dares say a word. Heavy silence envelops everyone at the table. Mari's cousins look at their mother, frightened. Heikki laughs faintly but immediately realizes how stupid it sounds. Mari looks at Anja in amazement. She looks at her mother, who is staring at her sister, numb. Mari sees Anja turn her head, slowly shifting her gaze from Heikki toward her sister. At that instant Mari sees something. She can see that her mother sees it, and she can see that Anja sees that her mother sees it. Mari isn't quite sure what it is — or maybe she doesn't want to know. She suddenly feels an irresistible desire to get up from the table and run away. She wants to call Julian, she wants nothing right now except to hear his voice. Julian, who's real. Who exists. Who belongs to her.

Her mother's thin voice breaks the silence. It's a request, almost a prayer. "Anja, will you help me with the dishes?"

Heikki's wife doesn't understand, offers to help.

"No," her mother says, her voice a bit stronger now. "Anja and I can do it."

## Anja

"DAMN IT," her sister said, trying not to let the tears start. "What in God's name are you planning?"

Anja stroked the fluted edge of a Villeroy & Boch plate with the fingers of her left hand, thinking about how to formulate her answer. Her sister was in a panic. Why was Marita acting this way? Was she losing her grip? Twice now in a rather short time Anja had seen that helpless, pleading look in her eyes. There was no backing out. She had to tell the truth. But with the right words, not revealing too much.

"Well," she began.

Her sister stood in front of her, stricken with terror, her hands held up as if she were ready to cover her ears so she wouldn't have to hear anything too painful.

"I've been thinking …" Anja began again.

Her sister groaned and lifted her hands to her face. "Don't say it. Damn it, don't say it out loud," she moaned from between her fingers.

"But I haven't said anything yet."

"I know what you're going to say," her sister whispered. "I know damn well what you're planning to do."

She looked at Anja, terrified. Anja could see a boundless

desolation in her eyes.

"There are some requests that have to be met," Anja said.

"Don't start that crap! What kind of ethics is that?"

"You don't understand. You never can. No one can."

"No, they can't. There's nobody who could understand what you're planning."

"Marita, honey," Anja tried.

Marita started to cry. She sniffled and scrubbed the dishes with raspberry-scented Fairy dish detergent, refusing to look at Anja.

Anja went over to her. Marita was at her weakest; her tear-streaked, angry face was open, naked. She had raised her right hand to emphasize her words, the yellow dishwashing glove covering a hand that still held the soapy scrub brush, water running down her arm to her armpit. When she was little, Anja thought, Marita would have thrown the brush at her in a situation like this. Now she just stood there and looked at her. Anja was flooded with tenderness. She took her sister by the shoulders.

"You can't understand. You can't understand what it's like to spend nights and days with the one you love when he's become a child again, crying because he can't remember."

"And you can't understand that as a doctor I can never accept that attitude." Marita's voice was a trembling whisper.

The scent of raspberry Fairy floated between them. Marita regained her confidence.

"I'm not stupid. I know it happens every day. But there have to be laws. Someone has to protect those boundaries. There have to be doctors who cherish life. What really happens is another matter. But as a doctor, I can never accept what you're saying."

"And as a person, I can never accept what you're saying," Anja answered.

Marita was quiet.

It was pointless to expect her to understand. There was nothing Anja could say that would make her sister change her point of view. She would have to experience the request, the extreme limit, and then perhaps she would understand.

She didn't comprehend it, couldn't comprehend it.

There it was — the thing that separated them.

# Mari

THE PHONE IS RINGING. Mari waits for Julian to answer. She's in her room, having slipped away upstairs, holding the phone tightly, her hand shaking, punching the letters J, U, and L into the search screen. It's eight o'clock. In a family with kids they must have opened presents long before eight. Julian's kids might already be asleep. So she has mustered the courage to call him. The phone continues to ring. Her heart pounds hard for a few beats, but it calms down by the third ring. She thinks he isn't going to answer. Then, after the fourth ring, she hears his familiar voice. A loving voice.

"Well, hi."

"Hi," Mari says, her own voice tender in spite of herself. "I'm not … I'm not calling for any particular reason. I just wanted to hear what … what …"

"I've been thinking about you all day."

"Why haven't you called me?" Mari asks, a tremble that promises tears already in her voice.

Julian is quiet for a second. The silence sounds like an accusation. Mari regrets her question. She shouldn't make demands. She just has to take whatever Julian's willing to give.

"We've been very busy with Christmas — housework and

everything," Julian gently explains. "I've been thinking about my dissertation topic, getting started on it. Are you upset?"

"Um," Mari says, feeling pleasure spread from behind her nose into her neck and shoulders and down, farther down.

"How can I make it up to you, if you're upset at me?" Julian asks, and the caress of his voice makes Mari wet. "My love," he whispers, and Mari sighs.

"Where are you? Are you in your own room?"

"Mm-hmm."

"Do you want me as much as I want you?" Julian whispers hoarsely.

"Yes," Mari says.

"I'm so hard."

"Can't your ... wife hear you?"

"No, I'm alone here. Tell me what you're wearing. Tell me how wet you are."

His voice is tender and husky, gentle yet commanding. Mari is aroused.

"Put your finger in your pussy," he says.

Mari moves the phone to her left hand and puts her right middle finger carefully inside her. It feels good. She moans as her finger sinks into her and touches the right spot. Julian moans on the other end of the line.

"Tell me how it feels, sweetheart. Is your pussy all stiff and wet?"

Mari starts to get into the story.

"I'm imagining that you're touching me ... that you're kissing my breasts and ... and coming inside me. Deep."

"Do you want me to fuck you?"

"Yes."

"Say it."

"Fuck me," Mari whispers.

"Louder. Say it again."

"Fuck me. Fuck me," she says.

"I love you."

"I love you."

Julian moans. There's a murmur on the phone. Then a rustle, then Julian's breathing gradually levels out. Mari takes her finger out of herself. She glances toward the door and only now realizes that her cousins could burst in at any moment. Julian still doesn't say anything. Mari sighs. Her breath is trembling.

"Are you still there?" Julian asks.

There's a gentleness in his voice again. It's not frightening now. Passion in his voice frightens her. A little. She nods, then realizes he can't hear her do it.

"I'm here," she says, hearing the same tenderness in her own voice.

"Would you like to go out to the country the day after Christmas? We have a house about an hour's drive from here. Just the two of us. A few days. I'm going in any case. Alone. I thought I could be alone and get some work done on my dissertation."

"Could I? Yeah, yes, I want to."

"I could pick you up in town. At one o'clock. Or maybe twelve-thirty — that'll give me time to heat up the sauna before it gets dark, once we get there. Meet me in front of the Sanomatalo. Bring lots of clothes. It can be cold there when the house hasn't been warmed up."

"Twelve-thirty," Mari says with a smile.

They say their goodbyes and Mari hangs up. Two more nights and she'll see Julian. She counts the hours. Forty hours.

She clings to the words he used. The L-word. Julian said that word, and with it, everything. Julian, who is hers. Julian, who is everything that means anything.

# *Julian*

ON CHRISTMAS EVE, Julian breathed a sigh of relief. The holiday was going better than he could have hoped. They did the housework together two days ahead of time. Luckily, the children's gifts had been taken care of earlier in the month. It was easy to buy presents for kids their age; their hopes were so clearly defined. He knew Ada wanted a doll that was all the rage with the girls at her kindergarten, a large-headed Barbie-like thing with bright-colored, trendy outfits. Julian asked the clerk at the toy store to help him find it. She knew what he meant. Anni's wish list included the same doll and a princess dress. Julian spent two hours in a children's clothing store and finally found a nice, moss-green dress. The clerk assured him that it had the princess look. He went with Ada and Anni to buy jewelry and a few books for Jannika. That's when he ran into the girl and her mother. The mother didn't guess a thing. He was sure of it.

CHRISTMAS EVE NIGHT went well, right up to the kids' bedtime. They went skating, and to the cemetery, and the kids built a snow fort in the yard before dinner. They opened their gifts without any emotional outbursts: the kids were satisfied, and Jannika's eyes lit up when she opened the jewelry. The books he gave her were also a hit.

They had a tradition of taking a sauna together on Christmas Eve, just the two of them, after the kids had gone to bed. It usually ended with them making love. Jannika would buy some scented oil and candles, and they would drink good champagne in bed after the sauna. Since Anni was born it had been their own little romantic game, with Anni away in her manger.

Now the game felt routine, half-hearted; felt in fact like it only served to underscore the atmosphere of mutual contempt. Jannika moved to the lower sauna bench when Julian tossed more water on the stove. She had always done that, but now it annoyed him exceedingly. Jannika's stupid, bony shoulders sinking in a heap, bent over like a martyr's to endure the steam. Julian was overcome with hopelessness thinking about them here like this for thirty more years, Jannika on the lower bench and Julian above her, throwing steam on the stove like a torturer. Everything turns out this way, he thought, trivial and resentful and backhanded. It starts as a blessed, vast, shared space that feels like a miracle, everything about the other person a pure promise of happiness. Then a year goes by, and another, five years turns into ten, and suddenly every little thing about the other person — the way she drinks her coffee in the morning, washes up in the evening, sits in a chair — they're all infuriatingly the same; the abject posture and expression like she wishes she were far away is so unbearable that desperation spills into your mind like a flood and covers everything. If only all of this could be exchanged for something else. If only he could have something different. He looked at his own shriveled penis and his desperation turned to shame. How could he sink so low, talking with the girl on the phone like that while his wife gave the children a bath? He'd jacked off like a fifteen-year-old. It had felt too good. He remembered that just as he was about to come he'd said he loved her. Why? It just slipped out, by accident. Or maybe it was true. He thought about her all the time. Who knows, maybe it was true.

Jannika straightened up on the lower bench, turned her head toward him, and leaned it against his sweaty legs. She stretched out her hand and stroked his wet thigh. Desire awakened.

"Shall we go?" she asked.

"Yes, let's."

SOMETHING CLICKED inside Julian. He saw his anger from the outside, an anger mixed with lust. The line between violence and pleasure was blurring. A person carries the knowledge of the existence of this line, and of its fragility, in everything he does. How easily a caressing hand can be lifted to strike, how easily a sigh of pleasure can turn into a groan of pain. A request to keep going can turn into a request to stop. Yes can turn into no. It's always being redrawn, this line that separates pleasure from agony. It's never in the same place. With every act, a person redefines his relationship to good and evil. The line that divides the two runs through each of us, and though it may seem to be settled between two people, everything you do can affect it. Nothing you do can ever resolve the question, can ever decide once and for all whether your role is essentially kind or cruel.

One minute Julian was kissing Jannika's back, the next minute he was slapping it. At first it was purely the dictate of passion. At first she moaned with pleasure. She was lying on her stomach, lifting her rear end toward him. He turned her over, her face red, striped from the folds of the pillow, slightly startled. Her face irritated him, its naked plea not to be hurt, a reminder of the weight of his responsibility.

"Are you a whore or are you my wife?" he heard himself ask. His voice was an angry hiss.

There was a strange haze in Jannika's eyes. She thought it was a game.

"I can be your whore today if you like," she whispered.

Julian pushed himself inside her. He could see that he was hurting her, but the knowledge only made him push harder.

"Look at me, cunt," he growled.

Jannika looked at him and he saw that her indifference had receded someplace far away, had been replaced with fear. She let him push hard, took his thrusts meekly, like a victim. There was fear in her face, but no desire to escape. Her submission made him feel a humiliating anger.

"Don't play the martyr. It's like your whole attitude is making fun of me," he gasped, overwhelmed with anger and passion.

He stopped moving and just held on to her. She still looked completely open.

"How am I making fun of you?" she whispered.

There was a glimmer of desolation in the question.

"By withdrawing. You're never there. It's never you anymore."

The situation had turned unreal. The scented candles flickered on the night table. His erection still throbbed insistently. He no longer knew how to judge whether his reactions were right or wrong. Where was this going? What was really happening?

Jannika tried to raise herself out of his grasp. Julian pressed her back down, too hard. Her head hit the headboard. She screeched. Julian lifted his hand. A thought flashed through his mind: All power is here. All meaning. All love and all hate. All of life.

Before he could move to strike her, or help her, she sat up and wrapped both arms around him. "Sshhh," she said, holding him close. He lowered his hand and sank into her embrace. He didn't know if he was sobbing or just shaking with the force of the gesture he'd just made. But Jannika was squeezing him tightly in her arms.

"I'm here. I've been here the whole time," she whispered, as if she were comforting a child after a bad dream.

# Anja

CHRISTMAS NIGHT. Snow falling quietly, the world silent.

Anja walked across the snow-covered courtyard of the nursing home and opened the door. The familiar night nurse nodded from the reception desk: visitors were always welcome here, even at night.

Anja opened the door of her husband's room and stepped inside without making a sound. She walked over to his bed and lay down beside him.

He started awake.

"Is that my girl?"

"Anja," she answered. "Just your girl Anja." She hugged him.

"It's Terri, isn't it? Terri, is that you?"

"No, it's not Terri. It's Anja, your wife. Your wife, Anja."

"Yes, of course. Anja. Just Anja," he said, and pulled her closer to him.

They lay there. Outside it was freezing and Christmas night was moving toward morning and there they lay, husband and wife, side by side in the too-narrow bed.

She thought about the first time he went to see the doctor.

IT'S APRIL. The doctor has a bushy beard, like a psychiatrist in a cheap television movie.

Her husband sits down opposite the doctor and tries to joke about the cost of the visit. He's always making jokes — it must be easier to breathe if he laughs now and then. The gravity of the situation is covered over with smiles.

"Well, doctor, what's the verdict? Will I remember my wife's name tomorrow, or should I write it down right away?"

The doctor laughs. His beard shakes with the laughter. "Go ahead and write it down, just to avoid trouble later."

"If you give me a piece of paper I'll make a note of it right now. Best to write it down right away, don't you think, Katariina?" he jokes, turning to Anja.

Anja doesn't laugh.

The doctor smiles again, then puts on his official expression. "But anyway. Back to the matter at hand. Why don't we give you a little memory test right now? That's the usual procedure. Completely routine. You're so young that I'm sure you can get through it without any problem. It's called the MMSE. The Mini-Mental State Examination."

"Mental state. So it's a psychiatric examination," her husband sputters.

"Yes, it is," the doctor says. "But it's a test that measures memory. I'll read you some questions, and you answer at your leisure, to the best of your ability. All right?"

"Sure. Let me have it," he says.

The doctor clears his throat. "What year is it?"

Her husband looks at the doctor and then at her with an expression of amused disbelief, and says the year.

"What season is it now?"

He laughs. "Has it occurred to you that your patients can

look out the window?" he asks.

Anja can hear the beginnings of annoyance in his voice.

The doctor laughs politely at his quip. "Do answer the question, though," he says.

"Spring," her husband says.

The doctor nods. "And what is today's date?"

Her husband shakes his head in mock amusement and states the date.

The tension in Anja's body starts to melt away.

"What country are we in?"

"Heck, the country and the date? I'm not that senile."

"Well," the doctor says with feigned amiability. "If you think the test is silly, that's no problem. We can just forget about it."

"Forget about it." He snorts. "Interesting choice of words. Let's keep going. Why not?"

The test continues with word repetition, naming objects, writing, drawing pictures. Anja watches her husband's face out of the corner of her eye. He writes something on the paper. Scratches his chin. Asks for an eraser. Writes something else. Draws a line through what he's written.

He looks at Anja, and that's when she knows.

He laughs.

"If I fail the test, do I get to take it over?" he says, handing the paper to the doctor.

The doctor takes a moment to read his answers.

Anja feels an overwhelming desire to take her husband's hand and walk out of the room, go to the cafeteria, run across the street, get on a bus, hide in a library or a museum or a movie theatre, somewhere no one can find them.

Maybe if they left now. What does it matter if he doesn't

remember everything? She can remember. Maybe they don't need to know the result of some test asking what country they're in or what today's date is.

The doctor clears his throat. His beard quivers.

"Right," he says. "I definitely would want to do another test on you. That's how this looks to me."

Her husband is silent for a couple of seconds, looking out the window.

"So that's the verdict," he says. "I flunked the test."

"I wouldn't say you flunked," the doctor says. "These things are always subject to interpretation. But perhaps you should come in for another test. We'll set up an appointment. And an appointment for a neurological exam. Check everything out at once just to be sure."

"Righto," her husband says. "Let's go, Katariina. There's nothing more for us to see here." He grins and gets up.

Anja gets up and registers two things. The doctor's expression: a serious, apologetic attempt at a smile, troubled under the surface; a look she knows she'll see from now on, on the faces of all the doctors who have no personal knowledge of loss in their own lives. And her husband's expression: an attempt to cover a deep, childlike bafflement, and the certain knowledge that this is the beginning of a string of humiliations from which he will never escape except through complete oblivion. She can see that he knows it.

He sees it.

WHEN THEY GET HOME, he leaves his coat on, goes into the kitchen with his shoes on, and sits down at the table. Terri comes up behind him and wags her tail. He pets her absentmindedly.

Anja stops in the doorway. Words fail her.

"It doesn't mean anything for sure yet," she tries. "It could be an incorrect result. Everybody forgets things sometimes."

"I didn't even remember what the hell the word is for wristwatch. I couldn't do simple addition, damm it."

"You were under pressure."

"Damn it."

"My love."

"Promise never to feed me."

"Stop it."

"Promise. Promise not to feed me like a baby. Not to leave gravy around my mouth."

"I promise."

# Mari

JULIAN DRIVES the car calmly, focused on the road. Mari watches him when he's not looking. She can't not watch him. Happiness gallops through her mind when she remembers the L word. He said it. She lifts her feet onto the seat and pulls her knees up to her chin. The grey mist of Boxing Day covers everything. They've traded Helsinki for rolling countryside. Red farmhouses, village schools, gentle brown marshes surrounding a lake covered in a thin crust of ice. Julian turns to her and smiles.

"Let's stop up here at the service station. I need to buy us some food and some oil for the lamps."

He stretches out a hand and strokes her cheek. Mari smiles. This is indisputably good. The gentle marshes, oil lamps, and Julian. The L word, said for her.

In the service-station bathroom Mari looks at herself in the mirror. What a miracle that suddenly she's the kind of woman who says that word. A woman. Because men like Julian don't love little girls. Her outline in the mirror seems to stand out in a completely new way. Whole. These are the eyes that Julian loves. These shoulders. This mole along her jaw. This nose.

It feels real.

THE HOUSE IS on the shore of the lake. The lake isn't separate from the sky — both are dream-white. The yard is its own world, a low enclosure bordered by spruce and oaks. A woodpecker somewhere is tapping. There's no echo — the snow swallows up every sound, leaving each tap a solitary syllable.

On the porch, Julian takes her in his arms and kisses her for the first time. The stubble on his chin is rougher, but his tongue is just as soft and slippery as before.

"Look," he says, and turns Mari around in his arms. She looks at the lake. "This is what I wanted to show you. Look at the colors. Light brown. The colors of winter. Soon it will be the blue hour. You can fall into it quite suddenly. The world turns in on itself. I want to fall into the blue hour with you."

THE HOUSE IS a little white villa — he says it's his family's ancestral home. Rag rugs, floorboards that creak when you step on them. There are two bedrooms upstairs and another off the kitchen. There are dried flowers from summer still on the windowsills, and one plump dead bee. It's cold and damp at first, but Julian lights a fire in the tile stove and the place warms up quickly. They light the oil lamps and the candles on the windowsill, and make the bed. It's a double bed. The sheets from the linen cabinet are cool and smell of lavender. Someone has ironed them and put a lavender sachet in with them. Julian's wife, perhaps.

THE SAUNA CABIN is at the edge of the lake, and has a small antechamber and a steam room. Julian lights a fire in pails of sand on either side of the sauna steps. Mari watches from the doorway. There's a spider's web on the door handle and a picture of a flower on the wall.

"Is that your daughter's drawing?"

"Yes. Ada's."

"What was the other one's name?"

"Anni."

"Anni," Mari repeats, and feels apprehension slice through her thoughts.

But Julian comes up behind her and presses against her. That's where they make love the first time that day, in the sauna dressing room. Mari watches through the window as the light disappears in a red glimmer beyond the lake. The only sounds are the spruce log popping as the fire slowly licks at its bark, and then Mari's sighs as Julian pushes his way deep into her, throbbing, biting her ear once, lightly. Some large animal is moving over the lake ice. A bear? Or is it a horse that's loose and is running toward the dim woods? She can't see clearly. Julian cups her breasts in the palms of his hands, thrusting into her rhythmically from behind. He moves his hands to her hips and she puts her knees on the bench so he can reach deeper. There, on the bench in the dressing room, Mari comes for the first time, rising and sinking all at once, not wanting to sink completely until she's sucked into that beautiful indifference that holds all meaning. She can still see the horse — it's a horse, not a bear — at the edge of the woods, her forehead pressed against the sparkling glass of the window. She hears her own voice moaning, it surprises her, and Julian, who knows how to be so gentle and rough at the same time, surprises her more than anything in the world. The horse raises its head, gallops into the woods, and disappears from view just as she closes her eyes and sees a hundred million stars streaking toward her.

Afterward, they take a sauna in the dark. It's more like

making love than taking a sauna. It's more like entering into each other than making love. More like becoming one person. It happens once in the sauna and again in the house, on the floor next to the warm tile stove, four times in the bedroom, until Julian is so tired and Mari is so tender inside that they just lie beside each other between the lavender-scented sheets.

Then Julian asks her directly, openly:

"Why do you cut yourself?"

Mari flinches. Julian strokes the smoothness of her thigh. The scars stand out like pale, narrow tracks. Mari puts her head against his chest and listens to his heartbeat and says out loud for the first time, "When I do it, I don't miss anything."

"Do you usually miss something? What do you miss?"

Mari is quiet for a second. Only one word comes to mind.

"Home."

"Where's your home?"

"Someplace else."

Julian gently moves her hand to his lower abdomen, and from there down through the thick trail of hair.

"Do you miss it now?" he asks in the tenderest of voices.

"No," she answers, her voice a mere whisper.

"Why not?"

"Because you draw my boundaries for me."

Julian doesn't speak for a moment. Mari feels complete. For the first time in her life it's absolutely clear that she exists. I'm here, she thinks. I'm me.

"You should be renamed," Julian whispers.

"Why?"

"Because a girl as amazing as you can't have such an ordinary name. You're Desiree. My Desiree. The object of desire."

He turns her on her back, encloses her hands in his. He

locks her there, in place. She knows she couldn't escape even if she wanted to. It feels exciting. He gets on top of her and looks at her, curious.

"Would it excite you if I thought of you as a horse?"

Mari tries to break free of his grasp. He pushes her arms down again. Anxious excitement shoots through her body. It occurs to her that he could hurt her if he wanted to. He could kill her. Or save her. Or tame her. Anything. Is it frightening, or exciting, or both? She's not sure.

He presses her thighs open with his knee, decisive but gentle, like hobbling a horse to be shod. He presses himself against the damp place between her legs and pushes into her.

Mari remembers the riding stables she went to when she was ten, the lush smell inside the barn and the horses shying away, carrying a secret inside them. She remembers how their movements held her attention, their undeniable reality, eating oats in their stalls, their canter controlled by her calves and her reins during her lessons, the way they rolled in the grass for the pure joy of it. And their secret was never disclosed, no matter how long you looked at them.

Julian turns her over, lifts her hips to the right angle, enters her from behind, puts his hands over her hands, his fingers between her fingers, and holds tight, bites her neck and fucks her, takes her as he wants to.

Mari thinks of when the farrier came to the stables, how the whole atmosphere in the barn changed on those days, from cheerfully busy to deadly earnest. Some horses meekly submitted to being shod and others resisted right to the end. You could see an absolutely demonic terror in their eyes as they shrieked in panic, not relenting until the farrier calmed them with a method that seemed like a kind of torture. He would let go of the horse, let it sprint disobediently into the corral, in the throes of terror, and then he would run it with his crop until it was exhausted. And when the horse was tired to the point of collapse, he would go up to it, push it down on the ground, and stand on it. Horses never lie down. Even when they sleep and foal they stand. A horse will only lie down when it's mortally ill. Unless it's being broken. Then it will lower its head, its knees will buckle, and it will bow down, first falling on its knees, as if to pray, then lying down on the ground. Mari can't remember ever seeing anything so mesmerizing — the farrier standing on the horse with all his weight; the horse covered in sweat, steam rising from its haunches, its breath coming from deep within its throat; and slowly, slowly, the demonic terror in its eyes changing to trust.

The rhythm of Julian's thrusts speeds up and Mari knows that it's almost time. He comes inside her for the seventh time, and then lets go of her. They lie side by side, completely silent. The night outside is mute and dark and the winter eternal. Julian falls asleep quickly and Mari thinks of horses a little longer.

She remembers summer evenings when all the horses in the barn were let out at once. The stalls were opened and you had to race to the other side of the fence when their thundering started. First they let out the stallions, which galloped into the pasture with their tails erect and their ears back. Then they let the other horses out in one rumbling herd — the geldings, unaware that they were neutered, blustering out first, then the wild mares and the unbroken foals. And everyone could see, even if they didn't say so, that the animals had all the power: they carried the knowledge of their power in every centimeter and every kilogram of their bodies, so self-evident that the idea that they were broken was meaningless. That instant when they were let out into the pasture always had a hint of a storm in it. For years it was the most beautiful thing that Mari could imagine.

IN THE MORNING, the world has become real again. Julian is drinking coffee at the kitchen table and Mari is absorbing his every gesture and expression. The weather has turned gray, damp. When he's finished his coffee, Julian goes around to the other side of the table and takes Mari in his arms. She presses her head tight against him. There are places that you want to stay, where you could live, for the rest of your life.

Mari likes it here.

"Will we see each other again this vacation? Or not until school starts?" she asks, although she doesn't want to hear the answer.

"When school starts. After vacation."

TINKA IS BURSTING with curiosity. M`ari keeps her secret to herself a little longer.

"Was it wonderful? How many times did you do it? Are you going to get married now? Just think: if you get married, you'll be a *stepmother*."

"Hmph. Julian's already married. He's not getting a divorce — at least not right away."

"How many times did you do it, though?"

Mari can't hide her smile any longer. Wonderful Julian, hers completely. She holds up her fingers to show how many. Tinka giggles.

"Did you do anything else?"

"Well, no. Not really." Mari laughs.

Tinka's expression turns serious and she gets up and comes over to Mari. She strokes Mari's hair with a perplexing look of affection in her eyes.

"I'm sorry if I was mean," Tinka whispers.

"No, no. It's all right," Mari says, flustered.

She looks at Tinka. Tinka seems sad.

"Would you be mad at me if I told you something?" Tinka says, fear in her eyes.

"What?"

"You're going to be mad."

"No, I won't. Tell me."

Tinka leans very close and for a second Mari thinks she's going to kiss her. But she's leaning over to whisper something.

"I've never been with a boy that way. I mean, I did touch one boy's dick once at this party, but it was so weird and disgusting that I didn't put out for him."

"Oh."

"Now you're mad."

"No, I'm not. I just thought ..."

"That I'd done it before."

"Yeah."

"I haven't."

"I see."

"But now you have," Tinka says, pursing her lips. "And you have to tell me what it feels like."

She smiles a little. Mari tries to put on a smile.

"Well ... it's kind of gross, but kind of wonderful."

"Mostly gross or mostly wonderful?"

"Wonderful," Mari says with a smile. "It's mostly wonderful."

Tinka smiles, too, and puts her hand in Mari's. They're silent. The silence troubles Mari. Tinka searches for Mari's gaze, and when Mari looks into her eyes, Tinka says sadly, "I love you. You know that."

Mari stares at Tinka, bewildered, and tries to find the trick or the joke in her eyes. But all she sees is immense loneliness on her bare face.

"I know," she answers carefully. "I do, too ... love you, I guess."

# Anni

ON NEW YEAR'S DAY Anni and Sanna make a snow castle. They put the dolls they got for Christmas on the snow bank next to the tea lights so they can watch.

The castle is big and cavernous. Dad and Sanna's dad help them with the digging. If you dig really deep, dig all the way to the ground and keep digging, you might end up in China. It would be fun to try to dig to China, Anni thinks. Next spring.

"Who's going to be the princess in the castle?" Sanna asks.

Anni already knows the answer. Sanna hardly needs to ask.

"You can be the princess," Anni says.

"Thanks," Sanna breathes, excited. "You can be the watchman. Or the castle's building superintendent."

"The superintendent lights all the candles," Anni says enthusiastically.

She knows that Sanna wants to light the candles.

Sanna looks at the still-dark window holes of the castle with a pout. "But the princess can light some of them, too. At least one."

"Well, all right — one," Anni says.

Anni digs a little deeper. It's actually fun to be the one doing the digging. Diggers are strong. Let Sanna be the princess.

The castle superintendent has lots of responsibility. She gets to light all the candles in the castle windows. There are a lot of windows.

Before it gets dark they go inside and have some frankfurts and potato salad. They look out the window at the snow castle and the tea candles. Sanna wants to try on the princess dress that Anni got for Christmas and wear it to play in the snow castle. Anni doesn't want to give it to her.

"You don't need it, you're the superintendent," Sanna says. "You're a sissy superintendent if you don't give it to me."

"OK."

The dress fits Sanna perfectly.

"Too bad it's green," she says, looking herself up and down in the mirror. "Real princess dresses are always red."

"They can be green, too," Anni insists. "In some castles. Some princesses have nothing but green dresses."

"Stupid." Sanna snorts. "That can't be right."

Then Anni has an idea. She can secretly be the queen of the castle. Sanna doesn't even have to know about it. The superintendent queen can have a secret royal cloak. Anni already knows what the superintendent queen will wear. She grabs the car keys off the table by the front door and runs out to the yard. She knows she can open the car door by putting the big black key in the driver's side door. Click — the door opens. Anni climbs into the back seat and opens the hatch that leads to the trunk.

There it is, in a brown cardboard box hidden under some plastic bags. A beautiful coat with wonderful, soft fur on the hood and cuffs. Anni knows whose coat it is. The girl with the beautiful eyes. She saw her wearing it before Christmas, when they met her crossing the street. Anni doesn't know why the coat is in the car. Maybe the girl forgot it there. A perfect cape for a queen disguised as a superintendent. Anni takes the coat and gets out of the car.

Now all she needs is a stick that she can use as a scepter.

She goes back inside and tries on the coat in front of the hall mirror. It's too big, reaches all the way to her ankles. The sleeves have to be rolled up a little. Otherwise it's a perfect queen's cape.

"Where'd you get that?" Sanna asks. Anni can tell she wants the fur-lined cloak for herself.

"Out of the car," Anni says, pretending not to care about it.

"Whose is it?"

"This one girl's."

"Oh."

"But you can't tell anyone about her."

"OK. But a superintendent can't have such a fancy coat," Sanna says. "It looks stupid. Superintendents wear coveralls." She takes Anni's pale blue snowsuit off the coat rack.

"A superintendent queen can wear it, though," Anni says.

Sanna snorts. "Stupid. There's no such thing as a superintendent queen."

"There can be in a snow castle," Anni insists.

Sanna turns silent, gloomy. Anni looks at herself in the mirror. She feels different. She thinks about the girl. Or is she a woman? It's hard to know what age girls become women. Anni can see in the mirror that she could be a woman like that someday. The coat reaches to her ankles and the sleeves are too long, but she can see that someday she'll be a woman like the girl she's not supposed to tell anyone about.

# Julian

THE SMELL OF her pussy lingered on his fingers all through the week between Christmas and New Year's. Or was it guilt that he smelled for days afterward? He washed his hands when he got back from the countryside, took his wedding ring off his finger and soaped it, too. When he'd dried his hands, he could smell it again. It was still on his fingers, that rich, tangy smell. Her smell was different from Jannika's — darker and softer, more exciting — and Julian feared that Jannika would smell it if he went near her. He washed his hands again.

He thought the girl might call him again and cause problems. He decided not to answer if she called. He felt he should just be with his family on New Year's, build a snow fort with his kids in the yard, try to normalize the situation.

He still didn't know what to make of what had happened on Christmas Eve. Something had turned hard, something inside him. Or he himself had turned hard, changed completely. So had Jannika. So had their family.

It had become difficult to breathe.

He watched Jannika hum as she prepared for their New Year's Eve party. Some friends were coming over. Jannika loved these kinds of get-togethers. Friends and wine and different kinds of cheeses and candles all over the place. On nights like these, her eyes shone as she talked about politics and literature; her whole being shone with the knowledge that anything was possible, with the children romping around and the adults laughing and the whole world within their grasp. On nights like these, it was easy to love Jannika. She was completely present.

The guests arrived at six. They always started out talking about the same things: news about their kids, holiday plans, disagreements at work, the progress of their careers. After a couple of glasses of wine they switched to discussing politics and art. The sameness of these conversations didn't seem to bother Jannika. Julian had begun to find it annoying. He always had the same feeling — here we are, after thirty years, pudgy, prosperous, drinking wine of a good vintage, making pseudo-clever witticisms about where the world is heading. We think we're unusual, intelligent, aware, but in reality we're just middle-class comfort seekers. Can't get a decent erection anymore, nothing can get it up, least of all our own wives. There's crud built up in our blood vessels, our opinions have dulled to trivialities, and we're starting to grasp at possessions because we have no real passion left.

Julian felt his heart beating at double time, an urge to flee wriggling in his belly. He nervously sipped his wine. The girl kept forcing herself into his mind. What did sixteen-year-olds do on New Year's Eve? A house party, drinking too much strong homemade wine and puking in a snow bank. Giving each other hickeys and passing out before the fireworks started.

The feeling of wanting to flee grew stronger. How had he got himself into this? She was a child. He gulped down the rest of his wine. He had to go into the kitchen, said he was going to fetch more wine and put some on to mull. He couldn't sit there listening to his wife talk excitedly about the state of the world when his hands smelled like a teenager's pussy and all he could think of was fucking her endlessly.

He got up and brushed Jannika's neck as he passed. When he got to the door he turned around and looked at the familiar mole on her neck. When they'd first started seeing each other he had nibbled at that mole every day, kissed it in the long, dark nights, loving Jannika more and more all the time. He'd had a habit of covering it with his thumb. His thumb fit perfectly within its outline. That indelible mark had aroused an amazing feeling of happiness in him, unbridled longing, an insatiable desire to be with her always. Suddenly he had the same feeling again. Nothing could be more real than that mole. Nothing could be more tender. Nothing could be more meaningful than the fact that there was a girl with that mole, and that now she was a woman, and the mother of his children, and still there was the same mole where the fuzzy down on her neck turned into the even forest of her hair. And he still had a thumb that fit perfectly within its boundaries.

Standing there in the kitchen doorway he was struck by intense guilt and shame. He had to end the whole relationship. Relationship? What kind of a damn relationship was it, anyway? An adult playing games with a child. He had to end it immediately. Not call her anymore, not answer if she called. This is my life, he thought. Infatuations happen — love, even — but they pass. This is my life.

# Anja

ANJA CLIMBED THE STAIRS to Johannes' apartment. She stood inside the front door without taking off her coat.

"What is it?" Johannes asked. "Aren't you going to come in?"

Anja took a breath to say what she had to say.

"No. I just came to tell you that this can't go on." She shifted her weight to her other foot, tried to calm her breathing.

"It's not as if anything's even started yet," Johannes said.

"I'm married. Whatever it is that has started can't continue. That's what I came to tell you."

Annoyance darted through her mind. He didn't seem to care that she was upset, closed the door behind her.

"Just come inside and have a cup of coffee," he said.

HE MADE THE ESPRESSO CAREFULLY — measured the water, ground the coffee beans in the hoarse roar of the coffee mill, rinsed the cups, dried them with a linen towel. As he poured the coffee into the cups, the kitchen was flooded with a calming aroma that settled somewhere near the back of her head, a dark, comforting pleasure that flowed down her arms.

He brought the cups to the table and sat across from her.

"You know," he said, "you're right about plans. That your plans stop when you can't remember. It may be the first sign. My mother stopped planning, too."

Her irritation had subsided momentarily, but now it pushed its way forward again. She remembered why she had come.

"Don't try to start a discussion," she said, striving to make her voice cold. "I came to talk about ending this thing."

"Aren't you alone?" Johannes said. "Aren't you lonely?"

She would have liked to answer him. Why couldn't she answer him, say it out loud? She didn't say it, put on a tense expression. "That has nothing to do with it. My loneliness has nothing to do with this."

He looked at her, sizing her up.

She tried to change the direction of the conversation.

"Do you have a wife? Or a girlfriend? Who do you think you are, coming into another person's life without permission?"

"I had a wife. She left me."

"Is that all?"

"What do you mean, is that all? It was a long time ago. Years ago."

She noticed that he was annoyed now. Having them both annoyed made the situation easier. It would be easier to end it with a quarrel. She wanted to annoy him some more.

"All my husband has is death," she said. "All I have is his death. But you have life. You can't deny it."

She turned to look out the window. She was starting to cry. Johannes didn't seem to know what to say; he kept quiet.

"How did you make that promise?" he asked suddenly.

Anja sighed. Tears pressed at the back of her eyes, made her breath tremble.

"Did he ask you?" Johannes said.

She answered grudgingly. "Until he stopped recognizing me, he asked me every day. Or every night. He would wake me up at night, every night, and demand that I promise."

"Did you promise?"

"I was never able to promise it out loud. I couldn't do it."

She looked across the table at Johannes. He looked back. He always looked at her like this, calmly, his eyes slightly squinted. A serious, knowing sort of expression, probing and measuring.

"Do you think you won't be able to carry out his request?"

The very idea made her impatient.

"I'm waiting for something," she said, hearing her voice break. "He wanted it to happen when he couldn't recognize me anymore. And now he can't, but I'm still waiting."

"What are you waiting for?"

For the first time, Anja admitted it to herself.

"For the turning point," she said slowly. "For that moment that will change the course of events and impose a meaning on everything so that I can keep my promise."

Johannes got up and came to her. It could be said out loud now, it could easily be acknowledged.

"The turning point will never come," Anja said, defeated. "I'm just waiting because I can't do it. It will never come because this is life. Turning points belong in tragedies, in the plots of dramas. But this isn't a tragedy, it's life. The turning point never comes. I'll just keep planning it endlessly, always intending to do it but never doing it. But I'll keep on planning to do it, for my own sake."

Anja slipped her hand into his. She couldn't not touch him. His hands were large, bigger than the ones she was used to. Men's hands had always brought out a tender feeling in her. They could look so clumsy, the fingers large, the nails cut flat.

But she knew when the clumsiness was an illusion. Strong hands, gentle and skillful when necessary, gentler than you might have guessed. She looked at his hands and knew that their clumsiness was an illusion, thought about how it felt when they found the right places, in the dark. Forearms that didn't seem to fit with the rest of his body somehow. Maybe that was from sports, from working out at the gym or something.

He pulled her into his arms. Now she said it.

"I am alone."

"But you're here now."

"This has to end."

"All right. But not today."

"I love him. I love him more than you can know."

"I can see that."

"We've been together for thirty years."

"That's longer than I can comprehend."

Suddenly she felt she knew Johannes, the way you know someone just before you fall in love. When you dream of him — that's how you fall in love, when you first begin to dream about him. You dream that he's a child, small, and absolutely known to you. A dream where you see him when he's sixteen, and you run together through the woods, through the shadows of tall spruce trees, and build a fort, and you take his hand and say *I've known you for a long time.*

This has to end, Anja thinks.

But not yet. Not today.

# Mari

IT'S WELL INTO JANUARY and she still hasn't heard from Julian. She doesn't have language and literature this semester. She doesn't dare to go to his classroom after class. She's been waiting for him to call. He'll call. He has to call eventually. Because he wants her all the time.

But he doesn't call, not even after the first week of February.

Mari calls him once. On a Monday night after six o'clock. She sits on her bed and listens to the plastic charm knock against her phone as her hand shakes. The phone rings seven times. Julian doesn't answer. She puts the phone down on the bedspread. The light on the phone goes off. That stupid bear logo appears on the display. She knows Julian isn't going to call her back. She can see her own reflection in the window, the way her face twists just before the tears come.

ON WEDNESDAY MORNING, the thirteenth of February, Mari puts on mascara, a flared skirt, and boots.

After her last class of the afternoon, she walks down the hallway to Julian's classroom and stops in front of the door. Students are still coming out of the room. She waits for all of them to leave.

Julian is wiping the blackboard, doesn't turn around until she's quite close to him.

Mari's afraid to look at him. Afraid that his face will immediately show her what she fears. But when he turns around, all she sees on his face is that familiar calm.

"Hi," he says.

A mere statement. A firm nod of the head and one neutral syllable.

"Hi," Mari answers.

Just saying hi exposes her uncertainty and fear, all her helplessness and desire not to be rejected. She can hear it herself. There's nothing she can do but admit it right away: all that matters hangs on that desire. She's so close to tears that she wants to run away.

"Why haven't you called me? Or answered my calls?" she says.

"Yeah," Julian says slowly, sitting down on the edge of the teacher's desk.

He looks out the window and sighs. Mari can tell already.

"What do you think about this situation?" he says.

All she can answer is, "I want to be with you."

"You're sixteen years old."

"What does that have to do with anything?" Her voice has started to tremble. A large tear rolls down her cheek.

Julian comes close to her and takes her in his arms. She presses her head against his shirt. Everything about him is so familiar and yet so strange. She starts to cry even more.

"Don't cry, sweetheart," Julian whispers.

He takes her face in his hands and kisses her cheeks. He kisses both of her eyes, then her lips. First lightly, then more deeply. She presses herself against him and eases her hand into his pants, feels his stiff penis.

"Wait, let me close the door," he whispers.

Behind the locked door, they do it again. Julian takes off her boots and stockings, lifts her onto the desk. He pushes himself into her and she thinks that maybe he'll want to be with her as long as she lets this happen, that she has to keep letting this happen over and over so that he'll remember her skin, and everything, and not want to let go of her even for a minute.

# Julian

HE KNEW she would come eventually. He couldn't stop her from coming. He saw at once that she had dressed up for him — her hair fluffed up and alluring, rouge on her cheeks, her lips glossed. A short skirt, well above the knee, that positively demanded to be lifted to her waist, high-heeled boots that made her legs gangly and coltish, irresistible. She was in a sad frame of mind. It awakened his affection at first, then his lust, overpowering.

She let him fuck her. All she did was lie still and look at the ceiling.

The entire act was sickening when he thought about it: a lecherous grown man consoling a teenager gets an erection and shoves it into her. Her behavior was pitiful, tepid, more indifferent than passionate. His own climax was an involuntary yelp followed by a shame-faced desire to get away from the entire grotesque scene. He looked into her eyes as he ejaculated and saw sadness there, submission, a bottomless pleading. He trembled a few times inside her and felt a deep humiliation and self-hatred. She unwrapped her legs from around him and sat up on his desk.

He hugged her reflexively. It was easier to hug her than to look in her eyes and see their plea.

He thought she might want to have a serious talk after the sex, but she was very quiet. They stood embracing for several minutes. Just one thought pulsed in his mind: this has to end, once and for all.

# Mari

IF YOU PLAY the death-thoughts game, it might suddenly come true. By accident. No, not by accident. It's been half serious all along, half in earnest — when is the thought of death ever a light one, ever merely a game? Maybe it always has this side to it. Maybe she's just been waiting for something to happen, something heavy enough, serious enough, something that will change the tone of the game and make it true. The death game itself waiting for a situation that will make it come true.

Now she has a reason. Suddenly her reality is heavy, her days have their full weight. The line is clearly drawn, right in front of her eyes. This is how it's going to be. Maybe it's inevitable that the game should turn heavy, come true.

She's been living on this line, seeing everything turn into its opposite, her self gone and something empty taking its place, filling it like a disease. Tilting the balance against any compromise, any acceptance of the existence of a "me."

EVERY DAY AT SIX, Mari sits on the edge of her bed and looks up a name in her phone, a name that has six letters. She first looks at the hideous reflection of her face in the window, the winter dark beyond it, cruel as ever. The face in the window is cruel, too — a ridiculous girl, a stupid girl. Is she really this girl, who wants to be someone else, to cease to exist?

She lets the phone ring seven times. Always seven times.

And Julian doesn't answer. Ever.

She opens the text-message inbox. The first two messages are ones he sent her. She deleted the others so that his would always be the first on the list. She opens the second message, sent on the third of December, and reads it for the thousandth time: *In my fantasies I'm making love to you night and day, fucking you in my dreams all the time.*

Mari holds the phone tight in her hand, looks at her reflection in the window, the shape of a stranger.

I'll give all my strength, all my power, to you. Draw my boundaries for me. Save me or I might as well just disappear. I might as well vanish completely. Kill me.

★

Now it's March. Everything on the edges has become meaningless. The emptiness is all that matters. Emptiness is sweet forgetting. Mari gets up in the morning, eats two slices of bread and cheese in the kitchen as always, drinks her cocoa. She washes her hair, makes the same cuts in her arm — the only thing that feels good all day. The wounds don't scar over anymore. That feels good, too, having open wounds all the time.

Walking to school in the bright sunshine, she thinks that maybe this has been her truth all along. Maybe it was clear from the beginning that this would happen, that she would be walking here like this, a husk, booming hollow in the shadow of each step, acting out the inevitable.

She opens the door of the school and Tinka immediately

comes to meet her. Tinka looks serious, worried. Mari can't bring herself to care.

"Hi," Tinka says, giving her the usual kiss on the cheek. The kiss is warm and wet. Mari feels like crying.

"Wanna go downtown after school?" Tinka says. "We could look for some new make-up. I want some green eyeshadow and some of that sparkly blush."

"I dunno," Mari says dully. "I have to study for the test."

"You've been studying all week."

Tinka looks at Mari. She comes closer and hugs her, not knowing that she's pressing against the open cuts under Mari's winter coat, making her flinch.

"What's the matter with you? You've been looking just like a ghost lately. Do you even sleep at night?"

She strokes Mari's hair. Mari can't stop the tears from coming. They flow silently, the only sign that she's alive. Mari turns her head away. The sun is shining outside, forming a wedge of light in the empty school corridor. Specks of dust dance in the beam of light.

"Is it because of Kanerva?"

"Ugh!" Mari says, not turning her head. "I can't stand him anymore. He's such a shithead now."

"Kanerva's a prick," Tinka says affectionately, pressing her nose against Mari's nose.

Draw my boundaries, fence off the fear, and protect me, Mari thinks.

Kill me.

★

OF COURSE it happens eventually. Half by accident, for a trivial reason, without warning. Her mother just gets it into her head to ask her about her coat all of a sudden. Mari has expected the question, has made up a somewhat lame explanation. But in spite of being prepared for it, she's filled with anxiety when it comes. Her mother's face is perfectly normal and the question perfectly innocent.

"Where's your other winter coat? The one with the fur trim?"

It's an expensive coat. Her mother bought it for her. Naturally she wants to know what's happened to it.

Mari looks away as she answers. "I dunno. Maybe I lost it somewhere."

Mari knows where the coat is. She brought two coats with her to the countryside in December. When they were getting ready to come back to town the weather changed, sleet started to fall, and she put on her lighter coat. The heavier one, the one with the fur trim, she forgot to bring home. She hasn't had the courage to ask Julian about the coat. Maybe he'll return it. She hopes he'll call her about the coat. Call about the coat and then ask her out to coffee. She hopes he'll call because he still wants her, wants her all the time.

"Where did you lose it?" her mother asks.

"I don't know," Mari answers curtly. "Wherever lost coats go. Maybe I forgot it someplace."

"How can you forget your coat someplace? I saw you wearing it in December. Did you leave it at Tinka's cabin?"

"What do you mean Tinka's cabin?"

"Didn't you spend a couple of days there? At Tinka's family's cabin?"

Mari remembers telling her mother this now. "Right, right. It must be there."

"Well, could you call Tinka, then, and ask her about it?"

"Sure."

"Or shall I?"

"No, that's OK. I'll do it."

Her mother looks at the cell phone on the living-room table. Mari thinks she should rush to the phone, pick it up, and run away with it. Her mother is near the table, reaches for the phone. Mari looks at her in horror. Her mother sees the look on her face.

"What kind of secrets are you hiding in here?" she says teasingly, holding the phone up in the air. "Love letters?"

The dangling charm, the little smiling plastic bear, clacks against the phone's case.

"Nothing," Mari says. "Nothing at all." She can hear her voice go thin, unrecognizable.

"Hey," her mother says, surprised. "It's OK for you to have a boyfriend. There's absolutely nothing wrong with it."

"I don't have any boyfriend," Mari says flatly.

"Then what are you …?"

Her mother looks at the phone again. Then she looks at Mari again. Mari looks at her. It's there, in the phone, the first two messages in her inbox. *In my fantasies I'm making love to you night and day, fucking you in my dreams all the time.*

"Don't, Mom. Really."

Mari takes two steps, grabs hold of the phone. Her mother holds it tightly and won't let go. "What are you doing?" she says, amused. "You don't really think …"

Mari takes the phone. Her mother looks at her, bewildered.

Mari puts the phone down on the table.

Why? Why did she do that?

Why did she put the phone down where her mother can

reach it? Why did she leave it there? Why didn't she take it upstairs, lock it up in her desk drawer?

Maybe she *wants* her mother to know about Julian; maybe she wants her to put an end to all of it. Or maybe nothing matters anymore, not really. Maybe everything's become so meaningless that she can leave the phone there in front of her mother. To tease her, to goad her.

Mari turns and walks out of the living room, walks away so she won't have to look at her mother's face. And then, from the kitchen doorway, she sees her mother blatantly, brazenly picking up the phone, without trying to hide what she's doing. She holds the phone and looks at Mari. Everything is my business, her face says. Everything inside you belongs to me.

Or is it just worry? Has it just been worry all along? Not disrespect but worry that makes her pry into Mari's life. Maybe Mari will be able to see that now. Maybe her mother could even be her lifesaver, if Mari would only agree to it, agree to see the worry. But she can't grasp the idea, because everything has become meaningless. She's drowning, surrendering to the arms of the cool water. Indifferent.

Suddenly Mari can see herself from the outside, her own feeble gestures. She takes two steps toward her mother, holding her hand out as if she might reach the phone from across the room. Then she freezes, lets her hand drop.

Her mother is reading the message.

Mari hears the silence, crackling at the edges like silk paper, a silence that hums and whistles. A moment that stretches out at the seams.

Mari registers two things. First, the sound of the dog's toenails on the floorboards, a happy, oblivious *click-click* as the dog walks across the hallway to the place where he sleeps, turns around three times clockwise, and lies down. Second, the look on her mother's face, a helpless, empty look, all amazement gone, leaving nothing but a pure, certain realization.

Mari also notices a few insignificant things.

She sees the tropical palm in the window, its verdant leaves reaching toward the light.

She sees a little bird in the flowerbed outside the window take two brisk hops, from one branch to the next and then to the ground.

The warm shimmer of the silk living-room curtains that promise no safety now, the clock that tick-tocks away the trivial seconds, the world that never seems to come to an end, the moment that never stops, the indifferent gleam of the floorboards and the knots in the Persian rug that knows no pity.

If there's no other escape then at least there's this: What does it matter? What does anything matter really? For a moment her mother doesn't say anything, doesn't move. At first her face is expressionless. She looks at Mari, pale, her lips trembling. The raised hand that still holds the phone is shaking, first slightly, then more, so that the plastic charm knocks against its case again. The phone drops to the floor. Her mother's whole body is trembling now. The phone breaks into pieces as it hits the floor. The bear charm rolls under the couch. Mari watches it tumble eagerly to stand next to the sofa leg. The bear stops there, standing next to the leg of the sofa, smiling a happy toy's smile, oblivious to the turn that events have taken.

Even after all this, in this soft vacuum of indifference, Mari makes an effort to lie. She can hear the panic in her own voice betraying her.

"It's nothing. It's really nothing. Just a joke. It's just a joke."

"J-Julian," her mother stammers.

Ju-li-an. When her mother says it, the brief whispered syllables, it sounds strange, foreign.

"Is that your teacher?" she asks in a choked voice, and immediately answers her own question. "It's your teacher."

"No. No, it's not," Mari says in a whisper.

"It is. It's your teacher."

Mari doesn't speak.

"What else have the two of you done? What other messages has he sent you?"

Mari can see that her mother wants her to say, *Nothing. I didn't do anything with him. Just text messages.* She would like to hear Mari say it, but she knows it isn't true.

And Mari doesn't say it. She doesn't have to, because her mother already knows.

Her mother sinks onto the sofa, puts her head in her hands. Mari stands there, looking at her. Then she turns and walks out of the room.

On the living-room threshold it occurs to her, for the first time, to tell the truth. To tell her mother that the thing that was a game has become real, floating in front of her, a fact.

She doesn't seriously wish her mother dead, or Julian. It's not their deaths she wishes for. Instead it's herself — this girl, this young woman, betrayed and rejected — she's the one who's dying.

The thought is clearer than ever. There are girls who die. There are girls whose lives end, and those they leave behind grieve for them. There are girls like that. Girls that remain forever beautiful, their innocence guaranteed, almost like saints. What else can Mari do? How else can all this end except by descending into the beauty of a silence that covers her entire being?

Here on the threshold, her mother standing speechless in the living room, Mari takes hold of her own fate. That's what's going to happen to her. Exactly that. A shiver of pleasure passes through her. Her mother can't prevent this. And Julian — he practically wants it to happen. This is what she has, the inevitable ending to her own story. There are girls who die. She takes hold of that thought and wraps herself up in it.

# Julian

AFTERNOON CLASSES were over. Julian was drinking coffee in the teacher's lounge. Tanskanen sat next to him, flirting with the Swedish substitute. Tanskanen always had some game going, always with a different woman. Julian was content to listen from afar. A great big kid, he thought as he watched Tanskanen.

Julian glanced carelessly at the door. His heart skipped a beat: it was the girl's mother, standing in the doorway. She was looking at him — staring at him with a face that demanded explanations. Withering. Hostile.

The school secretary went to ask her whom she came to see. The mother said something and looked at Julian. Julian got up. He felt cold. He knew he'd have to explain himself now.

Her gaze was filled with an icy anger.

"You're Mari's mother, aren't you?" Julian said, trying to hide his discomfort by looking her in the eye.

"Yes," the woman answered.

Julian extended his hand. She looked at it but made no move to take it. Julian could see what she was thinking: that hand has touched my daughter's breast.

"I thought I remembered you," he said, trying not to be flustered by her behavior.

"I want to talk to you in private," she said brusquely.

"Of course. Certainly. We can go to my classroom."

As SOON AS the classroom door clicked shut, she said what she had to say.

"You fucked my daughter."

Julian didn't answer, didn't know what to say. Should he deny everything? Probably not: she would just think he was making light of the situation, lying about something that was as clear as day. He was silent, neither denying nor confessing.

"What possible reason can you have for such disgusting behavior?" she asked, her twisted face showing all the hatred she felt for him.

"Are the reasons important?" Julian could hear his own voice from afar — it wasn't as relaxed as he would have liked it to be.

"Why did you do it?" she asked again.

He told her what had driven him to it, what he believed to be the reason, the justification: "I did it for the muses. The muses demanded that I not pass it by."

The mother's cool anger turned to flaming hatred. She stepped closer to him, right in front of his face. Julian didn't back away. Rage rushed like blood into her face and made her raised hands shake.

"Fuck your muses. Don't give me that shit."

Julian stepped back involuntarily and realized that the gesture revealed his doubt.

The woman's hatred was undisguised, ugly, almost smug.

There's always an element of pleasure in anger. As if you suddenly have the right to all manner of cruelty, even the kind that crosses a line beyond what you could have imagined. The right to cross the line, any line, rushing like blood into your head and feet, lifting your hand to strike the face before you, giving you the right to fire a gun. Somewhere at the heart of anger is an enjoyment of this righteousness. Nothing is forbidden because rage justifies itself and demands that you act. Anger, like desire, makes you part of its fire.

The rage had thinned the mother's voice to a whisper by now. "That attitude is a cover for the worst kind of violence."

"Don't you think your attitude of drawing a line dividing everything into good and evil is the worst violence of all?" Julian asked.

"You can accuse me of whatever you like. But you can't deny that you've hurt my daughter. You can't deny that."

"I'm sorry if I did. I ask your forgiveness. That wasn't my intention. But it's over now, I can promise you that."

"You can't get out of it that easily."

He watched the feeling of loathing spread over her face in a widening sea, blackening her eyes. She walked to the door, turned around once more to say her last words.

"I'll do what I have to do. Goodbye."

She walked out the door. Julian remained standing next to his desk. A feeling of nausea rose from somewhere in the pit of his stomach.

As HE OPENED the door to the teacher's lounge, Tanskanen came to meet him. Julian gave him a weak hello and tried to hurry past without looking him in the eye. Tanskanen seemed, in some strange way, to know what was going on, and he might try to pry into the details.

"Dude, what a dude," Tanskanen said.

"Dude," Julian said, still not looking him in the eye.

"Hey, what's the hurry?"

"Nothing. Just thought I'd go home."

"Let's go to the gym."

"I really don't want to right now."

"Come on."

"Well, maybe just for an hour."

"Good boy."

JULIAN DID ten pull-downs with the cable pulley, then let go. Tanskanen stood behind him critiquing his posture.

"You're pulling it too far down. You have to keep it close to the back of your head so it moves in an ergonomic line. Concentrate on keeping your shoulder blades together and don't worry about how far you can pull it down. It's more effective that way."

"Effective. Right," Julian said, not giving half a shit about Tanskanen's advice. "Just what kinds of effects are we talking about?"

Tanskanen grinned. "You tell me. From what I can tell, you know more about it than I do."

Julian's smile dimmed. "What do you mean?"

"Don't pretend you don't know what I'm talking about. I know you've been spreading your talents around." He eyed Julian defiantly.

"Fuck," Julian said.

"Precisely. What's that girl's name? Mari?"

Julian looked around. "Don't talk about that here. It's nobody's business."

Tanskanen's expression turned serious, instructive. "You're playing this game the wrong way. I'm just saying this as a friend."

Julian got up, annoyed, and took a few steps toward the locker room. "I'm not playing any game. I'm living my life."

"Listen to yourself. How old is she, sixteen?"

"That's over. For good."

"Should I believe you?"

"Believe what you like. Anyway, you're hardly in a position to give me advice about it."

"You're joking, right? I've never been with a sixteen-year-old, for one thing; and for another, I'm not married."

Julian picked up his water bottle and went to the locker room. The door slammed behind him more loudly than he had intended. Tanskanen was a silly little man. A great big kid. A big talker who knew nothing of the situation. It was best not to tell him anything more about it.

Tanskanen came into the locker room, still serious. Julian sat on the bench and drank from his water bottle so he wouldn't have to talk. Tanskanen sat down beside him.

Julian sighed.

What if he did talk? What did it matter now? Tanskanen was the only person who was even slightly on his side. He couldn't tell Jannika about it. The whole thing would be blown out of proportion if he told her. Maybe he'd tell her later, but not now. The girl herself was a child — there was no point in denying it anymore. She was a child. A mere child. A priest or a shrink, those were his only alternatives if he wanted to talk about it. And Tanskanen. He might as well admit it: Tanskanen was his only friend in this situation.

Julian gave a heavy sigh, and began. "What if I did it for love?"

Tanskanen looked at him in disbelief. "Well, did you?"

Julian turned away. "Her mother came to see me. Demanded explanations. I wonder, would it have made me less of a shithead in her eyes, less evil, if I'd told her I did it for love?"

"I hope you didn't go and say that."

"No. But what if I had? Would it make me any less evil if I'd said I was in love? Would it make any difference?"

"It seems to me you're confusing desire and love," Tanskanen said.

"Can the two things be separated?"

"If you don't see any difference between them, then I don't know what to tell you," Tanskanen said. He tapped his foot on the floor and rubbed his face. "It'll make you sad. If you did it for love, it'll make you sad."

"I'm in the soup," Julian said, letting his desperation show. "I don't know what I should do."

He glanced at Tanskanen, trying to read mockery, condescension, pity, on his face. This was humiliating.

Tanskanen plucked the words that were hanging in the air. "Are you asking for my advice?"

"I don't know. Should I?"

"If you are, I'd say that you have only two choices."

Julian knew that. "Well?" he asked anyway.

"You can wait and see if her mother reports it. If she does, you won't have much chance of getting out of it with your hide intact. You could hope that she'll let the matter drop."

It hadn't occurred to Julian that she might do that. If he didn't report it himself, he might have some time — days, perhaps even a few weeks. But it hadn't occurred to him that the girl's mother might drop the whole thing. "Why would she do that?"

Tanskanen took a swig from his water bottle before answering. Julian had an amusing thought: It's come to this. I'm asking for advice from Tanskanen. But maybe it was true — maybe Tanskanen did know this game.

"Well," Tanskanen said, weighing his words. "The girl

might suffer more if the matter became public. Gossip from other students, changing schools, all kinds of consequences. It might be that her mother wouldn't want her to go through that, so she'd let the matter drop."

"Do you think she would?"

"She might. With mothers and daughters you never know. But if you ask me, I wouldn't count on it. If it becomes public, you're a goner."

"Shit."

"The other choice," Tanskanen said emphatically, "is to report it yourself."

Julian shook his head. "It's all over for me if I do that. I don't think Jannika could bear it."

"You just have to have faith in her."

"Nobody has that kind of faith."

Tanskanen got up, looked at the door, and said what Julian already knew.

"What else have you got left? All you've got is faith."

JULIAN OPENED HIS front door and stepped inside. Jannika had already picked up the kids and was sitting at the kitchen table, absorbed in a book. Rice was steaming on the stove. He could hear the children playing in the living room, arguing about something.

He went to the kitchen door.

Jannika had her back to him. She was wearing an old shirt, an ancient t-shirt with the name of a band on it. She only wore it at home, on Sundays or in the evenings. Many times he had looked at her like this, come close to her, while she was brushing her teeth in the bathroom or reading on the sofa or writing something at her desk, come up to her and put his hand under her shirt, let down her hair.

Had he only imagined that she had changed? Familiar. That's what she was, absolutely familiar. And she had no idea. She might have noticed that something wasn't right, but she had no way of guessing about the girl. It would almost have made it easier if she had guessed it herself and asked him about it.

Now she turned and saw him and got up.

"What is it?" she asked.

Maybe she saw something in his face, realized that something was coming. Julian stood in the doorway, stock still.

Now, he thought. Now.

"Is something wrong?" Jannika asked.

Now or never. Now.

Jannika came toward him, swept back her hair, came closer, hugged him. There was still time. He could whisper it. The moment was passing, still hovering just beyond Jannika's shoulder. Now. It's not too late. Julian's arms felt heavy: he couldn't get them to lift at all, couldn't put them around her. The rice bubbled in the pot, the lid tapping a leisurely tempo as it simmered. The children's voices drifted in from the living room.

Julian let the moment pass.

He managed to lift his arms. They were heavy like they are sometimes in dreams, when it takes all your strength to move your arms and legs. He commanded his arms to lift, commanded them to embrace her. He held her, slipped a hand under her shirt. He brushed his fingers over her spine like it was a string of pearls, the way he always did.

"Is anything wrong?" Jannika asked.

The moment had passed. He had let it pass.

"Need any help with dinner?"

"You can make the salad," she said.

"I'll make the salad," he answered.

# *Mari*

OF COURSE her mother wants an explanation. It's no use denying it. It's no use to start by denying it and when that doesn't
work, assure her, insist that it's all over, and, in the end, beg.
None of it is any use. Her mother wants to settle the matter.
Mari is sitting on the living-room sofa. Her mother stands in
front of her, walks back and forth, stands still again.

Mari has only one thing to say to her mother, a sentence
mixed with tears, a desperate cry.

"You fucking shithead! My life is none of your business."

"Sweetheart," her mother says. "This is not a small thing."

"I know it isn't!" Mari yells. "It's my life, and it's none of
your damn business."

Her mother looks at her sadly. "Do you realize that laws
have been broken here? I could report this to the police.
Involvement with a minor would be punished with a fine, at
the very least. He'd lose his job ..."

"And you'll fucking do it, too! But if you do, you'll never
see me again!"

Mari tries to muster some bravado in her voice but she can
hear that her anger is nothing but a pitiful scramble to escape
the inevitable crumbling. Her cheeks are hot. Her words turn

viscous with tears. She's never felt such pure hatred of her mother before. She isn't my mother anymore, Mari thinks. Just the woman who gave birth to me.

Her mother looks at her with resignation. A look more tender than angry, Mari realizes. Why isn't she angry? It would be easier to yell at her if she yelled back.

"You know that I don't want something like that to happen. I don't want a break between us," her mother says.

"Well then, you know what to do."

Her mother's about to sit down, but she doesn't sit down, can't sit down, continues to pace back and forth in front of her. And then she says what Mari feared she would say.

"I went to see Julian."

There it is. The exposure, the destruction.

Mari begins to cry, more forlorn than before.

It's all over. She'll be exposed now. The whole school will know. If she goes to school, they'll laugh at her: there she is, the girl who stripped herself bare for the world. A stupid girl. Pitiful. A girl who thought she was important. And Julian — he'll never speak to her again. He'll hate her.

"No, Mom," she says from behind the curtain of tears. "What did you say to him?"

"I told him what I thought of him."

"Fuck. I hate you. Why are you torturing me? Why are you doing this to me?"

Her mother is sadder than before. "Because you're my daughter and I have to protect you."

Mari can barely speak anymore through the tears. Her mother doesn't understand. No one does.

"But I love him," she sputters.

"Sweetheart," her mother says in her gentlest voice. "You're sixteen years old. Try to understand."

"Well, I don't understand," she answers.

Her mother raises her voice over the crying. "Did you know that it's illegal?"

"Fuck."

Her mother sighs again. Resigned. Humble. "Please don't swear at me. This is a serious matter. I have to report this. I have to call the principal and the student counselor."

"Don't, Mom. I can't go to school if you call. I can never go there again."

Her mother sits down on the sofa facing her. "Maybe it would be best if you changed schools."

"No, Mom! No," she says, sobbing. "I'll die if you call them."

Her mother shakes her head. "I have to do it. It's the only right way to handle this."

"What will I have left then? I can't go to school anymore. No one will want to be my friend. If you report it, what will I have left?"

Her question breaks through her tears. It isn't really a question; it's an acknowledgment of the hopelessness of the situation. She won't have anything left, just emptiness.

Her mother doesn't care if she begs.

"You can start over at another school in the fall."

Mari sinks into despair. She has nothing left but a request: "Mom, let's just let it drop," she says, pleads.

It's all she has left. Her mother can accept it, give in to her request, if she wants to. It hangs there between them, the only thread holding them together. A taut thread, thin, fraying.

She looks at Mari without answering.

"Mom, I'm begging you," Mari says, more emphatic now. "Let's just drop it."

Her mother still doesn't answer. Mari can see that she can't answer. She's left alone with her request. Her mother looks at her, her expression hard, no sign of mercy, no answer. She won't give in.

Mari has nothing left. She's finally lost everything.

Her expression hardens too: her lips tighten, she wipes away the tears. She turns her back on her mother and walks out of the room without saying a word.

As she's walking out the door, out of her mother's sphere of influence, she invites a thought in, her own thought. She's going to fly through the air again, spread her arms, open her wings, and jump.

Or maybe not.

Suddenly her old thoughts seem silly to her, childish, the flimsy imaginings of a daydream. No — the game is real now. In the real world, she can't fly. There's nothing so beautiful and light as that in reality. Reality is crueler, rougher, more violent. It will happen, that's for certain, but in some other way.

When it does happen, it will happen all of a sudden, almost as if it were an accident. Girls like that, the kinds of girls who do it, think about it in secret. Maybe they don't even think about it, maybe they talk to their mom in the morning about ordinary things — their homework, their plans for the weekend, some new shoes they saw in a store window, the blueberry pie they're going to make tonight when they get home. But the blueberry pie never comes, not for them, not for the kinds of girls who do it. Girls like that get up from the table at breakfast, put their dishes on the counter and say thank you, put on their coat and shoes, and tell their mothers *see you later*. They say *see you later*, and then they open the front door and close it behind them like they have every day before, close the door and look at the trees in the yard and take the tram into town. Girls like that walk through town past the department store and see the shoes in the window, the ones they were talking about, walk past them as their own reflection shines from the surface of the glass, and they don't go to school. They go to the river, they climb on the roof, they walk along the railroad tracks to a spot with a steep drop over the rails.

That's how it happens.

*See you later.* No intention. No decision. The decision is just a whim that comes into their heads as their face is reflected in the shiny window of the department store. No shouts of passers-by. No flight tracing a beautiful arc across the blue fabric of the sky. Nothing beautiful. Reality is mute, random, and cruel. Violent. A mute thud, a voiceless shout that disappears in its own unimportance.

When the game becomes reality, that's how it happens.

Mute. Unremarkable. Random. Real.

# *Anja*

SPRING CAME UNEXPECTEDLY in the second week of April, without warning, as always. Just a week before, snow was still falling, the nights still freezing, then winter humbled itself before spring, disappeared into spring's shameless light. The sun was shining just enough to make the dirty, dreary piles of snow along the road begin to melt ever so slightly, but evening brought a touch of frost that froze the melted snow into rippling ruts. The sun painted the western sky red and there it was: the first spring evening, sudden and sure, a fait accompli.

The next day, the spring felt its way forward shyly, dripping from the eaves, stretching the dawn out longer than the day before. And then winter had already forgotten itself.

On Thursday, Anja left work at two o'clock.

She got on the tram at the corner of Senaatintori and rode toward Hakaniemi.

She felt light.

The free morning papers lay in rustling piles on the floor of the tram. A beer bottle rolled down the aisle and under a row of seats. A young boy was kissing a girl in the stairwell at the passenger door and a passenger from the suburbs was muttering to himself.

Anja got off at Hakaniemi and transferred to a bus heading home, but got off at the school of fine arts on a whim. She felt like walking the rest of the way.

She saw two little girls on a side street. They were bent over looking at something lying next to the road. As she came closer, Anja saw that they were poking at a dead hedgehog with a stick.

"It's dead," one of them said.

"Maybe it's paralyzed, or sleeping," the other one said, tapping her rubber boot against the hedgehog's side.

The hedgehog rolled onto its back. It was frozen in a sad little ball. Its paws were twisted and held out like it was begging for mercy, its mouth open and its eyes closed in a way that made it look human somehow. It was definitely dead. It held all the memories of its hedgehog life — forest moss, sunlight on a springtime boulder — but death had placed a mute seal over it. The hedgehog's body was another sign to those left behind of what death is: it had the knowledge of the other side and it wasn't sharing that knowledge in any way other than being stiff and motionless, small but proud.

Anja stopped next to the girls. "Hi," she said.

It felt like she ought to introduce herself. They had all ended up here, at the body of the dead hedgehog. Its body publicly required acknowledgment, demanded it, without asking permission, laid claim to the concept of death right in front of them, and brought them together for a brief moment. Suddenly, they were at a funeral. They were witnesses to the eternal riddle of death, and they had to fulfill the little body's demand that they not pass it by; they had to form a group, introduce themselves to each other.

"I'm Anja," Anja said.

"I'm Sanna and that's Anni," the braver girl said.

The shy one, Anni, nodded solemnly, awed by events greater than herself.

"Look at it," Sanna said to Anja, and pointed at it with the stick in her hand.

"Is it dead?" Anni asked, although her face showed that she knew the answer.

Anja could see in the eyes of both girls a brimming fascination with the mystery of death. There was no doubt that both of them hoped the hedgehog was dead and not just paralyzed. Not because they wanted the little animal to lose its life, but because death itself was something they were at a loss to explain, something whose secret they longed to understand.

"Yes, it's dead," Anja said calmly.

"How do you know?" Anni asked.

"Look," Sanna said, and poked it with the stick. "Dead things are very quiet and they don't move at all."

"That's right," Anja said. "That's how you know."

"What should we do with it?" Anni asked.

"Bury it!" Sanna exclaimed.

"Where?" Anni asked.

"In the woods. Under the moss."

They used sticks to move the dead hedgehog away from the road, rolling it carefully into the outer edge of the woods. Anni lifted a soggy mat of moss while Sanna gathered pebbles to mark the grave. Anja used two sticks as gentle tongs and carried the hedgehog to its mossy grave.

They stood around the grave and let the fact of death and the placing of the grave marker etch themselves in their minds.

"Why do people bury dead things?" Sanna asked.

Anja hesitated. "It's important to bury the dead. That way

the people who are still alive understand what death means. So we know what's coming. You have to make a point of the fact that the dead aren't here anymore, that they only live in memory."

"Don't dead people live in heaven?"

"Maybe. But they live in our memories, too."

"Oh. But I think this hedgehog is in hedgehog heaven," Sanna said knowingly. "There's a lot of flowers there and other hedgehogs."

"You may be right."

They stood around the grave a little longer.

Sanna stared at the hedgehog and repeated the fact of death to confirm its reality: "Dead things are very quiet, and they don't move at all."

They said brief goodbyes and left in different directions. Anja turned and glanced back at the girls once. They were both wearing rubber boots, the shy one walking a step behind the bolder one, like a faithful lackey. The braver one beat the rhythm of their steps with the stick.

The little girls would go home, watch cartoons, maybe play with a pet hamster full of life, before going to bed and waking up the next morning to Barbie clothes, sugar cubes, plastic ponies, and barrettes. But the hedgehog would live in their minds; they would take it into their memories, carry it in their thoughts and dreams, and try to understand the incomprehensible. Maybe it was the first time they'd seen it, right here, on this road. Maybe it would be the first time they took in the knowledge that all life is limited, the knowledge of what inevitably awaits us all.

★

MAKING THE REQUEST was just as difficult as Anja had expected. Her sister was sitting in front of her, drinking coffee, talking of other things — her summer plans, putting up spring curtains. Marita could tell that something was coming, sped up her talk a little after each pause. Anja cut in at the next pause without hesitating.

"I want to ask you to arrange the funeral if I get caught."

Her sister looked surprisingly calm. She looked at her in silence for perhaps half a minute. "No."

"What, you won't do it?"

"No. I just can't promise to do it. I can't promise anything to do with criminal activity. I can't promise to be your accomplice."

"You don't understand."

"Yes, I do."

"No. No, you don't. What the hell do you think, that I want this? Do you think I wanted a life like this?"

Her sister didn't answer. She went to the window and plucked the dead leaves off the flower on the windowsill. Anja went up to her, and reached out and put her arm around her.

"Why do you have to do something like this?" her sister said.

Her voice was full of confusion, helplessness, fear. Everything that Anja wasn't used to seeing in her.

"Because he asked me to," Anja said without hesitation.

"Why did you say you would do it? How could you promise to do something like that, to break the law?"

Anja had only one explanation.

"Because he asked me to. I promised because he asked me to."

ANJA WAKES UP in the middle of the night and sees that her husband's side of the bed is empty. She sits up, sees the moon greeting her behind the curtains. A sliver of moonlight reaches into the corner of the bedroom.

Her husband is sitting in the corner, trembling.

The moon illuminates a face frozen in terror, reveals a fear that is no longer endurable. The fear is made up of a dread of his very existence, a pure desire for escape that gapes in his face, and an anguish at the thought that the possibility of escape is disappearing.

Anja opens her mouth to say something, but no sound comes out.

She gets out of bed and goes to her husband. He grabs hold of her as if for dear life, squeezes her neck and arm too hard. She's afraid he'll hurt her. He cries a broken, ugly sob, the kind of sound people make when crying is strange to them, a memory from childhood. He trembles and grips her as if seeking rescue.

She comforts him like she would a child.

"Help me," he says.

"How can I help you? Tell me how."

"I can't bear to go through this. Save me."

Anja holds him tightly, rocks him. She won't let go of him all night. She whispers slowly, humbled, helpless against the reality of her powerlessness, "I would save you if I could."

He holds her tighter, nearly shaking her, and says with a sob, "Save me. Kill me. Kill me and save me."

Anja pulls herself out of his grasp. She sees the expression on his face, the horror of the world to come, hears it at the outer edges of his voice.

"Don't. Don't ask me to do that," she hears herself saying.

He begins to cry even more disconsolately than before. "I'd do it myself if I dared to. But I'm a damn coward. I still want to see the days, to see if any good days come."

Anja takes hold of his sentence and uses it to weave herself a safety net.

"Well, that means that you don't want me to kill you."

He stops crying and grabs hold of her again. He shakes her shoulders, holds her in place, and says each word with emphasis.

"Yes, I do. I'm asking you. When there's nothing else left. Do it then."

Anja shakes her head. She doesn't want this moment. Even now, in this sliver of moonlight, in the corner of the bedroom, she knows that this will shape the weight of the coming years, make them heavy, true, impenetrable.

"For God's sake, don't ask this of me. You can't ask me to do this." She says it desperately, nearly shouts it.

Her husband stops trembling, takes her face between his hands in a gesture of certainty, holds her there, and says again, "I can't ask you to do this. But I am asking you. Kill me and save me."

A YEAR LATER, Anja's mind still couldn't grasp what she said, what she did. Did she nod? Did she give her consent and accept the request, or did she just stay there, look at him, the man she knew better than anyone in the world, and let him see consent in her face? Maybe she kissed him, maybe she stroked him and held him in her arms, said what she was supposed to say — that everything would be all right — and asked him to come back to bed. Maybe she did all this even though she consented to his request. Maybe she did both things — said no and yes. Because you can't promise a crime, promise damnation, to the one you love the most; and it's the one you love the most to whom you would promise anything, including breaking the law. Him more than anyone.

## Julian

A WEEK, a week and a half, two weeks. Julian still wasn't able to
tell her. But he did dare to think about it. Maybe things would
continue like this forever. Maybe the girl's mother would never
tell. At first it was a relief to think that. Then an annoyance:
this endless waiting, half afraid, a question in Jannika's eyes,
day after day the same question-shaped silence whenever she
came near him, touched him, took him between her legs and
inside her while their daughters slept in the next room. When
Jannika fell asleep, he lay awake. Was it a small price to pay, that
leaden moment before sleep, night after night?

And the girl. She had gone off the deep end. Julian could
see that. He'd sent her off the deep end. She was quiet and
pale. She was in his second-level language and literature
course. She came to class every day, sat in the middle row of
desks, participated in the group projects like she was supposed
to, and answered when she was asked a question. By the end
of class she would be looking out the window with a distant
expression. It seemed as if she were about to burst into tears at
any moment.

She didn't look at him anymore. When he asked a question
about something to do with literature or linguistics, she

almost always raised her hand. Sometimes he let her answer. It was hard to say her name when he called on her. "Mari," he would say with deliberate nonchalance, afraid that all the other students could hear the meaning of the name he was speaking. He waited for her to raise her eyes, trembling, her expression stripped of its indifference. But she would look at the floor, or past him, at the blackboard, put her hand down, and answer in a clear voice that showed no sign of emotion. She always answered correctly. If the question asked for an interpretation of literature, her interpretation was clear, original, and beautiful.

The course covered world literature, and Julian couldn't avoid putting the tragedies of Sophocles on the reading list. The students were placed in groups, and each group chose a work to explore in greater depth and then gave a presentation on it to the class.

Today was her group's turn to present their work. They had chosen *Antigone*. They took turns reading from it in front of the class.

When her turn to read came, they had reached the scene where Antigone gave her speech defending herself for breaking Creon's law. Mari had been standing aloof as the others read. Now she raised her eyes, unashamedly, publicly, and looked right at him, reciting Antigone's words, her voice steady:

*I knew that I must die;*
*E'en hadst thou not proclaimed it; and if death*
*Is thereby hastened, I shall count it gain.*

She didn't look away. They stared at each other. Julian was silent, watching her. The rest of the class had sunk into boredom. No one noticed what was happening.

But Julian knew what was happening.

He pulled himself together and asked the group to analyze the work, as he'd asked the other students to do. Their enthusiasm for critical analysis was lukewarm; it was just before lunchtime and everyone's concentration was flagging.

But then she raised her hand. She didn't look at him, just raised her hand.

He had to call her name.

"Mari," he said.

She turned her head, lowered her hand, and looked at him. It was a gaze of naked accusation.

"It's a mistake," she said in a clear voice.

"Oh? What is?"

"It's a mistake that Antigone chooses death."

"But does she choose? Isn't death inevitable in her situation? Death or Creon's law?"

"No. She should choose life," Mari insisted. "She should choose life no matter what."

Julian didn't know what to say.

"Thank you," he finally said.

Her gaze was clearly filled with anger now. She didn't want his thanks anymore. She didn't want another word out of him.

*Forgive me,* Julian wanted to say. He didn't say it.

She looked at him.

He felt longing and regret like an ache. She ought to be smiling and laughing, carefree and young, like other sixteen-year-olds. She ought to be with boys her own age, boys who didn't talk about desire or love. The kind of boys who went out for ice cream and cigarettes from the corner store between classes and talked about what they were going to do tonight, who made straightforward propositions, felt an unquestioned certainty of their place in the world. He should have left her in peace, left unsaid all the things he still wanted to say. *Desiree, my love, my desire. Forgive me.*

"If no one has anything to add, then let's finish up for the day," Julian said lamely.

He glanced at her again. She wasn't looking at him anymore. He felt like he had no influence over her. The students got up from their desks and clomped out the door. She stayed after they'd left. He could see that she was trying to act like nothing was happening, putting her things away without looking in his direction. He felt a surge of affection. The feeling was followed by a wave of passion: those lips and eyes and hair and legs. Those breasts.

Her friend stood in the doorway for a moment, asked if she was coming, then looked at him; and he could see that she knew what was going on. A protective look, almost hostile. How ridiculous it all was — her friend there to protect her from him. Hell. He should put an end to it. He should work this out with her, hope that her mother didn't pursue the matter, and put the whole thing behind him. The girl's friend looked at him again and then disappeared from the doorway. Julian waited to be sure she was gone before he spoke.

"Mari," he said. "Should we talk?"

"What about?"

She pretended not to know, still not looking at him. Her courage of a moment before was gone, replaced by an evasive gaze.

Julian tried to soothe her. "I was thinking that we could talk calmly about all this. Go somewhere, to coffee maybe."

She put on an impassive expression. "Is there anything more to say about it?"

"Mari," he tried again. "You know there is."

She brushed her face with the edge of her hand. Her expression seemed to melt. Julian stepped closer to her, quite close. He took her hand. A tear rolled down her cheek — just one, slowly, so slowly that he could have licked it off.

"Maybe we could see each other in town tomorrow, go have coffee. I have classes in the afternoon. Say three-thirty?"

"OK. Three-thirty tomorrow."

"I'll see you then," Julian said.

"See you then," she answered.

She took her hand out of his, turned, and walked out of the classroom.

# Mari

MARI WALKS OUT of Julian's classroom and thinks that this
would all be easier if she could cry. But no tears come. There
she is, the girl with no feelings. That's so weird, she thinks —
that there's this "she."

Mari looks at her hands. Their outlines are clear, but someone else has drawn them. A torturer. Her torturer, coming
back again and again to make her visible.

The torturer said thank you. But he didn't mean it. He
mostly meant to concede that events had come to an end.

TINKA'S WAITING OUTSIDE.

She looks at Mari. She can see. Mari doesn't have to say
anything. Tinka can see.

This is when the lifesaver arrives: Tinka sees Mari, sees
everything, all of it, all of a sudden. Or has it always been here,
has Tinka always known that it would come to this?

Tinka's lifesaving attempt is a simple suggestion, veiled in
innocence: "Let's go have some coffee."

Mari squeaks a brief reply that Tinka interprets as hesitance.
She coaxes.

"We can go get some coffee and an ice-cream cone. The first

ice cream of the year, with lots of scoops, and sprinkles on top."

"Nah."

"Come on," Tinka wheedles.

"No."

Tinka's quiet. For a second it looks like she's going to give up. How many noes does Mari have? But Tinka doesn't let her off, not yet. She comes closer, hugs her the way she always does. Apples, rose milk, lavender, all of Tinka's smells.

"I was thinking we could get a summer job together," she whispers. "At an amusement park or an ice-cream stand. Just think how fun it would be. We could eat as much ice cream as we wanted."

Mari doesn't answer. Tinka lets her go, loosens her hold.

"Should I call around about summer job openings?"

"Hmm."

"Should I?"

"Maybe."

Mari grants her that. Maybe. It means no. Because summer jobs aren't for girls like her, the kind of girls who say *see you later*, and then go out to the railroad tracks, to the river, the bridge, the highway, and look into the unsuspecting eyes of the cars' headlights just before it's all over.

Tinka can see that *maybe* means *no*.

That sadness. A sea of sadness. Mari can see it in Tinka's eyes. Tinka knows.

"See you later," Mari says.

"See you," Tinka says.

Mari turns to leave. There it is, a little hesitation. She can still turn back. Tinka, ice cream, summer plans.

"Mari," Tinka says.

Mari turns. A life buoy, one last try to get Mari to take hold of it.

"Call me," Tinka says. "If you want to go to coffee. Later today. Call me."

A lifeline, thrown for the last time. *Call me. If you want.* Mari doesn't take hold of it. She's sinking below the surface: nothing matters. How do you rescue another person? How can you do it if sinking is her decision, a decision made lightly, thoughtlessly? You can't.

Mari could still turn around. Tinka, ice cream, summer plans.

She doesn't turn around.

She walks to the door. She walks out the door.

SEE YOU LATER. She doesn't intend to see Tinka later. Or Julian. She's going to do something else instead. Because although the choice should be hers, she has no choice.

She only has this clear March day, and two hours until she's going to do the inevitable.

It's one o'clock. She's going to do it at three.

What do people do for two hours? What does a person do when there's not much time left?

Mari goes to the café on the top floor of Stockmann department store and buys a large dish of ice cream.

When there's not much time left, people eat.

She feels the whipped cream on the roof of her mouth and tastes the chocolate sauce all the way up to her nose.

This might be the best ice cream I've ever had, she thinks.

"Hi, Mari."

It's her mother's sister, Anja.

"Hi."

"Can I join you?" Anja asks, putting her coffee cup down on the table across from her without waiting for an answer. "How are you? You're eating that ice cream like it's your last day on earth."

*Your last day on earth.* How does she always know the right thing to say? Mari answers her question briefly, with a lie. "Fine. I'm fine ... I guess."

*I guess* is always an opening. It's an opening big enough to let some doubt through Mari's calm demeanor. *I guess.* Anja can take hold of it if she wants to.

"What do you mean, *I guess?*" she asks, sipping her coffee.

Of course. Anja knows this game. She takes hold of *I guess.* Now she's sitting there in front of Mari, drinking her coffee and demanding an answer to the greatest of all questions. Anja, who always has a twinkle in her eye, it seems. Is she even serious? Yes, she is. Her good-humored, ready questions are pierced with a ripple of worry. Mari can see it. Anja's worried. Suddenly, Mari considers telling her everything. She could say it all in one sentence, saving the biggest part for last. The plan.

But Anja speaks first. "Studying anything interesting at school?"

"Tragedy," Mari answers.

She knows then that she won't tell Anja about the plan. Anja's a literature professor and the mention of tragedy will no doubt make her forget all other questions. Mari makes a note of it, half carelessly: This is the turning point. She won't discuss her plan. Her last chance has passed. The plan will come true. There's no turning back. She feels a vague pleasure at the finality of it. Here it is again, a chance occurrence making her decision come true.

"Oh," Anja says, pleased. "What tragedy?"

"*Antigone.*"

"Ah! *Antigone.*" Anja sighs, with a hint of irony in her voice. "What do you think of *Antigone?*"

"I wonder if her solution is the right one. If death is unavoidable."

"What's your opinion?"

"Maybe it's unavoidable in her situation. Dying."

"Do you think the same principle applies to everyone? That fate is brought on by events and leads people to their inevitable end?"

Mari answers without hesitation. "Yes. It applies to everyone."

"That's the tragic take on things. Believing that fate determines your actions is an attitude that has all the hallmarks of tragedy. Interpreting situations as inevitable is an error of hubris. In a tragedy the characters have the weight of their families on them, so the choice isn't entirely in their hands. But in real life we have a choice."

Mari looks at her ice-cream dish. The ice cream has melted into a sad, white puddle in the bottom of her bowl. Only ten minutes left of this hour. Anja doesn't see. Mari doesn't let Anja see her plan, formed from a decision taken half carelessly, a plan that will be fulfilled when she goes to the river. The early spring river is flooding. She just has to go to the river and her plan will come true, effortlessly.

Anja looks at Mari. Mari looks back. Does she see? Does she? Anja always knows more than she lets on. Sometimes she sees everything.

Mari gets up. Anja touches her arm.

Mari turns. Anja doesn't say anything, just looks at her.

"Well, I guess I'll go now," Mari hears herself say.

"Bye, then," Anja says.

Mari turns to walk away, stops. Anja is still looking at her, and says, "It's possible to think that she chooses life."

"What?" Mari says.

"Antigone. She refuses to obey Creon's unjust law. You could think that by refusing to obey that unjust law, Antigone is actually saying yes to life."

"But she dies. Antigone dies."

"Yes, but she doesn't have a life of submission to Creon's law. She dies, but she chooses her life."

"But she says: *if death is thereby hastened, I shall count it gain.* How can she be choosing life if she wants to die?"

"The point is that there's a difference between tragedy and real life. In a tragedy it's possible to choose life through death — that conflict is possible. But in real life, death is the only possible option. Antigone chooses life by dying, because the nature of tragedy allows her to do that. That's the difference between tragedy and life."

Mari doesn't know what to say. She just turns and walks away without looking back.

MARI TAKES THE ESCALATORS to the first floor. She goes to the cosmetics department and on a whim sprays two different perfumes on her wrist. The scent is a comforting mix of sweet and spicy. She looks around one last time before walking past the smiles of the clerks and out the door to the bus stop. The bus comes right away. Her decision is approaching, just like it's supposed to, effortlessly.

Mute. Unremarkable. Random. Real.

HER PHONE RINGS. It's Julian. Another distracting interruption of her plan. What does he want now?

She answers the phone.

Julian is silent at first. One second, two.

"Hi," he says.

"Hi," Mari answers.

"You know," he says. "I just remembered that you left your coat at our place. Or in the car, I mean. On Christmas break."

Mari's heart skips a beat. "Oh, yeah."

Julian pauses for a second. The pause trembles with possibility. "Do you want to come and pick it up? At our house?"

"Is anyone else there?"

"My wife's away this afternoon and evening. The girls are at the neighbors'. It's all right if you come."

"OK. I guess I will."

"Do you know where we live?"

Mari's embarrassed to admit it. She looked his address up on a map. She's even gone by his house, on the chance that she might get a glimpse of him.

"Yes, I know where it is. I'll be right there. Maybe in half an hour."

"Right. Good."

Mari takes the thought of the river, picks it up. A gentle, comforting thought, her fate. She picks it up and shoves it to the back of her mind. The river will still be there. She can go to the river if she wants to. But first she'll go to see Julian.

Maybe he does want her after all. Maybe he wants her more than anything else.

# *Anni*

SANNA'S STUPID. Sanna is maybe the stupidest person in the whole world. Ada's stupid, too, because she doesn't want to play, she just wants to bake sweet rolls in the kitchen with Sanna's mom. Anni mopes in the kitchen doorway for a long time. Everyone is baking: Ada, Sanna, Sanna's mom. Stupid sweet rolls. Anni made a sweet-roll man that came out wrong when she baked it and Sanna called it a roly poly. Baking is stupid, Anni thinks as she stands in the doorway.

Nobody notices her.

She goes into the hallway, looks at herself in the mirror. She's a big girl now, not a baby anymore. But she has a game she plays that's just her own: she can turn into something else whenever she wants. All she needs is the coat. She thinks about the coat hanging in the hall closet at home underneath all the others. Anni hid it there. It's her royal cape. Mom can't know anything about it — not Mom or Dad. It's her own secret game.

She wants to be somebody else right now. She wants the coat.

Anni sneaks to the front door so Sanna and Sanna's mom and Ada won't hear her. She turns the latch quietly, opens the door, and steps outside. She walks close to the wall under the kitchen window, very quietly, then runs across the gravel yard to her front door. She opens the door with the key around her neck and listens: the house is empty.

Anni goes to the coat rack, rummages under the other coats, stops to smell the world of the coats. She could make a nest here, stay here and hide. No. It might be boring. She digs out her queen's cape, the secret one, the one that makes her someone else, the one for pretty girls. She puts it on. The sleeves are still too long, the hem still reaches to her ankles. But otherwise it's perfect.

Anni goes in front of the mirror and twirls a little, looking at herself.

This is what she is now: a big girl, a woman someday, maybe a beautiful woman.

This is what she is now: someone completely different.

Anni hears a muffled noise in the living room. It startles her at first, but then she realizes that it's Dad. She goes to the living-room door. It's closed. She opens the door a crack. Just a little bit.

Dad is there with the girl — the girl the coat belongs to. Anni watches what they're doing, some adult thing. She watches them for a minute. Then she closes the door and looks at herself in the mirror again.

This is what she is in this coat, in her royal cape: someone completely different.

She sneaks to the door, opens it, goes out and closes it behind her.

# *Julian*

WHY? WHY DID HE have to invite her into his home? Why bring the crime here? He had convinced himself that he just wanted to talk to her. *This has to end.* He said that over and over in his mind before she arrived. This has to end. He thought he would offer her some coffee; thought they would talk, bring the whole thing to a conclusion. Self-delusion.

It happened again, almost as soon as she arrived. First they looked for her coat in the car; it wasn't there. Julian didn't know where it had gone. It didn't matter. Maybe the coat was just an excuse, for both of them. Just an excuse all along.

She smiled at him a little. He whispered the words *Desiree, my Desiree* in her ear, and they kissed again. She sat down on the living-room sofa. Julian offered her some coffee or tea. She asked for juice. She never got around to drinking her juice — they kissed.

The sex was languorous, with a touch of melancholy. Tender. Julian knew even as they were doing it that the guilt would be greater than ever. She was in his arms. He was quick to climax: then the embarrassment, the thought of escape. She put her underpants and bra back on shyly, not looking at him.

"I'm sorry this happened again," Julian began.

She straightened up, put on her skirt, looked out the window, wrapped her arms around herself, didn't answer. Julian sighed. How difficult was this going to be?

"You know this has to end."

"Don't say that," she said, suddenly shrill.

"What?" Julian said, surprised. "You know that this is an impossible situation."

She muttered something.

"What?" he said.

"Kill me," she said, her voice clear now. "If you don't love me, then kill me. Rescue me or kill me."

Julian couldn't think of anything to say.

She started to cry. He got up and tried to approach her. She backed away, gathered her things, went to the front door. He followed her. He tried to touch her again, when he couldn't think of anything to say. She shoved his hand away.

"Leave me alone," she said, putting on her coat.

"Where are you going?"

"None of your business. Nothing's any of your business."

"Mari."

"Don't say that!" she yelled. "You have no right to say my name. No right. You have no right to say anything anymore!"

"Sweetheart ..."

Now she was crying so much that he couldn't make out what she was saying. She picked up her bag and wiped her tears away with the back of her hand, then she opened the door and closed it behind her. Julian didn't try to stop her. He sat on the chair by the door, sat there for a long time, listening to the silence. Fifteen minutes. Half an hour.

*Rescue me or kill me. Love me or kill me.* That's what she said.

He thought about what she said.

A suspicion entered his mind.
*Rescue me or kill me. Kill me.*
The suspicion grew stronger.
He got up and put on his coat.

# Anni

IT'S THE HORSES' FAULT. The horses made them go into the woods, to the riverbank. Or one horse did. Anni's not sure if the horse was even real. Maybe it was an imaginary horse. But she wants to believe in it. She saw its tracks on the trail, big hoof marks that disappeared and reappeared, as if the horse could sometimes take off and fly, like the horses with wings in stories.

ANNI WALKS A LITTLE WAYS along the edge of the woods, wearing her queen's cape. She's a queen who's been mistreated. No one understands her. No one knows that she's a queen. But soon everyone will find out and then there will be a party for her, the most wonderful party ever. Anni skips along the path. Do queens skip? No. No, she's sure they don't. Queens walk. Anni slows down. Her royal cape trails along the ground. Then she has an idea. Maybe she'll see a horse, here in the woods. There might be a horse behind any tree, watching her with its ears up. It might come walking onto the trail and then gallop away. Maybe Anni doesn't really see a horse. But she imagines she sees it. There it is, behind that rock. Yes, she decides: it's a horse. She's going to tell Sanna about it. Sanna has never seen a horse in the wild, she's sure of that.

When Anni gets back to the yard, Sanna is on the swing. Anni goes up to her. She thinks about the difference between a lie, a fib, and the truth. Good girls don't lie, of course. If you think about it, you might think that the story of the horse is a lie. On the other hand, it's not a *big* lie. A person *could* see a horse in the woods.

Anni decides she has seen a horse. It doesn't really matter that she's not sure if it was a real horse or an imaginary horse.

"I saw a horse," she tells Sanna, who's sitting on the swing, not bothering to look at her. "A wild horse, in the woods," she adds when Sanna doesn't seem surprised enough.

Now Sanna turns her head. She looks curious, surprised, just like Anni hoped she would.

"I don't believe you," Sanna says.

"I did," Anni insists.

Now Anni has started to believe it herself.

"I still don't believe you," Sanna says defiantly.

Anni answers in the same tone. "Would you believe it if you saw it?"

Sanna nods.

Anni hesitates. She's not allowed to go in the woods in the springtime. Because of the river. But if they stay on the trail ...

"Come on, then," she says.

It's bright in the woods. The sun is dancing in the branches of the spruce trees and the snow has melted off the path completely. Anni walks ahead, her queen's cape trailing on the ground, and Sanna trudges after her, complaining. She still doesn't believe Anni's story and she wants to go home.

"I know we'll find it soon. It's probably gone off the trail,"

Anni says hopefully. "Maybe it went to the river to eat some grass."

"We're not allowed to go to the river."

Anni feels like she's stronger than Sanna today. Usually it's Sanna who decides what they're going to play and who's the boss of the game. But today Anni thought up the idea of the horse and she's in charge.

"We're not going to go to the river," she says. "We're just going to go *near* it. There's a difference."

"I don't know," Sanna says. "The river can be dangerous."

"It's not dangerous. It's exciting."

They don't see the horse at the river, either. But there are a few hoof marks in the grass — at least, Anni thinks they're hoof marks.

The ice crackles thrillingly. The river is surging and the spring breeze flutters Anni's royal cape. She'd like to get closer to the river to see the ice breaking up. Suddenly it seems important to be braver than Sanna. Anni's afraid of the river, too, but not that much. She doesn't believe anymore that they're going to see the horse, but she can't let go of the story yet. Maybe the horse will help her tempt Sanna closer to the riverbank so they can watch the rafts of ice crash against one another.

"Aha!" Anni shouts. "Look! There it is. A big horse. A real one."

"Where?" Sanna says, alert.

"Over there, it went into the meadow."

"I didn't see anything," Sanna says, irritated. "Show me where it went."

Anni runs toward the river. Sanna follows.

They go to the stones on the bank. Anni knows that this is

a place they're not supposed to be. The rocks are dangerous. They can be slippery. But she's braver than Sanna now, for once. They stand on a big rock and watch the rushing river.

"I still don't see any horse," Sanna says impatiently. "Where did you say you saw it?"

"Over there," Anni says, and points down the river. "I saw it. I really did. They're so fast. It must have run away."

Sanna cranes to look. Anni looks down the river, too. They both crane their necks a little more, just a little more.

And then there's a splash.

Sanna falls in the river. Anni has just enough time to see Sanna's pink hood and her hat with the red pom-pom before she disappears under the water.

Anni tries to shout, but no shout comes out, just a strangled squeak. Sanna's hat floats on the river's current, gets stuck on a rock. She can't see Sanna anywhere: the river has swallowed her up.

# Mari

THE ICY MARCH WIND on the river shore gives everything clear edges. The river rolls and roars. The sun is shining as if it plans to spend all its rays on this one day. Mari walks under the naked birches toward the channel of the river. The water is surging; the ice is breaking up. The dock — that's where she's headed.

She looks at the water. She thinks of the swimming competition. The water is soothing, not scary at all. The water is the forgetting she's been wishing for, her liberation.

This has been her fate all along. The decision was easy, almost involuntary, just how you would imagine it.

Mari looks up at the open span of sky. If she stops to think now, she might feel doubt. If she looks at the birches along the river, she might get the idea that there's nothing inevitable about this. She looks at the birches. It's only a few weeks until the blackbirds will be singing. If she looks at the birches and thinks about it, it's a bit melodramatic being the unhappy girl. Unhappy as if there were no blackbirds waiting to sing. Unhappy as if there weren't going to be any apple blossoms.

No, Mari thinks. Her tormentor has driven her to this. A tormentor who loved her and then stopped loving her, drew her an outline and then left it empty. Not dead, just hollow.

That's why she's come here, she thinks, stretching her left foot out to step onto the dock. All she has to do now is stumble. It doesn't even have to be something she decides to do. One small, careless step and her fate will be fulfilled. She doesn't dare to move. If there is no stumble, is that a sign? If there's no stumble, all she has to do is close her eyes and lean forward and topple in. She waits another second.

No stumble.

But she hears a splash.

She sees a glimpse of a little girl in a pink hood and a red hat disappearing under the water. Another little girl is standing on a rock right over the river. It's Julian's daughter. The little girl looks at her, doesn't move. She's wearing Mari's coat, which reaches all the way to her ankles.

Mari pulls her telephone out of her pocket and calls the emergency number.

## Anni

A SECOND PASSES before Anni sees the girl. She's standing on the dock. She's looking at Anni. Now she's taking out a phone and calling someone. She finishes the call and waves her hand at Anni, then steps down off the dock and runs over to her. When she gets close, Anni realizes that it's the same girl she saw with Dad. The one with the pretty eyes. The one she's not supposed to tell anyone about.

"I called for help. I'm going to go get the lifebuoy from the dock and see if I can see your friend anywhere. You run home right now and get help. Tell them I've already called an ambulance. Can you do that?"

Anni nods.

She takes off at a run toward the houses on the other side of the woods. Her royal cape drags along the ground and she almost stumbles over it. The dry meadow is as high as her head, but she runs faster than she ever has before. She wants to stop, wants to cry. But she knows no tears will come because she has a big thing, an important thing throbbing in her head.

Anni's halfway across the meadow. And then Dad is coming toward her. He looks alarmed, strange.

Anni tries to tell him, but suddenly she can't speak. All that comes out are great big tears.

# Julian

JULIAN RAN through the woods, praying that he wasn't too late. Dry branches struck his face. *Kill me.* He knew what the girl planned to do, and he guessed that she planned to do it at the river. *Kill me. Rescue me.*

The meadow, then the river. Julian loped through the dry grass, crushing it under his feet.

He was halfway across the meadow when he saw Anni coming toward him.

He stopped and looked at his daughter. She gasped for breath, and burst into tears.

She was wearing Mari's coat.

"Help," she said.

The coat was dragging on the ground. Its hem was covered in mud.

"Help, Daddy," she said. "Help."

Julian looked at his daughter. He couldn't tear his gaze away. Help, she said. He stood there and let the excruciatingly clear image of Anni etch itself in his mind. A second passed, maybe half a second, a fleeting moment; and during that moment, everything acquired its real meaning.

"What's wrong? What happened?" he said.

Anni couldn't get the words out.

"Sanna fell in the river," she finally said. "Sanna fell in."

Julian scooped her up in his arms and ran again, toward the river.

He saw Mari there. She was bent over something. At first it looked like she was praying, kneeling on the ground, lifting and then lowering her head. Julian came a few steps closer and saw that she was giving CPR. On the ground in front of her lay Sanna.

# Mari

SHE FINDS THE GIRL floating in a bend of the river. The strings of her hood are tangled in her hair, her hair spread out over the surface of the water like a mermaid's. Mari bends over the slimy river rocks, manages to throw the lifebuoy around her, and pulls her to the shore. She can see immediately that the girl's been in the water a long time — maybe too long.

Mari learned CPR in first-aid class. She checks the girl's breathing, puts her head in the right position, and begins to blow.

She doesn't know how much time passes as she presses on the little girl's chest and blows into her mouth. The girl isn't breathing. It isn't until the ambulance comes that Mari stops and gets up. She sees that Julian is there. He's holding his daughter in his arms.

Julian is saying something. Mari can't hear him at first.

"Thank you," he says to her. "I was too late to help," he says to the emergency crew. "She revived her, by herself. I got here too late."

*Thank you.* That's what he's saying, her tormentor, her rescuer who didn't rescue her.

The ambulance drives away, leaving deep tire tracks in the

mud, crushing the willows along the trail with the sides of its broad body. It must be only a few weeks until the pussy willows are blooming.

Julian is saying something. Again Mari can't hear him. A rational thought, an objective point of view, comes to her: When a person's in shock, their senses don't work properly, their hearing can be weakened, their sight may be bad, their attention may be disrupted. When you're in shock, all you notice are the willows, the tire tracks, the rubber boots sinking into the soft mud. All speech becomes meaningless. Julian seems to be looking at her hands and saying something again. Mari looks at her hands. They're covered in mud. There are cuts, from the sharp rocks on the shore, on the backs of her hands, bleeding. She puts them behind her back. Julian repeats what he said.

"We're going to the hospital, in my car. Do you want to come with us?"

Mari nods. Of course. Of course she'll come.

In the car, no one speaks. Mari and the little girl, Anni, sit in the back. Julian doesn't look well; he's squeezing the steering wheel tight as he drives. Mari looks at him in the rear-view mirror. He looks back at her for a fleeting second, then turns away.

He drives to a service station. Mari thinks at first that he needs some gas, but he parks the car and gets out. Anni glances at her. Mari reads the worry in her eyes. Julian goes into the station for a moment, comes out, rips open a pack of cigarettes, takes one out, and lights it clumsily with a match. Mari didn't know he smoked. She's never seen him smoke before.

Julian leans against the side of the car and takes a drag.

Anni opens the car door and gets out. Mari sees the coat drag over the ground as Anni goes around to the other side of the car, to where Julian is. Anni says something. Julian answers, pats her head mechanically, his movements slow.

Anni gets back in the car. Julian leans against the car a little longer, puts out his cigarette, rubs his face. He looks ill. Mari notices that her right hand is bleeding. She has a deep gash along the edge of her hand from her little finger to her wrist. There are cuts on her left hand, too. They make Mari feel ashamed, as if they demand attention, as if she were demanding to be noticed, drawing attention to her own plight. She squeezes her hand into a fist. Maybe it will slow the bleeding.

Julian gets back in the car and starts it.

"Sorry," he says, and pulls out toward the highway.

*Sorry*, he says. Her tormentor. Sorry. Maybe he's apologizing for stopping, delaying their trip, or maybe he's apologizing for something else, she's not sure. Anni watches her father, watches him the whole time as he drives down the highway among the other cars, as if her gaze is the only thing keeping him from coming apart.

IN THE HOSPITAL PARKING LOT, the wind grabs Mari's hair. Julian grabs his daughter's hand. They walk ahead. Mari hangs back. Once again she's the intruder. Julian asks the receptionist where the little girl was taken. They're directed down the hall to a small waiting area. The woman at the reception desk looks at Mari, glances at Anni, tells Julian that the little girl's parents are on their way. Julian nods, doesn't say anything, and goes to sit in a faded chair. Anni sits next to him. Mari sits farther away, on the other side of the hallway, next to an old man.

The receptionist looks at her, says something to a nurse walking by.

"It looks like you could use some patching up," the nurse says in a friendly tone.

Mari looks at her hands. Blood is dripping silently onto the dark-blue linoleum floor. Mari's embarrassed.

"I'm sorry. I can clean it up. I'll wipe it up."

"Come with me and we'll see if you need any stitches."

ON THE OTHER SIDE of the swinging door of a treatment room, the nurse has her sit down in a chair, gives her a drink of water, and starts to clean the wounds with a smelly substance that stings. The smell reaches into Mari's nose, behind her nose to the back of her head, wraps around her eyes, and makes her start to cry.

A tear drops between her hands and rolls down onto the paper that covers the examination table, a centimeter from the nurse's thumb. First one, then another, then a third. The nurse looks her in the eye.

"Cry all you like. You're allowed to cry if you feel like it," she says.

The nurse smells like Miracle perfume. It's a comforting smell. Mari got the same perfume as a confirmation gift. The nurse is wearing a small silver pendant around her neck. Mari feels like taking it in her hand, feeling its cool, smooth surface against her palm. She can see down the nurse's shirt. A black lace bra covering perfect breasts that rise and fall lightly as she focuses on cleaning the wounds. An absurd idea occurs to Mari: Those breasts have been here the whole time. They've been here all along, but Mari didn't know about them. It almost happened that she never saw them.

That's where the line was drawn: almost. It almost happened that she never saw them.

But here she is, looking at the soothing curve of those unknown breasts, the sting of disinfectant in her nose. She's sitting here now, at this moment in time, and soon she'll get up and leave. The nurse will go home, say hello to her beloved, who will kiss her on the neck to greet her, press his lips against the cool surface of the pendant, take off her bra in the pale light of the spring evening and press his face between her breasts, these breasts, which are real, more real than anything.

The nurse covers the wounds in white bandages and wraps gauze around Mari's hand. "How old are you?" she asks.

"Sixteen. Almost seventeen. This summer."

The nurse smiles. "That's a good age. Soon it will be summer and you'll be seventeen. That's good. What do you plan to do this summer?"

"I don't know yet."

"Maybe get a summer job?"

"Maybe."

"Where at?"

"Maybe sell ice cream, with a friend of mine."

"Sounds like a good plan," the nurse says. "You'll get to eat as much ice cream as you want."

She looks at Mari's arm. Mari realizes what she's looking at and tries to tug her sleeve down to cover the cuts.

"What about these?" the nurse asks. "Shouldn't we do something about these, too?"

"They're nothing."

"Is that so?"

The nurse eyes her intently.

"Yeah," Mari answers.

She lifts her hands a little. They glow in their new white bandages.

"These are the only cuts I have. The only real ones."

The nurse looks at her. "OK," she says finally. "Those are the only ones."

THROUGH THE WINDOW in the swinging door Mari can see the little girl's mother coming down the hallway. It must be the little girl's mother. Mari sees Julian talking to her. It's like a film in slow motion, without sound. There's no sound for some reason. The girl's mother falls onto the floor like a rag doll that's been dropped. The look on her face is like a doll's, too, painted on, paralyzed, humble. The cry doesn't come until a second later. Like a child who's hurt herself and doesn't feel the pain for a moment, a child pausing in the center of the pain, surprised at the suddenness of it, the vividness. Her cry is like a child's, too. Like a child who's stepped on a nail on the path to the sauna. Crying in waves, rising and falling. The little girl's father is holding on to her, sitting on the floor and holding her. Julian is standing beside them. For the first time Mari can see him, really see him. There's nothing in the way. He's laid bare. Absolutely bare.

The nurse goes out of the room to see if the little girl's mother needs help.

The swinging door continues to swing after she leaves, forward and back and forward again. Mari can see Julian. Julian the predator, the rescuer. Her tormentor. The door swings again, hides him for a second, then shows him for a fraction of a second, then swings back again. Mari can see him. He's absolutely bare.

The nurse comes back into the room.

"The little girl," Mari asks. "Sanna, her name was? Is she dead?"

"No," the nurse says.

"Is she going to die?"

"We don't know yet."

Mari looks at her hands, the white bandages covering the wounds. "Can I go home now?"

"Yes, you can go home now."

MARI LEAVES, walks to the end of the hallway, to the door. Step by step all the things she's walking away from become more and more like a picture, frozen: the river, her in the river — the water falling, clinging to the thicket of hair — floating open in the arms of the river. Nothing but a picture. It's easy to leave behind, as easy as it was to pick up: without deciding to, almost by accident. Step by step these two pictures move farther and farther away from each other. Her in the river, her here. Julian is watching as she walks down the hallway. Mari turns to look before she opens the door and steps outside. Julian looks at her. There's a whole world between them. The distance between them is growing, second by second. He lets her go.

Bare. Completely bare, Mari thinks as she walks out the door.

# *Anni*

SANNA'S BEEN FOUND at the bend in the river. Anni can see her hair floating, spread out on the water like a mermaid's. She can see mud in her hair. Sanna is completely quiet.

The girl, the pretty girl, is blowing life into Sanna in powerful puffs. She was just in the living room with Daddy. Anni saw her, heard her voice, that strange rhythm when she was breathing heavily with Daddy in the living room.

Adult stuff.

Now she's breathing heavy breaths into Sanna's mouth and Anni thinks that the rhythm of her breath is as strange as it was before — scary again, but in a different way.

Adult stuff.

The girl with Dad before, now here, bent over Sanna, a Sanna who isn't breathing. Sanna before on the trail, on the river rocks, then in the river, in water that stopped her breathing. And now completely quiet.

The ambulance men come. They put Sanna in the ambulance. Dad holds Anni, she doesn't have to walk. They go to the car. The girl comes, too. Dad starts the car.

He stops at the service station and goes inside, comes out and lights a cigarette. Dad never smokes. Mom smokes sometimes, at parties, but Dad never does. Anni opens the car door and goes to him.

"Why are you smoking a cigarette?"

"I thought it might make me feel better."

"Do you feel bad?"

"Yes."

"Like you're going to throw up?"

"No. Maybe a little."

He pats her head. Anni feels scared. Dad never smokes.

At the hospital they go to the waiting area. Sanna is somewhere inside, they can't see her now. Anni would like to ask Dad about her. Is she dying? Is Sanna going to die? She'd like to ask him about it, but she's afraid to. Maybe Sanna might die because Anni asked about it.

Sanna's mom comes. She comes running down the hallway first, then Sanna's dad, who isn't running, comes after her. Sanna's mom hears that Sanna fell, stopped breathing, was under the water. Then Sanna's mom falls, too. She drops like a rag doll. Anni already knows that this image will stay in her mind, will make the years ahead heavy, solid, real: Sanna's mother on the floor, her arms lifeless beside her like a doll's.

Dad goes outside to smoke again. Anni runs after him. It's wet out. The gravel crunches under her rubber boots. But there's still some ice. Anni scratches at the wet ground with the heel of her boot. Maybe she'll make a dam. No, not a dam — a brook, so the water can flow and spring will come sooner. Dad takes her hand.

Anni wants to ask him. She decides to ask a different way, so nothing bad can happen from her asking.

"Is Sanna going to stay here?"

"Yeah."

"Are we going to stay, too?"

"We can stay for a little while."

"Is Sanna going to spend the night?"

"Yeah."

"And us, too?"

"No. We're going to spend the night at home."

Inside, in the waiting area, Sanna's mom is lying on a bench. That scares Anni, too. You're supposed to sit on the bench. The doctor's asking Sanna's mom if she wants anything. She answers, "All I want is a Coke. Just a Coke."

Anni thinks that mothers aren't supposed to want a Coke more than anything.

Sanna's dad has snot coming out of his nose. Maybe men cry like that, Anni thinks. Through their noses.

Anni skips along the tiles on the floor. Blue and green tiles. You have to stay on the blue tiles. You can't walk on the green tiles.

## Mari

WHEN MARI GETS HOME, her mother is sitting on the sofa like she always does on weeknights. Mari takes off her coat and shoes at the front door. She looks at her hands. She knows that if her mother sees the bandages she'll make a fuss, demand an explanation. The thought of explaining is exhausting. She gets a sweater, holds it so that the bandages don't show, and goes into the living room.

She stands in the doorway. Her mother doesn't say anything; her throat is tight with worry, squeezing the words in. Mari hasn't spoken to her in two weeks. Her mother hasn't spoken either, hasn't said anything about Julian. Mari has been waiting. She's sure it will happen, someday soon. Her mother will go and tell the principal, tell everyone.

That's what it is, the thing that separates them.

Her mother begins. What she says surprises Mari.

"I don't plan to report Julian. I'm not going to say anything."

Mari's quiet at first, silenced by surprise.

"Why not?" she asks.

Her mother's answer is simple. There's no trace of condescension or resignation in it. It's just an answer.

"Because you asked me not to."

MARI SITS DOWN beside her.

She sits there for a second, not touching her or speaking to her. One second. Another.

Her mother doesn't say anything. She just takes Mari in her arms.

Mari remembers waking up once in the middle of the night when she was twelve years old, shaking all over. Something had frightened her. She woke her mother up. Her mother said that there was nothing to be afraid of, took her in her arms, between her knees in a way that was almost embarrassing. Mari remembers how ashamed she was to be twelve years old and yet so afraid that she ran into her mother's arms like a little child. But her mother said people get scared like that sometimes, even adults. She said you never grow out of being afraid. Mari remembers the sleepiness that gradually came over her as the trembling slowly stopped and the fear faded.

Now she's sitting with her mother's arms around her in just the same way. Her mother sees the bandages on her hands, sees them immediately. And Mari tells her about the little girl who fell in the river, the other little girl who ran across the meadow and through the woods. She cries a little, lets the shock of the story wash over her. She can cry now. The little girl might not survive, she might die — Mari says it. Her mother says that everything that could be done has been done. Mari takes hold of that: She did everything she could.

She doesn't tell her mother why she was at the river. She plucks her thoughts about the river out of the story. They've become a picture, a different world; another, almost foreign idea: the river. Is it childish? Silly? It's a different world from this one, anyway. She can pick it up again if she ever wants to. But she won't pick it up today, not right now.

Mari doesn't tell her mother about Julian, either. She doesn't say anything about him.

The clock ticks the soothing seconds on the wall and she could fall asleep to it. There's nowhere she has to be. She remembers being with her mother on a dock when she was small. Her mother was in a bikini, her feet bare. On a whim, Mari bit her mother's foot — out of affection or to tease her, she couldn't remember. Her mother got mad, picked her up with both hands and lifted her into the air. She dangled Mari over the water, and for an instant Mari thought she was going to drop her. It was that kind of moment, a look of horror, eye to eye. But her mother took her in her arms, squeezed her tight, not saying anything, not even scolding her, just holding on tight.

# Anni

THAT EVENING, Anni rocks on Mustang's back. She thinks
about the snow castle she made with Sanna on New Year's Day.
Just last week she and Sanna were playing together at the half-
melted castle. They couldn't go inside it anymore. Dad said
they couldn't because the roof might fall in. The castle was still
there in the yard — almost melted, but still there. Anni could
see it from the window.

Sanna could die. Dad said that it could happen. Anni thinks
about what that means. Sanna. Dying. Maybe. Dead things are
very quiet, and they don't move at all.

Anni has two images. The girl in the living room, her heavy
breathing. And Sanna on the riverbank, not breathing, and the
girl's heavy breathing again, this time for Sanna, to bring Sanna
back to life. The girl in the living room; Sanna at the river,
motionless. These are the two images she has. A distinct line
is drawn between them. Anni has that: the line between these
two images.

# Julian

JULIAN STOOD in the living-room door and looked at his daughter. Anni was playing, sitting on the back of her rocking horse, rocking quietly, abstractedly. Then she sat on the floor and put a dress on her doll. Ada tried to coax her into playing Barbies. Anni noticed him watching them, tried to smile a little. The smile shrank and died away.

Jannika came up beside him. She came home as soon as she heard, picked Ada up from the neighbors', waited with her at home, and came to the door when they got back from the hospital. Jannika had hugged him at the door, as soon as he came in, the way you do when all your words are meaningless.

Now she was standing beside him in the living-room doorway, her hand resting on the tender spot on his back, where his sacral bone was, holding it there, like she used to do.

The girl had left the hospital, walked down the hallway and out the door. *Thank you*, Julian had wanted to say. *I'm sorry*. He wanted even more desperately to say that. He hadn't said it. Or maybe he had, hurriedly, without meaning, without emphasis. She had left, walked away, become more of a stranger with each step, looked back at him from the doorway, and stepped outside. He had let her go.

*I've been here the whole time.* That's what Jannika had said. She had been here the whole time, right next to him, with him all along. Jannika, who broke wineglasses in fits of anger. Jannika, who was sometimes so distant that they lived in different realities, but who came back again, more fervent, more real, came back to herself, complete and undeniable. Jannika, who had carried their two children, who read to them every night when they went to bed. Jannika, who had a mole the size of his thumb on her neck, whose every body part he knew like a pathway home, her spine a straight road, the heart-shaped depression at the small of her back, just above her butt.

This is my life, Julian thought. All this is real. It's just this life, with nothing behind it. What happens to reality when you're ready to accept it? Does it narrow, flatten out? There's just this reality, where thanks and requests for forgiveness go unsaid, or they are said, but in the wrong way.

Julian had this: his two daughters and his wife. Anni in the meadow. *Help*, she had said. And his wife, here beside him.

Soon the girls would go to bed. He would lie awake next to Jannika before falling asleep. That heavy moment before sleep, ponderous, solitary. Every night the same heavy moment. Lying awake, beside his wife, waiting for sleep. He could do that. It could go on forever. He didn't ever have to tell her, he could leave the whole thing behind. The girl's mother hadn't told anyone. The first week had passed, then another. He could easily leave the whole thing behind him, effortlessly, the same way it had begun — like a game.

He could do that if he wanted to.

But he didn't want to. He'd known it when he came home, when Jannika came to meet him at the door.

Jannika went over to the girls and sat down, picked up

one of the Barbies without hesitation and started dressing it. Julian watched from the door as his wife and daughters played on the living-room floor in the pale spring-evening light, the way mothers and daughters play together, with wordless understanding, wrapped in mute tenderness.

Julian waited a minute longer. The light played through the window. A thin light, a dwelling place for the promise of summer. Julian picked up the light, the bird in the tree outside the window, and let them into his mind.

He went to Jannika. He reached out a hand to support her as she stood up. Jannika took his hand, looked in his eyes. A kind of trust that can't be put into words. It always surprised him how big that trust was between them, always bigger than he realized, always incomprehensible, as big as life.

"Come," he said. "I have something I want to tell you."

# Anja

ANJA WENT TO Johannes' house one more time. This would be the last time; she knew that. It was a May evening, the wind was coming off the sea, the seagulls screeched, and the still-cool weather already had a hint of summer in it. This would be the last time.

Neither of them said anything, at least not anything important. They were the kinds of moments that have too much meaning, too heavy on the tongue, too weighty for words, the kinds of moments that are filled with talking about the weather, pointing out how the light is becoming fuller day by day, how each day lingers longer in the arms of the evening, how the seagulls have already arrived and the birches are making their leaves.

They both knew, even without saying it.

Johannes made dinner — fried fish with the juice of a lemon squeezed over it, ground pepper, and a sprinkle of salt. Anja sat on the terrace and watched him cook. Potatoes boiled unhurriedly in their pot. Johannes chopped some spring onions and added them to the potatoes. A seagull was flying in a placid arch far off across the cold, blue sky.

They'd formed a habit of this leisurely, gentle ritual: Johannes made dinner, Anja watched, maybe tore some salad greens into a bowl or opened the wine. But mostly she watched. One of them would say something — Johannes would talk about his research or Anja about hers; they would compare travel stories about cities in the world they'd both visited.

After dinner they would drink some more wine, watch the angle of light and the apple tree blooming brightly in the yard, promising summer.

As the sun set and it became too cool to sit outdoors, they would go back inside. By unspoken agreement they would go into the bedroom, undress each other, slowly, greeting each other's nakedness again.

Anja found the tender spots on Johannes' skin with her tongue, pressed his quickly hardening penis between her lips, and sucked. After that, Johannes got up and took off her bra. Aside from their breathing, the muffled rustle of the bedspread was the only sound. The bedspread fell to the floor as Johannes lifted her onto the bed, got on his knees, laid her on her back, lifted her hips to the right angle, laid both his hands possessively on her lower abdomen, as if marking his territory, and entered her. A half-formed thought: How did he know that specific touch, in exactly the right place? He pressed lightly on her stomach. Am I too old for this? Anja thought until she really broke free for the first time and let the climax come.

At the climax was bliss and desolation.

A person is built of something inaccessible to comprehension, something unattainable. A kind of original melancholy that can only be seen at brief, surprising moments — like now, at the centre of bliss.

She had been with her husband for so many years, so many summers; slow, lingering summers with timid beginnings, like this one. She could see her husband as a young man, practically a boy. She could see the first time they made love — how many years ago was it? She couldn't remember, but she remembered how it felt. They had gone to his apartment. His roommate had been sleeping, or pretending to sleep, in the next room. He took his shirt off, revealing a slim boy's body that seemed perfect in every part. Anja had a startlingly lucid thought: This is the man I will marry. The shape of this body will become familiar to me. I will make these rises and hollows and ridges of bone under the skin my home. And she remembered the unbridled joy that bubbled up within her at the instant he climaxed inside her the first time, the boundless tenderness she already felt toward this man with a boy's body. The kind of tenderness that contained gratitude and sadness. A feeling that all of life was in that feeling, all the years to come.

After the climax, they lay side by side and let their breathing level off.

Anja looked at Johannes' birthmark, just above his breast-bone. If two straight lines were drawn from it toward each collarbone, it would form a perfect triangle. Or if two straight lines were drawn from his collarbones down to his xiphoid, it would form another, sharper triangle. A person's body is a wonderful geometric plan realized, complete in each small detail.

"We've been so happy, my husband and I," Anja whispered.

"Isn't that enough?" Johannes asked.

Anja nodded. "Yes. We've been so happy for so many years that you couldn't ask for greater good fortune."

"It's enough," Johannes said.

"It's enough."

THEY MUST HAVE fallen asleep, because it was already night when Anja roused herself. She got up, put on her clothes, combed her hair. Johannes woke up, too, and followed her to the door.

"I guess this is goodbye," he said.

"Yes, it is," Anja said.

Johannes held her in his arms a little longer. Then he loosened his hold and they said goodbye briefly. Anja stepped into the hallway and closed the door behind her.

She walked under the apple trees into the cool spring night and didn't look back.

We've been so happy for so many years, she thought. So happy that you couldn't ask for greater good fortune.

It's enough.

★

IN THE END, she thought of it as music. She had to make this journey one last time. It was the end of May: wood anemones in the laps of the trees, a virgin green veil among the still, darkly delineated limbs of the birches, the penetrating evening song of the nightingale. That certain kind of forest — stepping into its arching rooms, lying outstretched on a bed of moss with young ferns stroking your forehead, closing your eyes.

But Anja knew that she would stay on the path, take this journey again one more time, open the door, and hear her footsteps in the hallway.

She got off the bus a few stops early, walked along the edge of the woods. A placid certainty and quiet rhythm, on a violin or a piano, a peaceful march, an almost sedate tempo before the first drama. Andante, peace, and in the centre a mute grief, absolute.

Even now, when her whole life and all its meaning were here, she withdrew for a moment, saw the trees, the large crow that flew like a shadow over her head, heard the soft flapping of its wings, and thought how there had been the same noise when she was a child. She thought of the sheets hung out after they were washed, and she and her sister running under them, sheets that smelled like purity; remembered sitting under a sheet as her mother and father stretched it out between them. That same soft sound, like the beat of the crow's wings overhead. The sheet, she and her sister and the pure smell after the washing, a Monday evening at the beginning of spring years ago, when she was a child. The moments were always like this; they were never completely bare, completely present. Never bare. Here, walking, noticing the sound of the crow's wings, the trees, remembering the sheets and their smell, looking at the early spring green along the road, seeing the clouds, walking down this road one more time.

HER HUSBAND WAS SLEEPING. It had been a good day. He had eaten his meal with a good appetite. He didn't speak anymore, just used single words.

He did have one sentence, though, just as Anja was about to say hello.

"You're well liked here."

That's what he said. The words came out falteringly, hoarse, and a little mechanical, like an old phonograph skipping. He repeated the words. *You're well liked here. You. Well liked.*

The nursing home had called that morning to tell her that her husband had been given an intravenous drip. Always the same troubles.

That's when the music started to play in Anja's mind.

He didn't get up when she came now. She touched his hand, sat down next to him, and waited, listened. She didn't feel the panic anymore.

I will always remember you. I will carry you in my mind into the evenings and the mornings to come, the summer and the fall and the years to come. I will always remember you.

He breathed fitfully. Anja waited twenty more minutes, until he opened his eyes and woke up.

She walked to the door and locked it.

She took the bottle of sleeping powder out of her purse and put it down on the table.

"My love," she said. Her voice was a whisper.

He answered with a brief sigh.

"Let's sit you up," she said, adjusting the bed into an upright position.

She put a pillow under his back.

He looked at her without recognition.

"I brought you some chocolate pudding. The kind you like best."

He looked at the can of chocolate pudding on the night table.

Anja opened the lid and put a spoon in it. She picked up the sleeping powder, opened the lid, and poured the powder into the pudding. It formed a pale layer on the soft pudding and she mixed it in until it was invisible. She mixed it some more.

He looked at the pudding and opened his mouth like a baby bird.

Anja took a large spoonful and fed it to him.

He chewed the pudding as if it were bread, and swallowed.

"Good," he said.

"Yes," Anja said. "I bought the kind you like best."

Anja fed her husband the pudding, spoon by spoon, finally scraping the sides of the container clean.

He kept opening his mouth after the pudding was gone. Anja smiled and kissed him on the mouth.

She put the pudding container, the spoon, and the empty medicine bottle into her purse. She got up, opened the window to let in the sounds of the May evening, the nightingale and the blackbird; and the smell of the summer's first cutting of the grass came in on the breeze that fluttered the curtains. Then she unlocked the door. She left it unlocked, but closed. She sat next to her husband, took his head in her hands, stroked his thin hair, breathed with him, and waited.

ANJA WOKE UP. She didn't know how much time had passed. She looked at her husband and realized that it had been enough. She sat there a little longer, kissed him again on the mouth, the nose and cheeks and hair, then got up and went out of the room, walked down the hallway to reception where the nurses were watching the evening news, and told them.

"Antti died."

The nurses looked at her. She repeated what she had said.

"My husband Antti. He died."